Cambridge University of

Musae Seatonianae

A Complete Collection of the Cambridge Prize Poems...

Cambridge University of

Musae Seatonianae
A Complete Collection of the Cambridge Prize Poems...

ISBN/EAN: 9783744764063

Printed in Europe, USA, Canada, Australia, Japan

Cover: Foto ©Andreas Hilbeck / pixelio.de

More available books at **www.hansebooks.com**

Musæ Seatonianæ.

A COMPLETE

COLLECTION

OF THE

CAMBRIDGE PRIZE POEMS,

FROM THE

FIRST INSTITUTION OF THAT PREMIUM BY

The Rev. Mr. THO. SEATON, in 1750,

TO THE PRESENT TIME.

TO WHICH ARE ADDED,

TWO POEMS,

LIKEWISE WRITTEN FOR THE PRIZE,

By Mr. BALLY and Mr. SCOTT.

LONDON:

PRINTED BY T. WRIGHT FOR G. PEARCH;
J. JOHNSON, AT NO. 72. IN ST. PAUL'S
CHURCH-YARD; AND J. & T. MERRILL,
CAMBRIDGE.

M.DCC.LXXII.

C O N T E N T S.

CONTENTS.

The Two following Poems were written for the Prize, but rejected.

Just Published,

In Four Volumes Small Octavo, Price 14s. bound,

The SECOND EDITION of

A COLLECTION OF POEMS

By SEVERAL HANDS;

Being a Proper SUPPLEMENT to Mr. DODSLEY's COLLECTION.

Printed for GEO. PEARCH: and Sold by J. JOHNSON, No. 72 St. Paul's Church-Yard.

ADVERTISEMENT.

IF the present Age is not celebrated for Poetical Genius, it is remarkable for Poetical Taste, even the most refined. Numerous Poems might be adduced in proof of this, but none with greater propriety than those contained in the following Collection.

A DESIGN was formed some time ago to collect all the Poems which gained Mr. SEATON's Prize; but it was either interrupted or neglected. The design was too laudable to be entirely laid aside; we have therefore resumed it. We felt for the cause of Literature when we saw scattered in obscure corners, Poems which have done so much honour to their Authors, and which have so faithfully answered the intention of the

pious

pious Donor, by inculcating and embellish-
ing the great truths of the Chriſtian Religion.

It may be neceſſary to obſerve, that the
following is a complete collection of all the
Prize-Poems, ſome of which were become
very ſcarce. In the years 1766, 1769, and
1771, no Poems were publiſhed for the Prize.
We have added Two Poems to the Collection which were written for the Prize, but,
in the eſtimation of the Judges, were not
ſuppoſed to deſerve it. The Poems, how-
ever, have great merit, and as ſuch we thought
them intitled to the ſtation they poſſeſs.

We deemed this no improper opportunity
to give the world ſome account of Mr.
Seaton ; a man who is generally known to
it only by his liberality in the cauſe of Religion and the Muſes ; but our reſearches have
been unequal to the taſk. It is remarkable,
that the hiſtory of a public-ſpirited Man
ſhould have been ſunk in the ſhallow gulph

of

of little more than twenty years; for the Anecdotes of his life which are known are but few, and indeed not very interesting.

THE Reverend Mr. THOMAS SEATON was born at Stamford, in Lincolnshire, about the year 1684; and, after passing the usual time at the usual studies, was admitted, in 1701, a Sizer of Clare-Hall in the University of Cambridge, under the tuition of Mr. Clarke, the then Bedel of the University. Three years after, while Bachelor of Arts, he was admitted Scholar of that College, and at the end of the subsequent three years he acquired a Fellowship. Here he resided fifteen or sixteen years; in the course of which he wrote, among other little things, a Pamphlet against Whiston on the Eternity of the Son of God. In 1721 he resigned his Fellowship, and went to reside at his living in Northamptonshire, to which he had been presented by the late Lord Nottingham, whose Chaplain he was. Here he married,

and

and poſſeſſed the univerſal good-wiſhes of his pariſh till his death. He was a man aſſiduous in promoting the cauſe of Religion, becauſe he loved it ; and he gave no ſmall teſtimony of his attachment to it in his Will, from which the following clauſe is extracted :

"I give my Kiſlingbury eſtate to the
"Univerſity of Cambridge for ever; the
"rents of which ſhall be diſpoſed of yearly
"by the Vice-Chancellor for the time being,
"as he the Vice-Chancellor, the Maſter of
"Clare-Hall, and the Greek Profeſſor for
"the time being, or any two of them, ſhall
"agree. Which three perſons aforeſaid ſhall
"give out a ſubject, which ſubject ſhall, for
"the firſt year, be one or other of the Per-
"fections or Attributes of the Supreme
"Being, and ſo the ſucceeding years, till
"the ſubject is exhauſted; and afterwards
"the ſubject ſhall be either Death, Judg-
"ment, Heaven, Hell, Purity of Heart,
"&c.

" &c. or whatſoever elſe may be judged by
" the Vice-Chancellor, Maſter of Clare-Hall,
" and Greek Profeſſor, to be moſt conducive
" to the honour of the Supreme Being and
" recommendation of Virtue.   And they
" ſhall yearly diſpoſe of the rent of the
" above eſtate to that Maſter of Arts,
" whoſe Poem on the ſubject given ſhall
" be beſt approved by them.   Which Poem
" I ordain to be always in Engliſh, and to
" be printed; the expence of which ſhall
" be deducted out of the product of the
" eſtate, and the reſidue given as a reward
" for the Compoſer of the Poem, or Ode,
" or Copy of Verſes."

ON THE

ETERNITY

OF THE

SUPREME BEING.

BY

CHRISTOPHER SMART, M. A.

M DCC L.

B

ON THE

ETERNITY

OF THE

SUPREME BEING.

HAIL, wond'rous Being, who in power fupreme
Exifts from everlafting, whofe great name
Deep in the human heart, and every atom
The Air, the Earth, or azure Main contains,
In undecypher'd characters is wrote——
INCOMPREHENSIBLE !—— O what can words,
The weak interpreters of mortal thoughts,
Or what can thoughts (tho' wild of wing they rove
Thro' the vaft concave of th' ætherial round)?
If to the Heaven of Heavens they wing their way
Adventurous, like the birds of night they're loft,
And delug'd in the flood of dazzling day,——

B 2

May

May then the youthful, uninfpired Bard
Prefume to hymn th' Eternal ; may he foar
Where Seraph and where Cherubin on high
Refound th' unceafing plaudits, and with them
In the grand Chorus mix his feeble voice ?

He may—if Thou, who from the witlefs babe
Ordaineft honour, glory, ftrength, and praife,
Uplift th' unpinion'd Mufe, and deign'ft t'affift,
GREAT POET OF THE UNIVERSE, his fong.

Before this earthly Planet wound her courfe
Round Light's perennial fountain ; before Light
Herfelf 'gan fhine, and at th' infpiring word
Shot to exiftence in a blaze of day ;
Before " the Morning-Stars together fang,
And hail'd Thee Architect of countlefs worlds ;
Thou art—all-glorious, all-beneficent,
All Wifdom and Omnipotence thou art.

But is the æra of Creation fix'd
At when thefe worlds began ?   Could aught retard
Goodnefs, that knows no bounds, from bleffing ever,
Or keep th' immenfe Artificer in floth ?
Avaunt the duft-directed crawling thought,
That Puiffance immeafurably vaft,

And

And Bounty inconceivable, could reft
Content, exhaufted with one week of action—
No—in th' exertion of thy righteous power,
Ten thoufand times more active than the Sun,
Thou reign'd, and with a mighty hand compos'd
Syftems innumerable, matchlefs all,
All ftampt with thine uncounterfeited feal.

But yet (if ftill to more ftupendous heights
The Mufe unblam'd her aching fenfe may ftrain)
Perhaps wrapt up in contemplation deep,
The beft of Beings on the nobleft theme
Might ruminate at leifure, Scope immenfe
Th' eternal Power and Godhead to explore,
And with itfelf th' omnifcient mind replete.
This were enough to fill the boundlefs All,
This were a Sabbath worthy the Supreme !
Perhaps enthron'd amidft a choicer few,
Of fpirits inferior, he might greatly plan
The two prime Pillars of the Univerfe,
Creation and Redemption—and a while
Paufe—with the grand prefentiments of glory.

Perhaps——but all's conjecture here below,
All ignorance, and felf-plum'd vanity—
O Thou, whofe ways to wonder at's diftruft,

B 3

Whom

Whom to defcribe's prefumption (all we can—
And all we may—) be glorified, be prais'd.

A Day fhall come, when all this Earth fhall perifh,
Nor leave behind ev'n Chaos ; it fhall come·
When all the armies of the elements
Shall war againft themfelves ; and mutual rage,
To make Perdition triumph ; it fhall come
When the capacious atmofphere above   : ·
Shall in fulphureous thunders groan, and die,
And vanifh into void ; the earth beneath
· Shall fever to the center, and devour
Th' enormous blaze of the deftructive flames·
Ye rocks, that mock the raving of the floods,
And proudly frown upon th' impatient deep,
Where is your grandeur now ? Ye foaming waves,
'That all along th' immenfe Atlantic roar,
In vain ye fwell ; will a few drops fuffice
To quench the inextinguifhable fire ? ·
Ye mountains, on whofe cloud-crown'd tops the cedars
Are leffen'd into fhrubs, magnific piles,
'That prop the painted chambers of the heavens,
And fix the earth continual ; Athos, where ;
Where, Tenerif's thy ftatelinefs to-day ?
What, Ætna, are thy flames to thefe ?—No more
Than the poor glow-worm to the golden fun.

Nor

Nor ſhall the verdant vallies then remain
Safe in their meek ſubmiſſion ; they the debt
Of nature and of juſtice too muſt pay.
Yet I muſt weep for you, ye rival fair,
Arno and Andaluſia ; but for thee
More largely and with filial tears muſt weep,
O Albion, O my country ! Thou muſt join,
In vain diſſever'd from the reſt, muſt join
The terrors of th' inevitable ruin.

Nor thou, illuſtrious monarch of the day ;
Nor thou, fair queen of night ; nor you, ye ſtars,
Tho' million leagues and million ſtill remote,
Shall yet ſurvive that day ; Ye muſt ſubmit,
Sharers, not bright ſpectators of the ſcene.

But tho' the earth ſhall to the center periſh,
Nor leave behind ev'n Chaos ; tho' the air
With all the elements muſt paſs away,
Vain as an ideot's dream ; tho' the huge rocks,
That brandiſh the tall cedars on their tops,
With humbler vales muſt to perdition yield ;
Tho' the gilt Sun, and ſilver-treſſed Moon
With all her bright retinue, muſt be loſt ;
Yet Thou, Great Father of the world, ſurviv'ſt
Eternal, as thou wert : Yet ſtill ſurvives

The foul of man immortal, perfect now,
And candidate for unexpiring joys.

    He comes ! He comes ! the awful trump I hear ;
The flaming fword's intolerable blaze
I fee ! He comes ! th' Archangel from above.
" Arife, ye tenants of the filent grave,
" Awake incorruptible and arife :
" From eaft to weft, from the Antarctic pole
" To regions Hyperborean, all ye fons,
" Ye fons of Adam, and ye heirs of Heaven—
" Arife, ye tenants of the filent grave,
" Awake incorruptible and arife."

    'Tis then, nor fooner, that the reftlefs mind
Shall find itfelf at home ; and like the ark,
Fix'd on the mountain-top, fhall look aloft
O'er the vague paffage of precarious life ;
And, winds and waves and rocks and tempefts paft,
Enjoy the everlafting calm of Heaven :
'Tis then, nor fooner, that the deathlefs foul
Shall juftly know its nature and its rife :
'Tis then the human tongue new-tun'd fhall give
Praifes more worthy the Eternal ear.
Yet what we can, we ought ;—and therefore Thou,
Purge Thou my heart, Omnipotent and Good !

Purge

Purge Thou my heart with hyssop, left like Cain
I offer fruitless facrifice, and with gifts
Offend and not propitiate the Ador'd.
Tho' Gratitude were bleft with all the powers
Her burfting heart could long for, tho' the fwift,
The fiery-wing'd Imagination foar'd
Beyond Ambition's wish—yet all were vain
To fpeak Him as he is, who is INEFFABLE.
Yet ftill let Reafon thro' the eye of Faith
View Him with fearful love ; let Truth pronounce,
And Adoration on her bended knee
With heaven-directed hands confefs His reign.
And let the Angelic, Archangelic band
With all the Hofts of Heaven, Cherubic forms,
And forms Seraphic, with their filver trumps
And golden lyres attend :—" For Thou art holy,
" For Thou art One, th' Eternal, who alone
" Exerts all goodnefs, and tranfcends all praife."

ON

✳ 〰〰〰〰〰〰〰〰〰〰 ✳

ON THE

IMMENSITY

OF THE

SUPREME BEING.

BY

CHRISTOPHER SMART, M. A.

M DCC LI.

✳ 〰〰〰〰〰〰〰〰 ✳

ON THE

IMMENSITY OF THE SUPREME BEING.

ONCE more I dare to roufe the founding ftring,
THE POET OF MY GOD—Awake, my glory,
Awake, my lute and harp—myfelf fhall wake,
Soon as the ftately night-exploding bird
In lively lay fings welcome to the dawn.

    Lift ye ! how Nature with ten thoufand tongues
Begins the grand thankfgiving, Hail, all hail,
Ye tenants of the foreft and the field !
My fellow-fubjects of th' Eternal King,
I gladly join your Mattins, and with you
Confefs his prefence, and report his praife.

    O Thou, who or the Lambkin, or the Dove,
When offer'd by the lowly, meek, and poor,
Prefer'ft to Pride's whole hecatomb, accept
This mean Effay, nor from thy treafure-houfe
Of Glory' immenfe the Orphan's mite exclude.

What

Next to Pegu or Ceylon let me rove,
Where the rich ruby (deem'd by Sages old
Of Sovereign virtue) fparkles ev'n like Sirius,
And blufhes into flames.   Thence will I go
To undermine the treafure-fertile womb
Of the huge Pyrenean, to detect
The Agat and the deep-intrenched gem
Of kindred Jafper—Nature in them both
Delights to play the Mimic on herfelf;
And in their veins fhe oft pourtrays the forms
Of leaning hills, of trees erect, and ftreams
Now ftealing foftly on, now thundering down
In defperate cafcade, with flowers and beafts,
And all the living landfkip of the vale:
In vain thy pencil, Claudio or Pouffin,
Or thine, immortal Guido, would effay
Such fkill to imitate—it is the hand
Of God himfelf—for God himfelf is there.

Hence with the afcending fprings let me advance
Thro' beds of magnets, minerals, and fpar,
Up to the mountain's fummit, there t' indulge
Th' ambition of the comprehenfive eye,
That dares to call th' Horizon all her own.
Behold the foreft, and the expanfive verdure
Of yonder level lawn, whofe fmooth-fhorn fod

No

No object interrupts, unlefs the oak
His lordly head uprears, and branching arms
Extends—Behold in regal folitude,
And paftoral magnificence, he ftands
So fimple! and fo great! the under-wood
Of meaner rank an awful diftance keep.
Yet Thou art there, yet God himfelf is there
Ev'n on the bufh (tho' not as when to Mofes
He fhone in burning majefty reveal'd).
Nathlefs confpicuous in the Linnet's throat
Is his unbounded goodnefs—Thee her Maker,
Thee her Preferver chaunts fhe in her fong;
While all the emulative vocal tribe
The grateful leffon learn—no other voice
Is heard, no other found—for, in attention
Buried, ev'n babbling Echo holds her peace.

Now from the plains, where th' unbounded profpect
Gives liberty her utmoft fcope to range,
Turn we to yon enclofures, where appears
Chequer'd Variety in all her forms,
Which the vague mind attract and ftill fufpend
With fweet perplexity. What are yon towers,
The work of labouring man and clumfy art,
Seen with the ring-dove's neft?—On that tall beech
Her penfile houfe the feather'd Artift builds—

C

The

The rocking winds moleſt her not ; for ſee,
With ſuch due poize the wond'rous fabric's hung,
That, like the compaſs in the bark, it keeps
True to itſelf, and ſtedfaſt ev'n in ſtorms.
Thou ideot, that aſſerts there is no God,
View, and be dumb for ever —
Go bid Vitruvius or Palladio build
The bee his manſion, or the ant her cave—
Go call Correggio, or let Titian come
To paint the hawthorn's bloom, or teach the cherry
To bluſh with juſt vermilion—Hence away—
Hence, ye prophane ! for God himſelf is here.
Vain were th' attempt, and impious to trace
Thro' all his works th' Artificer Divine—
And tho' nor ſhining ſun, nor twinkling ſtar
Bedeck'd the crimſon curtains of the ſky ;
Tho' neither vegetable, beaſt, nor bird
Were extant on the ſurface of this ball,
Nor lurking gem beneath ; tho' the great ſea
Slept in profound ſtagnation, and the air
Had left no thunder to pronounce its maker ;
Yet man at home, within himſelf, might find
The Deity immenſe, and in that frame
So fearfully, ſo wonderfully made,
See and adore his providence and power—
I ſee, and I adore—O God moſt bounteous !

O in-

O infinite of Goodnefs and of Glory!
The knee, that thou haft fhap'd, fhall bend to Thee;
The tongue, which thou haft tun'd, fhall chaunt thy praife;
And, thine own image, the immortal foul,
Shall confecrate herfelf to Thee for ever.

ON

ON THE

OMNISCIENCE

OF THE

SUPREME BEING.

BY

CHRISTOPHER SMART, M. A.

M DCC LII.

ON THE

OMNISCIENCE OF THE SUPREME BEING.

ARISE, divine Urania, with new ſtrains
To hymn thy God ! and thou, immortal Fame,
Ariſe, and blow thy everlaſting trump !
All glory to the Omniſcient, and praiſe,
And power, and domination in the height !
And thou, cherubic Gratitude, whoſe voice
To pious ears ſounds ſilverly ſo ſweet,
Come with thy precious incenſe, bring thy gifts,
And with thy choiceſt ſtores the altar crown,
Thou too, my Heart, whom He, and He alone
Who all things knows, can know, with love replete,
Regenerate, and pure, pour all thyſelf
A living ſacrifice before his throne !
And may th' eternal, high myſterious tree,
That in the center of the arched Heavens
Bears the rich fruit of Knowledge, with ſome branch
Stoop to my humble reach, and bleſs my toil !

C 4

When

When in my mother's womb conceal'd I lay
A senseless embryo, then my soul thou knew'st,
Knew'st all her future workings, every thought,
And every faint idea yet unform'd.
When up the imperceptible ascent
Of growing years, led by thy hand, I rose,
Perception's gradual light, that ever dawns
Insensibly to day, thou didst vouchsafe,
And taught me by that reason thou inspir'dst,
That what of knowledge in my mind was low,
Imperfect, incorrect—in Thee is wond'rous,
Uncircumscrib'd, unsearchably profound,
And estimable solely by itself.

What is that secret power, that guides the brutes,
Which Ignorance calls instinct? 'Tis from Thee,
It is the operation of thine hands
Immediate, instantaneous; 'tis thy Wisdom,
That glorious shines transparent thro' thy works.
Who taught the Pye, or who forewarn'd the Jay
To shun the deadly nightshade? Tho' the cherry
Boasts not a glossier hue, nor does the plum
Lure with more seeming sweets the amorous eye,
Yet will not the sagacious birds, decoy'd
By fair appearance, touch the noxious fruit.
They know to taste is fatal, whence alarm'd

Swift

Swift on the winnowing winds they work their way.
Go to, proud reas'ner philofophic Man,
Haft thou fuch prudence, thou fuch knowledge?— No.
Full many a race has fell into the fnare
Of meretricious looks, of pleafing furface;
And oft in defart ifles the famifh'd pilgrim
By forms of fruit, and lufcious tafte beguil'd,
Like his forefather Adam, eats and dies.
For why? his wifdom on the leaden feet
Of flow Experience, dully tedious, creeps,
And comes, like vengeance, after long delay.

The venerable Sage, that nightly trims
The learned lamp, t'inveftigate the powers
Of plants medicinal, the earth, the air,
And the dark regions of the foffil world,
Grows old in following what he ne'er fhall find;
Studious in vain! till haply, at the laft
He fpies a mift, then fhapes it into mountains,
And bafelefs fabrics from conjecture builds:
While the domeftic animal, that guards
At midnight hours his threfhold, if opprefs'd
By fudden ficknefs, at his mafter's feet
Begs not that aid his fervices might claim,
But is his own phyfician, knows the cafe,
And from th' emetic herbage works his cure.

Hark,

Hark from afar the feather'd matron * screams,
And all her brood alarms ! The docile crew
Accept the signal one and all, expert
In th' art of Nature and unlearn'd deceit :
Along the sod, in counterfeited death,
Mute, motionless they lie ; full well appriz'd,
That the rapacious adversary's near.
But who inform'd her of th' approaching danger ?
Who taught the cautious mother, that the hawk
Was hatch'd her foe, and liv'd by her destruction ?
Her own prophetic soul is active in her,
And more than human providence her guard.

When Philomela, ere the cold domain
Of crippled Winter 'gins t' advance, prepares
Her annual flight, and in some poplar shade
Takes her melodious leave, who then's her pilot ?
Who points her passage thro' the pathless void
To realms from us remote, to us unknown ?
Her science is the science of her God.
Not the magnetic index to the North
E'er ascertains her course, nor buoy, nor beacon :
She, Heaven-taught voyager, that sails in air,
Courts nor coy West nor East, but instant knows
What Newton † or not sought, or sought in vain.

Illus-

* The Hen Turkey.   † The Longitude.

Illuſtrious name ! irrefragable proof
Of man's vaſt genius, and the ſoaring ſoul !
Yet what wert thou to Him, who knew his works
Before creation form'd them, long before
He meaſur'd in the hollow of his hand
Th' exulting Ocean, and the higheſt Heavens
He comprehended with a ſpan, and weigh'd
The mighty mountains in his golden ſcales ;
Who ſhone ſupreme, who was himſelf the light,
Ere yet Refraction learn'd her ſkill to paint,
And bend athwart the clouds her beauteous bow.

When Knowledge at her father's dread command
Reſign'd to Iſrael's king her golden key,
O ! to have join'd the frequent auditors
In wonder and delight, that whilom heard
Great Solomon deſcanting on the brutes,
O ! how ſublimely glorious to apply
To God's own honour, and good will to man,
That wiſdom he alone of men poſſeſs'd
In plenitude ſo rich, and ſcope ſo rare.
How did he rouſe the pamper'd ſilken ſons
Of bloated Eaſe, by placing to their view
The ſage induſtrious Ant, the wiſeſt inſect,
And beſt œconomiſt of all the field !
Tho' ſhe preſumes not by the ſolar orb

To

To meafure times and feafons, nor confults
Chaldean calculations, for a guide;
Yet confcious that December's on the march,
Pointing with icy hand to Want and Woe,
She waits his dire approach, and undifmay'd
Receives him as a welcome gueft, prepar'd
Againft the churlifh Winter's fierceft blow.
For when, as yet the favourable Sun
Gives to the genial earth th' enlivening ray,
Not the poor fuffering flave, that hourly toils
To rive the groaning earth for ill-fought gold,
Endures fuch trouble, fuch fatigue, as fhe;
While all her fubterraneous avenues,
And ftorm-proof cells with management moft meet
And unexampled houfewifcry fhe forms:
'Then to the field fhe hies, and on her back,
Burden immenfe! fhe bears the cumbrous corn.
'Then many a weary ftep, and many a ftrain,
And many a grievous groan fubdued, at length
Up the huge hill fhe hardly heaves it home:
Nor refts fhe here her providence, but nips
With fubtle tooth the grain, left from her garner
In mifchievous fertility it fteal,
And back to day-light vegetate its way.
Go to the Ant, thou fluggard, learn to live,
And by her wary ways reform thine own.

But

But if thy deaden'd fenfe, and liftlefs thought
More glaring evidence demand; behold,
Where yon pellucid populous hive prefents
A yet uncopied model to the world!
There Machiavel in the reflecting glafs
May read himfelf a fool.   The Chemift there
May with aftonifhment invidious view
His toils out-done by each plebeian Bee,
Who, at the royal mandate, on the wing
From various herbs, and from difcordant flowers,
A perfect harmony of fweets compounds.

Avaunt, Conceit, Ambition, take thy flight
Back to the Prince of vanity and air!
O! 'tis a thought of energy moft piercing;
Form'd to make Pride grow humble; form'd to force
Its weight on the reluctant Mind, and give her
A true but irkfome image of herfelf.
Woeful viciffitude! when Man, fall'n Man,
Who firft from Heaven, from gracious God himfelf
Learn'd knowledge of the Brutes, muft know, by Brutes
Inftructed and reproach'd, the fcale of being;
By flow degrees from lowly fteps afcend,
And trace Omnifcience upwards to its fpring!
Yet murmur not, but praife—for tho' we ftand
Of many a Godlike privilege amerc'd

By

By Adam's dire tranfgreffion ; tho' no more
Is Paradife our home, but o'er the portal
Hang in terrific pomp the burning blade ;
Still with ten thoufand beauties blooms the Earth
With pleafures populous, and with riches crown'd,
Still is there fcope for wonder and for love
Ev'n to their laft exertion—fhowers of bleffings
Far more than human virtue can deferve,
Or hope expeϗ, or gratitude return.
Then, O ye People, O ye Sons of Men,
Whatever be the colour of your lives,
Whatever portion of itfelf his Wifdom
Shall deign t' allow, ftill patiently abide,
And praife him more and more ; nor ceafe to chaunt
" ALL GLORY TO TH' OMNISCIENT, AND PRAISE,
" AND POWER, AND DOMINATION IN THE HEIGHT !
" And thou, cherubic Gratitude, whofe voice
" To pious ears founds filverly fo fweet,
" Come with thy precious incenfe, bring thy gifts,
" And with thy choiceft ftores the altar crown."

ΤΩ   ΘΕΩ   ΔΟΞΑ.

ON THE

POWER

OF THE

SUPREME BEING.

BY

CHRISTOPHER SMART, M. A.

M DCC LIII.

ON THE

POWER OF THE SUPREME BEING.

" TREMBLE, thou Earth!" th' anointed poet faid,
" At God's bright prefence, tremble, all ye mountains!
" And all ye hillocks on the furface bound!"
Then once again, ye glorious thunders, roll!
'The Mufe with tranfport hears ye; once again
Convulfe the folid continent! and fhake,
Grand mufic of Omnipotence, the ifles!
'Tis thy terrific voice, thou God of Power,
'Tis thy terrific voice; all Nature hears it
Awaken'd and alarm'd; fhe feels its force;
In every fpring fhe feels it, every wheel,
And every movement of her vaft machine.
Behold! quakes Apennine; behold! recoils
Athos; and all the hoary-headed Alps
Leap from their bafes at the godlike found.
But what is this, celeftial tho' the note,

D

And

And proclamation of the reign fupreme,
Compar'd with fuch as, for a mortal ear
Too great, amaze the incorporeal worlds?
Should Ocean to his congregated waves
Call in each river, cataract, and lake,
And with the watry world down an huge rock
Fall headlong in one horrible cafcade,
'Twere but the echo of the parting breeze,
When Zephyr faints upon the lily's breaft,
'Twere but the ceafing of fome inftrument,
When the laft lingering undulation
Dies on the doubting ear, if nam'd with founds
So mighty! fo ftupendous! fo divine!

But not alone in the aërial vauft
Does He the dread theocracy maintain;
For oft, enrag'd with his inteftine thunders,
He harrows up the bowels of the earth,
And fhocks the central magnet—Cities then
Totter on their foundations, ftately columns,
Magnific walls, and heaven-affaulting fpires.
What tho' in haughty eminence erect
Stands the ftrong citadel, and frowns defiance
On adverfe hofts, tho' many a baftion jut
Forth from the rampart's elevated mound,
Vain the poor providence of human art,

And

And mortal ſtrength how vain! while underneath
Triumphs his mining vengeance in th' uproar
Of ſhatter'd towers, riven rocks, and mountains,
With clamour inconceivable uptorn,
And hurl'd adown th' abyſs.   Sulphureous pyrites
Burſting abrupt from darkneſs into day,
With din outrageous and deſtructive ire,
Augment the hideous tumult, while it wounds
Th' afflictive ear, and terrifies the eye,
And rends the heart in twain.   Twice have we felt,
Within Auguſta's walls twice have we felt
Thy threaten'd indignation ; but ev'n Thou,
Incenſ'd Omnipotent, art gracious ever ;
Thy goodneſs infinite but mildly warn'd us
With mercy-blended wrath : O ſpare us ſtill,
Nor ſend more dire conviction! We confeſs
That thou art He, th' Almighty : we believe.
For at thy righteous power whole ſyſtems quake,
For at thy nod tremble ten thouſand worlds.

Hark! on the winged whirlwind's rapid rage,
Which is and is not in a moment—hark!
On th' hurricane's tempeſtuous ſweep he rides
Invincible, and oaks and pines and cedars
And foreſts are no more.   For, conflict dreadful!
The Weſt encounters Eaſt, and Notus meets

D 2

In

In his career the Hyperborean blaft.
The lordly lions fhuddering feek their dens,
And fly like timorous deer; the king of birds,
Who dar'd the folar ray, is weak of wing,
And faints and falls and dies;—while He fupreme
Stands ftedfaft in the center of the ftorm.

   Wherefore, ye objeЅs terrible and great,
Ye thunders, earthquakes, and ye fire-fraught wombs
Of fell volcanos, whirlwinds, hurricanes,
And boiling billows, hail! in chorus join
To celebrate and magnify your Maker,
Who yet in works of a minuter mould
Is not lefs manifeft, is not lefs mighty.

   Survey the magnet's fympathetic love,
That wooes the yielding needle; contemplate
Th' attraЅive amber's power, invifible
Ev'n to the mental eye; or when the blow
Sent from th' eleЅric fphere affaults thy frame,
Shew me the hand that dealt it!—Baffled here
By his Omnipotence, Philofophy
Slowly her thoughts inadequate revolves,
And ftands, with all his circling wonders round her,
Like heavy Saturn in th' etherial fpace
Begirt with an inexplicable ring.

If

If such the operations of his power,
Which at all feasons and in every place
(Rul'd by eftablifh'd laws and current nature)
Arreft th' attention ; Who! O Who fhall tell
His acts miraculous ? when his own decrees
Repeals he, or fufpends, when by the hand
Of Mofes or of Jofhua, or the mouths
Of his prophetic feers, fuch deeds he wrought,
Before th' aftonifh'd Sun's all-feeing eye,
That Faith was fcarce a virtue. Need I fing
The fate of Pharaoh and his numerous band
Loft in the reflux of the watry walls,
That melted to their fluid ftate again ?
Need I recount how Sampfon's warlike arm
With more than mortal nerves was ftrung t' o'erthrow
Idolatrous Philiftia ? Shall I tell
How David triumph'd, and what Job fuftain'd ?
—But, O fupreme, unutterable mercy !
O love unequall'd, myftery immenfe,
Which angels long t' unfold ! 'tis man's redemption
That crowns thy glory, and thy power confirms,
Confirms the great, th' uncontroverted claim.
When from the Virgin's unpolluted womb
Shone forth the Sun of Righteoufnefs reveal'd,
And on benighted reafon pour'd the day ;

Let

" Let there be peace (he faid) !" and all was calm
Amongft the warring world—calm as the fea
When, " O be ftill, ye boifterous Winds !" he cried,
And not a breath was blown, nor murmur heard.
His was a life of miracles and might,
And charity and love, ere yet he tafte
The bitter draught of death, ere yet he rife
Victorious o'er the univerfal foe,
And Death and Sin and Hell in triumph lead.
His by the right of conqueft is mankind,
And in fweet fervitude and golden bonds
Were ty'd to him for ever.—O how eafy
Is his ungalling yoke, and all his burdens
'Tis ecftacy to bear ! Him, bleffed Shepherd,
His flocks fhall follow thro' the maze of life
And fhades that tend to Day-fpring from on high ;
And as the radiant rofes after fading,
In fuller foliage and more fragrant breath
Revive in fmiling Spring, fo fhall it fare
With thofe that love him—for fweet is their favour,
And all Eternity fhall be their fpring.
Then fhall the gates and everlafting doors,
At which the KING OF GLORY enters in,
Be to the Saints unbarr'd : and there, where pleafure
Boafts an undying bloom, where dubious hope

Is certainty, and grief-attended love
Is freed from paſſion—there we'll celebrate,
With worthier numbers, Him, who is, and was,
And in immortal prowefs King of Kings,
Shall be the Monarch of all worlds for ever.

O N

Is certainty, and ... rewarded love;
Is like a garden ... well cultured;
With ever-springing flowers, ... and ...
And in immortal ... Life ...
Shall be the Home ...

ON THE

JUSTICE

OF THE

SUPREME BEING.

BY

GEORGE BALLY, M. A.

M DCC LIV.

ON THE
JUSTICE
OF THE
SUPREME BEING

BY

GEORGE BLAIR, M.A.

ON THE

JUSTICE OF THE SUPREME BEING.

O Thou, whofe Juftice awes the moral World,
Dread Judge, and Governor fupreme ! thine eye,
Thro' the vaft amplitude of fpace diffus'd,
No action 'fcapes, no thought that bubbling fprings
In the heart's troubled deep.   In vain the Wretch,
Specious in borrow'd vizor, lifts his front
Triumphant : Thee no artificial glofs
Deceives : the Monfter walks beneath thy ken
Foul with unnumber'd fpots.   His deeds are noted
In thy eternal volumes to confound
His guilt : tho' now perhaps he wanton bafks
In Fortune's funny fmiles, and laughs difdainful
At Virtue, pin'd with penury and cold.
Nathlefs, when this dark fublunary plot,
Which now with feeming intricacies mocks
Our bufy fearch, amazingly to view

Shall

Shall ſtand unravéll'd in th' all-cloſing ſcene,
The Caítiff, at the curtain's fall, ſhall bleed;
And Men and Angel-Choirs applauſive laud
Th' unerring rectitude of all thy ways.

O may the Poet then, whoſe faltering tongue
Liſps theſe rude ſtrains, and trembles while he ſings
What aſks a Cherub's note, a Seraph's glow,
This mundane polity by Thee ſuſtain'd
On the firm baſis of eternal right,
O King, that reign'ſt for ever! may He then,
When Thou the ſcatter'd Particles ſhalt call
His Soul's demoliſh'd manſion to rebuild,
Approach thy dread Tribunal unappall'd;
May Mercy o'er that Juſtice then prevail,
Which here his humble verſe eſſay'd to paint!

With ſcanty line ſhall Reaſon dare to mete
Th' immeaſurable depths of Providence?
On the ſwoln bladders of Opinion borne
She floats awhile, then floundering ſinks abſorb'd
Within that boundleſs ſea ſhe ſtrove to graſp.
Shall Man, here ſtation'd to revere that God
Who call'd him into being from the duſt,
His moral ſcheme implead, and impious cite
Th' Almighty Legiſlator to the bar

Of

Of erring intellect; too weak his fight
To trace each hidden link that knits the chain
Stupendous ?   Hence he labours to depofe
Jehovah from his fovereignty, and lifts
A blind ideal phantom to the throne.
Things oft inverted in this turbid mafs
Strike his difgufted eye, and fhake his Faith,
Too prone to fhift her compafs.   Vice he fees
With gems and Tyrian purple fparkling gay,
And Virtue mouldering in a dungeon's gloom.

 " Say, is This fitting (cries the doubting Sage) ?
" Do thefe unequal difpenfations fpeak
" A wife impartial Ruler of the World ?
" Shall earth, fhall air, and every element
" Be tax'd to furnifh the blafphemer's meal,
" While Heaven's beft votary, who in fervent pray'r
" Exhales his foul, the fcantieft offal wants
" His macerated body to relieve ?"
Thus Man, whofe mind's too narrow to contain
The vaft dimenfions of th' harmonious whole,
From parts, uncomely if afunder view'd,
Decifive fentence gives.   Thou laugh'ft above,
Dread ELOHIM, to fee him ftudious weigh
Thy meafures in his balance :   Thou whofe grafp
The waters, and whofe fpan the heavens compriz'd.

T•

To judge aright how Providence conducts
The moral fyftem, where a clue is lent
T' unwind the myftic maze, with cautious fteps
Man muft purfue ; each nice gradation fcan ;
Obferve how parts, erft oppofite, confpire
In one illuftrious concord of defign.
Then every jarring ftring, which, fingly touch'd,
Grated harfh diffonance on Reafon's ear,
Will fpeak the graces of th' Almighty hand,
And in a fweet-ton'd Diapafon clofe.

The Sun of Juftice may withdraw his beams
Awhile from earthly ken, and fit conceal'd
In dark recefs, pavilion'd round with clouds :
Yet let not Guilt prefumptuous rear her creft,
Nor Virtue droop defpondent : foon thefe clouds,
Seeming eclipfe, will brighten into day,
And in majeftic fplendor He will rife
With healing, and with terror on his wings.

Things in progreffive motion cheat our eye,
Unmark'd the deftin'd goal, to which they tend.
Mofes' all-powerful rod, amazing fight!
A ferpent crawls, and darts its forky tongue ;
But in his hand refum'd, to Ifrael's fons
Difpenfes bleffings, bids th' imprifon'd ftream

Gufh

Gush from the stricken rock, th' obedient sea
Drive back its refluent waves, and stand a wall
Condens'd, to yield a passage to his host.
Thus what we view abhorrent as deform,
And inconsistent with that faultless rule,
By which a sapient God each act should square,
In th' issue will its frightful aspect lose,
And leave th' all-righteous Sovereign unimpeach'd.

What eye but melts with pity, when it sees
Joseph's defencelefs piety and youth
To leagu'd fraternal hate a prey expos'd?
Shall Israel's darling, nay what's more, shall God's
With complicated ills be doom'd to strive?
Shall a pit yawn for him, yet none for those
Who plot against his life? The bargain's struck;
Unnatural bargain, where a Brother's sold!
The seven-mouth'd Nile receives him: here the sky
Fallacious smiles, to make the gathering cloud
Burst heavier on his head: the slighted charms
Of an enamour'd Mistress glow with ire
Fierce and impetuous as her former lust:
That stubborn heart must bleed, which would not melt.
Are chains the meed of Innocence? Does God
Exalt his enemies to thrones, deprefs
His friends to dungeons? Impious plaints, away!

And

And to that Hell, from whence ye rife, repair!
O'erblown the ftorm, which only rag'd to fpeed
Heaven's chofen veffel to the deftin'd port,
The Hebrew bright emerges. -Quick the fcene
Is fhifted from a dungeon to a throne.
Next to the proud Egyptian King he moves
In his high orb refplendent: lives to ftrain
Old Ifrael in his fond encircling arms,
To fee the typic fheaves in marfhall'd ranks,
His brethren, erft with other paffions warm'd,
Submiffive bow their vaffal heads before
His fheaf, that rears aloft it's lordly ftem.

    Silenc'd be every tongue, that dar'd to breathe
The rank exuberance of a fenfual heart
In fceptic murmurs: Reafon, ftand abafh'd,
And, whom thou canft not comprehend, adore!
If Virtue fuffers, 'tis to prove her faith,
To make abafement glorioufly confpire,
Like Jofeph's, to her rife: each ftroke fhe feels,
But adds new luftre to her maffive crown.
If Vice, unthank'd his feeder, gluts his maw.
With ftudied dainties, and with riot fwells,
'Tis but a victim fatten'd for the fword
Of Juftice, edg'd to drink his guilty blood.
A guileful Haman brooding o'er the fate

Of blamelefs Mordecai, when raptures high
Stretch every vein, and elevate the foul,
When glows the waffel moft, and fparkling joy
Laughs in each offer'd cup, O dire reverfe!
Shall from the royal banquet to the grave
Be dragg'd unpitied, on that tree expire,
Which for wrong'd innocence his hands had rais'd.

The fcheme of Providence, tho' knots perplex'd
O'er the unfolding texture feem to caft
Unpleafing fhades, at large difclos'd appears
With lucid order, and coherence crown'd.
So in the folded tapeftry, where parts
With gradual openings meet the paufing eye,
Here fprouts a leafy branch, a human foot:
There marks the woven ground: all feems a wild,
Mifhapen chaos of disjointed forms:
Yet, when in full expanfe the web entire
Shews the mixt groupe in orderly array,
The figur'd hiftory well-pleas'd we trace,
Each feveral part applaud, but moft the whole.

Shall counfels, plann'd by Wifdom infinite,
And by Omnipotence conducted, fail?
Sooner the Heavens, the fabric of his hands,
Shrunk their extenfive cope like fhrivell'd parchment,

E

Melted

Melted to viewlefs air fhall difappear,
Yea all things into primitive nothing fall,
Than God's eternal and all-wife decrees
One jot fhall be abolifh'd.   Flight of days,
The world obfcuring with their fhadowy wings,
Shall o'er his grand defigns a luftre throw;
Shall clear that wondrous, foul-abforbing text,
Which poring Seraphs puzzles and confounds.

 Righteous are all thy ways, O Power Supreme,
Whether thy patience ftruggling with thy wrath
Arrefts th' uplifted thunderbolt, that longs
To lance deftruction on the head accurs'd:
Or whether Piety, to purge her drofs
By fharp affaying fires, thou feeft permiffive
Crufh'd by Oppreffion's iron arm, or torn
By racking maladies, inteftine war.
Orb * within orb involv'd, Thy myftic Wheels,
On which this politic machine is whirl'd
Inceffant, with no giddy devious flight
Precipitate their courfe: with eyes they glow
Diftinct, and in a meafur'd orbit move.

 To right thy injur'd friends, and blaft thy foes,
Thou counterwork'ft Man's purpofe, and from ill

Educeft

* See Ezekiel, chap. i.

Educeft good : as erft thy potent voice,
Omnific, from the womb of night abhorr'd
Call'd forth that light, which glads th' invefted world.
A Pharaoh's Daughter, by thy impulfe led,
Shall in a Hebrew babe unweeting rear
Ifrael's Redeemer, and her Father's fcourge.
When Jacob's Seed, befide Euphrates' flood,
With groans refponfive to his murmurs, fwell
The current with their tears, and Sion's pride,
Illuftrious Sion wail, in afhes loft ;
The ravenous Eagle * from the Eaft fhall urge
His rapid flight, and in his talons bear
Jehovah's thunder : Babylon's tower'd creft
Shall fink beneath his fwoop, while he full-gorg'd
O'er the Affyrian prey fhall clap his plumes,
Victorious Minifter of wrath divine.

Thy throne, O Lord, eftablifh'd on the bafe
Of Juftice, how tremendous, how benign ! ·
Here foft-ey'd Cherubim with wings difpred
The mercy-feat infold, and beam on Man,
Repenting man, compaffion and meek love :
There flamy Seraphs from their pinions fhake
Horror and dire difmay : Thy awful fword,

E 2   Fierce

* Cyrus, fee Ifaiah, chap. xlvi.

Fierce as a comet, blazes in their grafp
High-wav'd, to flafh the harden'd rebel dead.

Who can abide thy terrors, Judge fevere,
When by repeated provocations warm'd
Thy anger burns, and Mercy ftrives in vain
To interpofe her fhield betwixt thy bolt!
Thy trampled laws, bright tranfcript of Thyfelf,
And the lefe Majefty of Heaven's high King,
Who pardon offer'd; pardon but contemn'd!
Bare thy red arm, and edge the vengeful brand.

Who in his milder governance difclaim'd
The living God, fhall feel him in his dread
Vindictive Attribute, and trembling own
That Power, whofe nod obedient Nature waits,
With all her armaments of fnow and wind,
Of battering hail, or wide-devouring fire,
To execute his vengeance: who can forge
The meaneft creatures into fwords, to foil,
The boafts of Kings, and wither all their ftrength.
What! tho' his wrathful vials in the clouds
Sufpended ftand awhile, nor burft, as once
O'er a devoted Sodom, or a World,
Whofe ftains a deluge fcarcely wafh'd away;
Yet is His arm not fhorten'd:——Thou'rt the fame,

JE-

JEHOVAH, thro' eternity unchang'd,
Thy eyes too pure, too beamy to behold
Iniquity's foul mift: each thought profane,
Each vile affection muft be far remov'd,
Ere we approach thy Sanctuary and live.

Tremble, ye Heavens, and Earth, but chief O Man,
Apoftate Man, before a God incens'd!
Juftice exacts the debt, but Nature fails,
Mere Human Nature; bankrupt and undone!
God muft be righted, or Mankind be loft;
For ever loft, unpitied, unrepriev'd.
Dreadful alternative! heart-chilling thought,
That leads to Defperation's flippery brink!
Who fhall the price immenfe, the ranfom pay,
Commenfurate to Guilt, and Worth divine?
Who but the King of Kings, the Lord Himfelf,
The Coeternal, Coeffential Son!
He, to appeafe infinity of wrath,
Muft quit the bofom of paternal blifs,
And in a flefhly tabernacle fhroud
His plenitude of light. Lord! what is Man,
Corruption's heir, and brother to the worm,
That Thou fo kindly labour'ft in his weal?
Oh! the exceffive depth, th' amazing height
Of Heavenly Wifdom! Juftice how fevere!

E 3

Mercy

Mercy how tender! from the clouds of ire
Omnipotent diſtilling balmy dew!

Shall then th' all-perfeƈt and unſpotted Lamb
For our tranſgreſſions bleed, to death reſign
His broken frame, to heal us with his wounds?
Shall the Son groan in bitterneſs of ſoul,
Implore his angry Father to remove
The baleful cup, empoiſon'd with the ſins
Of a whole World, and yet ſhall Man tranſgreſs,
Man by His death aſſerted into life?
O! let us turn repentant to our Sire,
Shake off our ſordid luſts, thoſe thorns which gor'd
Our Saviour's temples, and thoſe ſpikes obſcene
That nail'd his ſinleſs body to the croſs.
Let God's ſeverity our hearts appall,
Ev'n whilſt his kindneſs claſps us in its arms.
Elſe will that vocal Blood, which pleads above,
Cry loud for vengeance, and its cries aſcend
High as the dread judicial Court of Heaven.

That awful Court who ſhall eſcape? The Dead
And Living there ſhall wait their final doom.
Methinks I ſee from th' empyrean ſkies;
Preceded by his bright Angelic Hoſt,
The Judge deſcend: how chang'd from Him who late

The

The thorny crown, and reedy fceptre bore!
Glory arrays him; from his countenance beams
Splendor ineffable: ftars cluftering weave
A rich tiara for His head, who gave
Their beauteous lamps to fhine.   Look, Ifrael, there
Affrighted, and with dire conviction own
Thy King triumphant in his cloudy car!
See the Crofs glitter thro' th' enfanguin'd air,
Proud enfign of his conqueft, and thy fhame!

Hark! thro' Heaven's wide reverberating vault
The clanging Trumpet founds th' awakening peal.
Obedient tombs expand their marble jaws,
And every fad repofitory hears
The quickening voice, and renders back its truft
To light and life; each particle difpers'd
Crowds to a heap, and builds th' identic Man.
Chang'd are the living, and alive the dead.
Lo! cited myriads fill th' extended plain,
And trembling to the Grand Tribunal prefs.

The Book is open'd, and the feal remov'd;
The adamantine Book; where every thought,
Tho' dawning on the heart, then funk again
In the corrupted mafs, each act obfcure,
In characters indelible remain.

E 4

How

Mercy how tender! from the clouds of ire
Omnipotent diftilling balmy dew!

   Shall then th' all-perfect and unfpotted Lamb
For our tranfgreffions bleed, to death refign
His broken frame, to heal us with his wounds?
Shall the Son groan in bitternefs of foul,
Implore his angry Father to remove
The baleful cup, empoifon'd with the fins
Of a whole World, and yet fhall Man tranfgrefs,
Man by His death afferted into life?
O! let us turn repentant to our Sire,
Shake off our fordid lufts, thofe thorns which gor'd
Our Saviour's temples, and thofe fpikes obfcene
That nail'd his finlefs body to the crofs.
Let God's feverity our hearts appall,
Ev'n whilft his kindnefs clafps us in its arms.
Elfe will that vocal Blood, which pleads above,
Cry loud for vengeance, and its cries afcend
High as the dread judicial Court of Heaven.

   That awful Court who fhall efcape? The Dead
And Living there fhall wait their final doom.
Methinks I fee from th' empyrean fkies,
Preceded by his bright Angelic Hoft,
The Judge defcend: how chang'd from Him who late

The

The thorny crown, and reedy fceptre bore!
Glory arrays him; from his countenance beams
Splendor ineffable: ftars clustering weave
A rich tiara for His head, who gave
Their beauteous lamps to fhine. Look, Ifrael, there
Affrighted, and with dire conviction own
Thy King triumphant in his cloudy car!
See the Crofs glitter thro' th' enfanguin'd air,
Proud enfign of his conqueft, and thy fhame!

Hark! thro' Heaven's wide reverberating vault
The clanging Trumpet founds th' awakening peal.
Obedient tombs expand their marble jaws,
And every fad repofitory hears
The quickening voice, and renders back its truft
To light and life; each particle difpers'd
Crowds to a heap, and builds th' identic Man.
Chang'd are the living, and alive the dead.
Lo! cited myriads fill th' extended plain,
And trembling to the Grand Tribunal prefs.

The Book is open'd, and the feal remov'd;
The adamantine Book; where every thought,
Tho' dawning on the heart, then funk again
In the corrupted mafs, each act obfcure,
In characters indelible remain.

E 4

How

How vain thy boaft, vile Caitiff, to have 'fcap'd
An earthly Forum, now thy crimfon ftains
Glare on a congregated World, thy Judge
Omnifcience, and Omnipotence thy Scourge!
Thy mafk, Hypocrify, how ufelefs here,
When by a beam, fhot from the Fount of Light,
The varnifh'd faint ftarts up a ghaftly fiend!

But Ye of manners blamelefs, faith approv'd,
Who a long toilfome warfare have endur'd,
By flefhly wiles affail'd, yet unfubdu'd;
Ye who have fair Religion's caufe maintain'd,
Tho' Princes frown'd, and Flames encircling rag'd,
With front erect approach the throne auguft.
See how your Saviour bends his gracious head,
Smiling unutterable love! The choir
Of Saints congenial beckon you to blifs,
And all the glorify'd Affeffors burn
To add your fteady phalanx to their roll.

Soon are their wifhes, and your labours crown'd:
For now, your virtue's teft, your trial o'er,
Where every bafhful grace, that bloom'd unfeen,
Too delicate to bear the ruffling breath
Of worldly praife, is brought to light before
Its beft applauders, Angels and their Lord,

The

The Judge with accent mild cries : " Come, Ye Blefs'd,
" Share the unfading pleafures of my realm,
" Coheirs of blifs, my Sire's adopted fons."
Strait at that found the Pious, like a flock
Of harmlefs doves, are rapt with ardent wing
To meet their dear Redeemer in the clouds.

The bellowing convex ecchoes to the Trump,
And lo ! the yelling Wicked crowd the bar.
Settled Defpair, and pale Dejection dim
Each louring afpect : Beauty hides her face,
And fain would hide her guilt : curs'd Mammon's flave
Laments his treafures were not there fecur'd,
Where neither moth corrupts, nor ruft devours :
Grim-vifag'd Murder with reluctance lifts
Th' accufing hand, which Oceans ne'er could blanch ;
And, like a hunted panther, ftarts to fee
His horrid deeds emblazon'd in his fpots.
Confcience, God's dread official here below,
Too oft her friendly whifpers drown'd in noife,
Now rings her loud alarum in their hearts,
Their fears awakens, and foreftalls their doom.

Methinks I hear a felf-convicted Wretch
To his affociates vent his anguifh'd foul :
" Yonder He fits, whofe mercies we have fpurn'd,
" Whofe

" Whose laws we have profan'd, whose sides we oft
" Have pierc'd with Blasphemy's envenom'd spear :
" How shall we now confront his awful eye,
" That melts all Nature with a darted glance ?
" Or whither from His dreaded presence flee ?
" O that some rock would fall, some mountain yawn
" To bury us for ever in its womb !
" Vain hope, alas ! these mountains and these rocks
" Soon will be gone ; the Heavens and Earth dissolv'd ;
" And nothing for His fiery wrath remain
" To prey on but ourselves, immortal only
" To suffer an eternity of pain."

The Process stern commences : silence deep,
And dreadful expectation sits on all.
Each hidden fraud, each word, and thought impure,
Each overt violence, or slander dark,
From out th' omniscient registers produc'd,
Blaze in the view of Angels, and a World.
The heart now bar'd before its Maker's eye,
Evolv'd its mazes, and its filth expos'd,
How loath'd a spectacle the Villain stands !
The Virtuous look with horror down to see
Now first in genuine colours Vice appear,
And shudder at deformity so foul.
Conscience incessant plies her scorpion-whip,

And

And makes th' abominable mifcreants add
Self-accufation to their charge, and own
God's Juftice in the rigour of his Wrath.

    And now the Judge with vifage all inflam'd,
At which the molten mountains fhrink like wax,
With voice that fhakes the pillar'd firmament,
The dire award pronounces : " Go, Ye Curs'd,
" To fire, as everlafting as your fouls,
" For Satan, and his impious Hoft, prepar'd."
Strait from the inmoft center of the earth
Flames burft in fpiring eddies to the fkies :
Trembles the ground convuls'd, feas boiling roar,
And dafh yon crackling canopy with foam.
Creation finks beneath th' enormous blaze.
Myriads now burning, with th' Archangel's Trump,
The growling thunder of th' expiring Heavens,
And with a falling World's tremendous groan
Mingle their hideous yell ; and vainly wifh
They, like thofe Elements, could be no more.

    His Equal Ways illuftrioufly reveal'd
In Vice's torments, and in Virtue's blifs,
Th' Almighty rifes from his throne, and wings
To heavenly Zion his triumphal car.
Th' Angelic Hierarchy with loud acclaim

Accompany

Accompany their King ; with warbled Hymns
The ranfom'd Saints their bleft Redeemer greet.
Unnumber'd voices in fweet concord cry :
" Hofanna to the Lamb that fits above,
" To the World's honour'd Judge ! how juft his ways !
" How Everlafting Glory crowns them all !"

ON

ON THE

GOODNESS

OF THE

SUPREME BEING.

BY

CHRISTOPHER SMART, M. A.

M DCC LV.

ON THE

GOODNESS OF THE SUPREME BEING.

ORPHEUS, for fo the Gentiles * call'd thy name,
Ifrael's fweet Pfalmift, who alone could'ft wake
Th' inanimate to motion ; who alone
The joyful hillocks, the applauding rocks,
And floods, with mufical perfwafion drew ;
Thou who to hail and fnow gav'ft voice and found,
And mad'ft the mute melodious ! — greater yet
Was thy divineft fkill, and rul'd o'er more
Than art and nature ; for thy tuneful touch
Drove trembling Satan from the heart of Saul,
And quell'd the evil Angel : — in this breaft
Some portion of thy genuine fpirit breathe,
And lift me from myfelf, each thought impure
Banifh ; each low idea raife, refine,

Enlarge,

* See this conjecture ftrongly fupported by Delany, in his Life of
David.

Enlarge, and fanctify;—fo fhall the Mufe
Above the ftars afpire, and aim to praife
Her God on earth, as he is prais'd in heaven.

Immenfe Creator! whofe all-powerful hand
Fram'd univerfal Being, and whofe eye
Saw like thyfelf, that all things form'd were good ;
Where fhall the timorous Bard thy praife begin,
Where end the pureft facrifice of fong,
And juft thankfgiving ?—The thought-kindling light,
Thy prime production, darts upon my mind
Its vivifying beams, my heart illumines,
And fills my foul with gratitude and Thee.
Hail to the chearful rays of ruddy morn,
That paint the ftreaky Eaft, and blithfome roufe
The birds, the cattle, and mankind from reft !
Hail to the frefhnefs of the early breeze,
And Iris dancing on the new-fall'n dew !
Without the aid of yonder golden globe
Loft were the garnet's luftre, loft the lily,
The tulip and auricula's fpotted pride ;
Loft were the peacock's plumage, to the fight
So pleafing in its pomp and gloffy glow.
O thrice-illuftrious ! were it not for Thee
Thofe panfies, that reclining from the bank,
View thro' th' immaculate, pellucid ftream

Their

Their portraiture in the inverted heaven,
Might as well change their triple boaft, the white,
The purple, and the gold, that far outvie
The Eaftern monarch's garb, ev'n with the dock,
Ev'n with the baleful hemlock's irkfome green.
Without thy aid, without thy gladfome beams
The tribes of woodland warblers would remain
Mute on the bending branches, nor recite
The praife of Him, who, ere he form'd their lord,
Their voices tun'd to tranfport, wing'd their flight,
And bade them call for nurture, and receive :
And lo ! they call ; the blackbird and the thrufh,
The woodlark, and the redbreaft jointly call ;
He hears and feeds their feather'd families,
He feeds his fweet muficians,—nor neglects
Th' invoking ravens in the greenwood wide :
And tho' their throats coarfe rattling hurt the ear,
They mean it all for mufic, thanks and praife
They mean, and leave ingratitude to man,—
But not to all,—for hark the organs blow
Their fwelling notes round the cathedral's dome,
And grace th' harmonious choir, celeftial feaft
To pious ears, and med'cine of the mind ;
The thrilling trebles and the manly bafe
Join in accordance meet, and with one voice
All to the facred fubject fuit their fong.

F

While

While in each breaſt ſweet Melancholy reigns
Angelically penſive, till the joy
Improves and purifies; the ſolemn ſcene
The Sun thro' ſtoried panes ſurveys with awe,
And baſhfully with-holds each bolder beam.
Here, as her home, from morn to eve frequents
The cherub Gratitude; behold her eyes!
With love and gladneſs weepingly they ſhed
Ecſtatic ſmiles; the incenſe, that her hands
Uprear, is ſweeter than the breath of May
Caught from the nectarine's bloſſom, and her voice
Is more than voice can tell; to Him ſhe ſings,
To Him who feeds, who clothes, and who adorns,
Who made, and who preſerves, whatever dwells
In air, in ſtedfaſt earth, or fickle ſea.
O He is good, He is immenſely good!
Who all things form'd, and form'd them all for man;
Who mark'd the climates, varied every zone,
Diſpenſing all his bleſſings for the beſt
In order and in beauty :—riſe, attend,
Atteſt, and praiſe, ye quarters of the world!
Bow down, ye elephants, ſubmiſſive bow
To Him, who made the mite! Tho' Aſia's pride!
Ye carry armies on your tower-crown'd backs,
And grace the turban'd tyrants, bow to Him
Who is as great, as perfect, and as good

In

In his lefs ftriking wonders, till at length
The eye's at fault, and fceks th' affifting glafs.
Approach and bring from Araby the Bleft,
The fragrant caffia, frankincenfe, and myrrh,
And meekly kneeling at the altar's foot
Lay all the tributary incenfe down.
Stoop, fable Africa, with reverence ftoop,
And from thy brow take off the painted plume ;
With golden ingots all thy camels load
T' adorn his temples, haften with thy fpear
Reverted, and thy trufty bow unftrung,
While unpurfu'd thy lions roam and roar,
And ruin'd towers, rude rocks, and caverns wide
Remurmur to the glorious, furly found.
And thou, fair Indian, whofe immenfe domain
To counterpoife the Hemifphere extends,
Hafte from the Weft, and with thy fruits and flowers,
Thy mines and med'cines, wealthy maid, attend.
More than the plenteoufnefs fo fam'd to flow
By fabling bards from Amalthea's horn
Is thine ; thine therefore be a portion due
Of thanks and praife : come with thy brilliant crown
And veft of furr ; and from thy fragrant lap
Pomegranates and the rich ananas * pour.
But chiefly thou, Europa, feat of Grace

F 2

And

* Ananas, the Indian name for pine-apples.

And Chriſtian excellence, his Goodneſs own,
Forth from ten thouſand temples pour his praiſe;
Clad in the armour of the living God
Approach, unſheath the Spirit's flaming ſword;
Faith's ſhield, Salvation's glory,—compaſs'd helm
With fortitude aſſume, and o'er your heart
Fair Truth's invulnerable breaſt-plate ſpread;
Then join the general chorus of all worlds,
And let the ſong of Charity begin
In ſtrains ſeraphic, and melodious prayer.
" O all-ſufficient, all-beneficent,
" Thou God of Goodneſs and of Glory, hear!
" Thou, who to lowlieſt minds doſt condeſcend,
" Aſſuming paſſions to enforce thy laws,
" Adopting jealouſy to prove thy love:
" Thou, who reſign'd humility uphold,
" Ev'n as the floriſt props the drooping roſe,
" But quell tyrannic pride with peerleſs power,
" Ev'n as the tempeſt rives the ſtubborn oak:
" O all-ſufficient, all-beneficent,
" Thou God of Goodneſs and of Glory, hear!
" Bleſs all mankind, and bring them in the end
" To heaven, to immortality, and THEE!"

ON

ON THE

WISDOM

OF THE

SUPREME BEING.

BY

GEORGE BALLY, M. A.

M DCC LVI.

F 3
ON

ON THE

WISDOM OF THE SUPREME BEING.

ONCE more the Muſe, with pious ardor rapt,
Spurns the dank Earth, and trembling ſoars aloft
To hymn her God, JEHOVAH Only-Wiſe.

O for a beam from th' uncreated Fount
Of Light to pierce the gloom, that hov'ring damps
The briſk etherial Particle, which longs
Unmanacled and free to trace the ſteps
Of Wiſdom, and at diſtance to adore!
O Thou, who from the ſtamm'ring lips of babes
Mak'ſt heav'nly Truths diſtill to ſhame the pride,
The letter'd pride of reaſ'ning erring Man;
Who, when the full Maturity of Time,
From endleſs ages preordain'd, arriv'd,
Did'ſt from the dregs of Ignorance elect
Promulgers of thy Knowledge, O vouchſafe
Thy gracious aid to theſe my labour'd ſtrains,

F 4

Which

Which fain would fwell the choral fymphony
Of Angels and Archangels evermore
Glowing with love intenfe, and warbling fweet
Their fongs of joy with praifes intermixt !
O let Thy Impulfe guide Me, whilft I range
Nature's wide field of Wonders, where impreft
On ev'ry atom fhines creative Skill,
And ev'ry humble fhrub proclaims a God !
Without Thy Influence fpiritlefs would flow.
Thefe Numbers, as a tinkling cymbal's found ;
And much, I ween, would Folly's babbling tongue
Profane that Wifdom, fhe prefum'd to fing.

Shall boaftful Reafon, the minuteft ray.
Beam'd from the felf-exiftent Sire of Lights,
Difdain fubjeftion, and refufe to bring
Her incenfe to the throne of God ? Inftead
Of Admiration, which His Works exaft,
Works where tranfcendent Art difplays her pow'rs,
Shall fhe, with impious triumph flufh'd, retort
Her wanton cenfure, infidel reproof ?
Say, Sceptic, can thine eye pervade the whole,
See Syftem on dependent Syftem verge,
And Caufes with Effeéts connefted all
In one unbroken chain ? Did Science ever
Lend Thee a Seraph's flamy wing to mount

Above

Above th' empyreal Sphere? There did'ft thou view
The golden Balance which the Mountains weigh'd,
Ere their afpiring foreheads pierc'd the clouds?

Proud philofophic fool! thy airy flight
Sufpend awhile, and drop into Thyfelf:
Attentive fcan the texture of thy Frame
How fearfully contriv'd! the vifual orbs
Remark, how aptly ftation'd for their tafk;
Rais'd to th' imperial Head's high citadel
A wide extended profpect to command.
See the arch'd outworks of impending Lids
With hairs, as palifadoes, fenc'd around
To ward annoyance from without. The Nofe
Its intervening wall projects, the Cheeks
Swell with a gentle eminence, to fhield
The Body's gay irradiating Beam.
Who taught the rays, refracted from the bright
Chryftalline Convex, in a central point
To join their confluent ftreams, and paint each form
Of Dedal Nature in the fund opake,
Ill copied by Apelles' happieft fkill?
Who but th' Omnifcient Architect! who bade
The univerfal Eye, th' illuftrious Sun,
From Chaos' darkfome womb his fplendors dart
T' enlighten and refrefh the new-born World.

The

The channel'd Ear with many a winding maze
How artfully perplext, to catch the found,
And from her repercuffive caves augment !

When the crude fhapelefs Mafs imprifon'd lay
In its maternal cell, what plaftic pow'r
Appropriate figure to each part affign'd,
And gave th' envelop'd Animal t' expand ?
Whofe Nod controll'd the work abftrufe, infus'd
All-quick'ning vigour, and each motion fway'd ?
Who in the dark the vital flame illum'd,
And from th' impulfive engine caus'd to flow
Th' ejaculated ftreams through many a pipe
Arterial with meandring lapfe, then bring
Refluent their purple tribute to their Fount ?
Who fpun the finews' branchy thread, and twin'd
The azure veins in fpiral knots to waft
Life's tepid waves all o'er ; or Who with bones
Compacted, and with nerves the Fabric ftrung ?
Their fpecious form, their fitnefs, which refults
From figure and arrangement, all declare
Th' Artificer divine. —— 'Twas Thou, O Lord,
Who in the deep recefs did'ft mould the clay
Obfequious to thy will ; the procefs dark
Thou faw'ft, and Nought efcap'd thy piercing Eye.
Ere yet I was, in thy eternal Rolls

Each

Each bone was written, and each fibrous chord,
All-perfect Models of my future Frame.

And yet shall Man, who bears a World inclos'd
Of Wonders in Himself, though on his mind
Conviction flashes like a flood of Day,
In voluntary gloom benighted sit ?
With intellectual faculties endow'd,
Stamp'd on thy soul Thy Maker's signature,
In this magnific sky-roof'd Temple plac'd
High-Priest of Nature, to return to Heav'n
Due Incense, and articulate the praise
Of thy mute vassals, dar'st Thou, Wretch ingrate,
The Gift accept, the Giver leave unthank'd ?
See feeble Instinct with unvaried aim
Guide thy brute subjects to their Being's end,
Reproach to Reason's over-weening pride !
Their task enjoin'd they chearfully perform,
And laud the best they can their bounteous God.
With deep-ton'd praises roars the Wildernefs,
The Groves with Melody refound ; All Nature
Upbraids the thankless silence of her Lord,
Rebel to Him, whose delegate he reigns.

How fightless foars Philofophy, whene'er
She quits the beaten track that Nature points,

And

And Reafon, yet with prejudice unting'd ;
When impious fhe affumes creative pow'r,
And builds a World without an Architect !
In vain does Epicurus, borne aloft
Beyond the flaming barriers of our fphere
Into th' illimitable Void, command
His marfhal'd atoms, and direct their flight.
Whatever courfe he gives them, ftraight, oblique,
They never could, though ages they had fped
Their fwift career, have met in Space immenfe,
And each concurring with his like coher'd.

    Illufive Dreams, and ravings of a Brain
Unpurg'd with Ellebore ! to think that fmall
Unguided particles, at random floating
Through fhorelefs feas of Emptinefs diffus'd,
Could haply clafh, and flide into an orb !
Say, Grecian Dotard, did thy idol Chance,
Of Worlds expert Artificer, e'er bid
A fudden palace deck the wond'ring wafte ;
Did ftones and timber, trooping to her call,
Leap to a finifh'd pile, and ftand felf-rang'd ?

    When firft thy atoms with a ceafelefs fhow'r
Rufh'd from th' Expanfe tumultuous, fay what Mounds,
Rais'd in the thin vacuity t' arreft

Their

Their progrefs, check'd them in midway, and made
Them fettle to a Mafs? Could they unknowing
Determine where to fix, and there in fpite
Of Gravity's accelerating force,
Lull'd in the Air's foft ambient bofom reft?
What counteracted Nature's gen'ral laws,
And gave th' inflected bias? Did they call
A Council ere they fally'd from the goal,
And for each troop a rendezvous appoint?
Here Reafon fails You, and your wife reply
Amounts to nothing more than fo it chanc'd
That this our Planet with th' unnumber'd Orbs,
Which perfect the ftupendous artful Whole,
After repeated conflicts, and a war
Of thwarting particles, their ftrife compos'd,
Did ruffled into Harmony fubfide.

That philofophic tow'r, from whence You boaft
To look all Nature through, and pity Man
Bewilder'd in the mazy vale below,
Shook with each flight interrogation nods:
And, when the ftorm of Argument affaults,
The treach'rous bafis finks, and down it falls.

Duration's bounds Stagira's bolder Sage
O'erleaps, and lefs'ning to the view a World

Amidft

Amidſt Eternity's vaſt trackleſs wilds
Explores.   But what ſuccefs, what glorious meed
Rewards th' adventure ? Merits He for this
The Realms of Science with deſpotic ſway
'To govern, and his tyranny uſurp'd
Deep in our vaſſal intellects to found ?
Let this high-vaulting Genius from his flight
Tranſcendent ſtoop, and to enquiring Senſe
A ſober anſwer give, why, if for ever
'Things in the ſame unvaried tenor flow'd,
If Battles from eternity were fought,
And Polities in endleſs ſeries plann'd,
No direful tumults ſwell'd th' Aonian Trump
Before the war of Thebes, or ſiege of Troy :
Why from no higher ſpring hiſtoric Truth
Rolls down through ages her memorial ſtores :
Why Arts ſlow-rip'ning in the womb of Time
So late attain'd their growth : why from the Eaſt
But yeſterday her orient beam diſplay'd
Emerging Science, and with Heav'n's bright Lamp
In radiant progreſs journey'd to the Weſt.
Did one eternal torpor chill the brain
Of infinite ſucceſſions ? Unalert
Was Nature, nor yet ſtrong enough to form
An Ariſtotle's all-pervading Mind ?

In

In vain your routed clan of Vot'ries fly
To Deluges.   For where embofom'd fleeps
Sufficient mafs of Moifture to diffolve
The Globe, and from its faded place to blot
Each faithful Monument ? If this exceeds
Nature's weak pow'rs, they'll ceafe to roufe at will
The Waters from their bed, left unawares
They conjure up an Agent they difclaim.
If Nature can atchieve the feat, Ye Wits
Illumin'd, fay, why in a round immenfe
Of unbeginning Years it always chanc'd
That indifcriminating Floods fhould fpare
A chofen Few, to ftock the defert World :
Why, when the Deep its riven jaws difclos'd,
And Defolation o'er the proftrate Ball
Wide-wafting fwept along, not All Mankind
Once in the oft repeated Wrecks was loft,
And Your Eternal Race expung'd for ever.

If Particles obnoxious to decay
The univerfal Frame compofe, amidft
The ceafelefs ravage of unmeafur'd Years
Earth on her Axis had no longer mov'd
Vertiginous, long fince a mould'ring heap
Of Duft : the Sun, fo prodigal of light,
His golden urn exhaufted whence the Stars

Imbibe

Imbibe their gleam, had ſpent his lateſt ray,
And ſcatter'd in looſe atoms roam'd the Void.

　　Thus with Sifyphian toil miſguided Wit
The ſtone reluctant up the ſteep high Cliff
Urges : with violent recoil the Maſs
Ruſhes precipitous, and mocks their pains.
Though Mountain pil'd on Mountain threat'ning ſtands,
Confuſion follows, and their Babel drops.
Philoſophy's but Folly in diſguiſe,
A glitt'ring Ignorance, a fev'riſh Dream,
Unleſs from Earth, the Footſtool of her God,
She leads like Jacob's Ladder to His Throne.

　　To trace the Wiſdom of th' all-knowing Mind
In the World's ample Volume to our view
In ſhining characters diſplay'd, to glow,
Like Seraphs, as we turn th' amazing page,
And magnify the glorious Author's name,
This, This is to be Wiſe beyond the School
Of Epicurus, or Lyceum fam'd.

　　What human tongue can worthily record
The treaſures of Eternal Intellect,
The Fair archetypal, whence beams deriv'd
Each Good delectable, each beauteous Form,

That

That Nature's fpacious Theatre adorns ?
How fhall fublim'd Imagination dart
Into th' unlimited circumfluous deep
Of Chaos drear and dark, there fee Heav'n's King
Borne on Cherubic Wings enounce the Word
Omnific ? Wild Uproar hears, and is ftill,
And Circumfcription checks Infinity !

How all-accomplifh'd Sapience blaz'd abroad
Confpicuous in each grand proportion'd Work,
When the Divine Geometrician ftretch'd
Th' immeafurable level through the Void,
And to the canton Syftem bounds ordain'd !
What Hand could fcoop the Sea's capacious bed,
But His, who grafp'd the Waters in his palm ?
Who could expand the Curtains of the Sky,
And tinge with Blufh of Day their gorgeous Skirts,
But the ineffable I AM, who reigns
In fplendor unapproachable enfhrin'd ?
What placid fmiles of fweet complacency
In the Creator's radiant afpect fhone,
When He furvey'd his Workmanfhip, and faw
Utility and Grace diffus'd throughout !
With admiration rapt of Heav'nly Skill
The Sons of Phofphor hail'd the dawning World
With fhouts triumphant ; every harp was tun'd

GAngelic

Angelic to His praise, who Order call'd
From tumult, and from Nothing All educ'd.

    Where'er We turn our eyes, above, below,
The Deity confronts Us, and reveal'd
Flames in each Bush, and sparkles in each Star.
Where could the Platform of this complex Frame,
But in th' Eternal Mind's abyss, exist?
What but a Wise Omnipotence the Plan
Illustrious could so splendidly complete?

    The Sun, when with a vig'rous Bridegroom's heat
He sallies from the chambers of the East,
His Maker in his silent course proclaims.
Look up, vain Sceptic, and derive a ray
Thence to thy darken'd Soul; yon glorious Orb
Perpend, the Persian's Mithras, who ascrib'd
Th' emaning Good, by Providence devis'd
Omniscient, to th' unconscious Instrument,
Absorpt his Senses in the dazzling Beam.
Thou more sagacious hence infer a God,
Who launch'd in Air the Planet, and prescrib'd
An Orbit to His Ends benign most fit.
See! at due distance from Our Globe dispos'd
With warmth attemper'd to her Womb he chears
Th' all-fruitful Mother, and each Birth matures.

                                        Had

Had he, where sluggish Saturn rolls, been plac'd,
What defolation had deform'd this fcene
Now fo profufe of ev'ry boon ! Undeck'd
With mantling Grafs her lap, defpoil'd her meads
Of laughing harvefts, Earth had ftood untrod
By Man or Beaft, an icy Wildernefs.
If nearer he had wheel'd his flamy car,
His torrid rays had cleft the folid Rocks,
Exhal'd the Lakes, and drain'd the briny Deep.
The molten furface had to afhes turn'd,
Or whirl'd in eddying fands obfcur'd the Sky.

See ! how declining from the way direct
He winds obliquely through th' Ecliptic road
His courfe unwearied.　Hence the Seafons rife,
And glad with fweet viciffitude the Year,
Could Chance atchieve thefe Wonders, and imprefs
Such conftant movements that, fince Time began
His meafur'd race, not once the Sire of Day
Should ftart forgetful from the track, and bring
Chill Winter into Summer's flow'ry reign ?
Or where fuch Counfel, fuch Defign are feen,
Muft We not call an All-directing Mind
To folve th' amazing Knot ? Th' Opificer
All-pow'rful and All-wife alone could frame
For Ufes multiform an Orb, without

G 2

Whofe

Whose vital beams All Nature would expire,
And Darkness be the Burier of the Dead.
He the projected Motion gave : His Arm,
Unshorten'd still, restricts the rapid whirl
Of Planets to their Centre, and with Chains
Of Gravity and firm Cohesion binds
Each struggling atom, which would else unhing'd
Fly off, and ruin scatter through the Void.

Who sees a Sphere, where mimic Wit displays
The site, the number, and the size of All
Yon rolling Worlds, and how in figur'd dance
They glide harmonious, at first glance assents
That Reason sway'd the cunning Artist's hand.
Yet when he sees the wond'rous Archetype,
The Heav'ns themselves, with swift rotation urg'd,
Invariably each grateful Change revolve
Conducive to the Welfare of the Whole,
Doubts he that this by Reason is perform'd,
By Reason All-surpassing and Divine ?

Though Man were silent, th' azure Firmament,
The Moon, and all the glitt'ring Host of Stars,
Fix'd and erratic, would with one accord
Blazon Almighty Wisdom, and declare
The Marvels of His Finger, who, for ends

Subservient

Subfervient to His Glory and Our Good,
Bade their gay Splendors gild the brow of Night.

If to this lower Planet we advert,
Seat of our Birth and Nurture, proofs abound
Of infinite Contrivance, matchlefs Skill.
Whether the fite or figure we regard,
Or diftribution of the various parts
Perfective of the Syftem, Strokes appear
Too exquifite for bungling Chance to hit
With erring implements.   A Mind alone,
Where Models of Perfection treafur'd lay
From All Eternity, could call the fair
Exemplar into being when it will'd.

A form orbicular how fit to weigh
The golden gift of Light and Heat to all
The fcatter'd diftricts with impartial fcale !
Hence too the Waters, thofe meandring veins
O'er the Earth's body interfpers'd, with juft
Partition flow falubrious.   To the Winds,
Balmy refiners of the winnow'd Air,
This moft commodious Figure yields a pafs
Free, unobftructed.   Had another fhape
Been giv'n, impeding Angles had oppos'd

G 3

The

The breezy Currents, and Mankind had droop'd
Sickly and faint from th' intercepted Gale.

What made the humid Particles recede
From the dry land, and wear a furrow'd bed
Capacious of their ſtreams? Could aught but Art
The blended Maſs ſo ſkilfully disjoin?
Thou, Thou alone, with whom enthron'd on high
Sits coeſſential Wiſdom, bad'ſt ſubſide
The Vallies, and the Mountains from amidſt
Th' o'erwhelming moiſture heave their brow ſublime.
The liquid troops, obedient to Thy Voice,
Fled to th' appointed ſtation. Thou a bound
Haſt ſet they cannot paſs; nor ever ſpread
Their flowing Mantle o'er th' inveſted Earth:
Thou to the Sea ſay'ſt, Hitherto advance,
And here thy proud licentious waves be ſtay'd.
In various ducts, as Thou ordain'ſt, diſperſt
The Globe-encircling Waters draw their train,
And health and vigour as they glide impart.

Yet here raſh Man Thy Counſels dares implead,
And blames the vaſt diffuſion of the Deep
As uſeleſs and deform. He thinks that thrift
In dealing out the Treaſures of th' Abyſs,
And a more lib'ral dole of needful Land,

Had

Had spoke a wife Difpenfer of his ftores.
Vainly he cries, " Half th' Ocean might be fpar'd,
" Superfluous Wafte ! and added to domains
" Too ftrait for Man, who, by continual wars
" T' inlarge his frontier, feems to breathe but ill,
" As in a Prifon's narrow limits pent."

Blufh, futile Caviller, who Nature's Lord
Arraign'ft, unread in Nature's myftic lore.
For know that Vapours on their dufky wings
In due proportion to the Surface rife
Sublim'd.   Had then thy frugal fcheme prevail'd,
And the fhrunk Ocean flow'd with leffen'd wave,
Inftead of plenteous ftreams which now refrefh
Earth's faturated womb, but few had roll'd
Their fcanty fluid o'er the thirfty glebe :
Eve had not fhed profufe her trickling balm,
Nor Clouds dropt fatnefs on the labour'd field.

Thus in the nat'ral as the moral World
The ftricteft fcrutiny but ferves t' unveil
New Riches in the deep exhauftlefs Mine
Of heav'nly Wifdom : What is beft, the ftamp
Of Deity, occurs in ev'ry work.
His Providence the floating vaft Machine
Steers with unerring hand.   Hence 'midft the flight

G 4

Of

Of Ages ne'er one jarring atom broke
The nice adjuftment of confpiring parts,
Or clogg'd the motion of the fmalleft wheel.

   Sceptic, no more the dazzling beams withftand,
Bright emanations of a fapient God,
But, taught by Nature, Nature's Lord adore:
From known Effects of Order and Defign
Rife to the felf-exiftent Caufe Supreme:
The Depths of Wifdom, far as human Ken
Can penetrate, explore; and here attain
A foretafte of that Knowledge, which perhaps,
With Angels poring o'er the Text abftrufe,
And in ecftatic admiration loft,
Will in Eternity's unceafing round
The intuition of thy Soul abforb,

ON

* ～～～～～～～～～ *

THE

DAY of JUDGMENT.

BY

R. GLYNN, M. D.

M DCC LVII.

* ～～～～～～～～～ *

THE
DAY OF JUDGMENT.

T HY Juſtice, heav'nly King ! and that great Day,
When Virtue, long abandon'd and forlorn,
Shall raiſe her penſive head ; and Vice, that erſt
Rang'd unreprov'd and free, ſhall ſink appall'd ;
I ſing advent'rous.——But what eye can pierce
The vaſt immeaſurable realms of Space,
O'er which Meſſiah drives His flaming car
To that bright region, where enthron'd He ſits
Firſt-born of Heav'n to judge aſſembled worlds,
Cloath'd in cœleſtial radiance ! Can the Muſe,
Her feeble wing all damp with earthly dew,
Soar to that bright Empyreal, where around
Myriads of Angels God's perpetual choir
Hymn Hallelujahs ; and in concert loud
Chaunt ſongs of triumph to their Maker's praiſe ?——
Yet will I ſtrive to ſing, albeit unus'd

To

To tread Poetic Soil.   What though the wiles
Of Fancy me enchanted ne'er could lure
To rove o'er Fairy lands ; to fwim the ftreams
That through her vallies weave their mazy way ;
Or climb her mountain tops ; yet will I raife
My feeble voice, to tell what Harmony
(Sweet as the mufic of the rolling Spheres)
Attunes the moral world : That Virtue ftill
May hope her promis'd crown ; that Vice may dread
Vengeance, though late ; that reas'ning Pride may own
Juft though unfearchable the ways of Heaven.

Sceptic ! whoe'er thou art, who fay'ft the foul,
That divine particle which God's own breath
Infpir'd into the mortal mafs, fhall reft
Annihilate, 'till Duration has unroll'd
Her never-ending line ; tell, if thou know'ft,
Why every nation, every clime, though all
In Laws, in Rites, in Manners difagree,
With one confent expect another world,
Where Wickednefs fhall weep ? Why Paynim Bards
Fabled Elyfian plains, Tartarean Lakes,
Styx and Cocytus ? Tell, why Hali's fons
Have feign'd a Paradife of Mirth and Love,
Banquets, and blooming Nymphs ? Or rather tell,
Why, on the brink of Orellana's ftream,

Where

Where never Science rear'd her facred Torch,
Th' untutor'd Indian dreams of happier worlds
Behind the cloud-topt Hill ? Why in each breaft
Is plac'd a friendly monitor, that prompts,
Informs, directs, encourages, forbids ?
Tell, why on unknown evil grief attends ;
Or joy on fecret good ? Why Confcience acts
With tenfold force, when Sicknefs, Age, or Pain
Stands tott'ring on the precipice of Death ?
Or why fuch Horror gnaws the guilty foul
Of dying Sinners ; while the Good Man fleeps
Peaceful and calm, and with a fmile expires ?

Look round the world ! with what a partial hand
The fcale of Blifs and Mifery is fuftain'd !
Beneath the fhade of cold obfcurity
Pale Virtue lies ; no arm fupports her head,
No friendly voice fpeaks comfort to her foul,
Nor foft-ey'd Pity drops a melting tear ;
But, in their ftead, Contempt and rude Difdain
Infult the banifh'd Wanderer : on fhe goes
Neglected and forlorn : Difeafe, and Cold,
And Famine, worft of Ills, her fteps attend :
Yet patient, and to Heav'n's juft will refign'd,
She ne'er is feen to weep, or heard to figh.

Now turn your eyes to yon fweet-fmelling Bow'r,
Where flufh'd with all the infolence of wealth
Sits pamper'd Vice! For him th' Arabian Gale
Breathes forth delicious odours; Gallia's Hills
For him pour Nectar from the purple vine.
Nor think for thefe he pays the tribute due
To Heav'n: of Heav'n he never names the name;
Save when with imprecations dark and dire
He points his Jeft obfcene.   Yet buxom Health
Sits on his rofy cheek; yet Honour gilds
His high exploits; and downy-pinion'd Sleep
Sheds a foft opiate o'er his peaceful couch.

See'ft thou this, righteous Father! See'ft thou this,
And wilt thou ne'er repay? Shall Good and Ill
Be carried undiftinguifh'd to the Land
Where all things are forgot?—— Ah! no; the Day
Will come, when Virtue from the cloud fhall burft
That long obfcur'd her Beams; when Sin fhall fly
Back to her native Hell; there fink eclips'd
In penal Darknefs; where nor Star fhall rife,
Nor ever Sunfhine pierce th' impervious gloom.

On that great Day the folemn Trump fhall found,
(That Trump which once in Heaven on Man's revolt
Convok'd th' aftonifh'd Seraphs) at whofe voice

Th' un-

Th' unpeopled Graves shall pour forth all their Dead,
Then shall th' assembled nations of the Earth
From ev'ry Quarter at the Judgment-Seat
Unite ; Egyptians, Babylonians, Greeks,
Parthians ; and they who dwelt on Tyber's banks,
Names fam'd of old : or who of later age,
Chinese and Russian, Mexican and Turk,
Tenant the wide Terrene ; and they who pitch
Their tents on Niger's banks ; or where the Sun
Pours on Golconda's Spires his early light
Drink Ganges' sacred stream.   At once shall rise
Whom distant ages to each others sight
Had long denied : Before the Throne shall kneel
Some great Progenitor, while at his side
Stands his Descendant through a thousand Lines.
Whate'er their nation, and whate'er their rank,
Heroes and Patriarchs, Slaves and sceptred Kings,
With equal eye the God of All shall see ;
And judge with equal love.   What though the Great
With costly pomp and aromatic sweets
Embalm'd his poor remains ; or through the Dome
A thousand tapers shed their gloomy light,
While solemn organs to his parting soul
Chaunted slow orisons ? Say, by what mark
Dost thou discern him from that lowly Swain
Whose mouldering bones beneath the thorn-bound turf

Long

Long lay neglected ?——All at once shall rise ;
But not to equal glory : for, alas !
With howlings dire and execrations loud
Some wail their fatal birth.——First among these
Behold the mighty murth'rers of mankind ;
They who in sport whole kingdoms slew ; or they
Who to the tott'ring pinnacle of power
Waded through seas of blood ! How will they curse
The madness of ambition ; How lament
Their dear-bought Laurels ; when the widow'd wife
And childless mother at the Judgment-Seat
Plead trumpet-tongu'd against them !——Here are they
Who sunk an aged Father to the Grave ;
Or with unkindness hard and cold disdain
Slighted a Brother's suff'rings.——Here are they
Whom Fraud and skilful Treachery long secur'd ;
Who from the infant Virgin tore her dow'r,
And eat the Orphan's bread :——who spent their stores
In selfish Luxury ; or o'er their gold
Prostrate and pale ador'd the useless heap.——
Here too who stain'd the chaste connubial Bed ;——
Who mix'd the pois'nous bowl ;——or broke the ties
Of hospitable Friendship :——And the Wretch
Whose listless soul sick with the cares of life
Unsummon'd to the presence of his God
Rush'd in with insult rude.   How would they joy

Once

Once more to vifit earth ; and, though opprefs'd
With all that Pain or Famine can inflict,
Pant up the Hill of Life ? Vain wifh ! the Judge
Pronounces doom eternal on their heads,
Perpetual punifhment.   Seek not to know
What punifhment ! for that th' Almighty Will
Has hid from mortal eyes : And fhall vain Man
With curious fearch refin'd prefume to pry
Into thy fecrets, Father ! No : let him
With humble patience all thy works adore,
And walk in all thy paths : fo fhall his meed
Be great in Heav'n, fo haply fhall he 'fcape
Th' immortal Worm and never-ceafing Fire.

But who are they, who bound in ten-fold chains
Stand horribly aghaft ? This is that Crew
Who ftrove to pull Jehovah from His throne,
And in the place of Heav'n's eternal King
Set up the Phantom Chance.   For them in vain
Alternate feafons chear'd the rolling year ;
In vain the Sun o'er Herb, Tree, Fruit, and Flow'r
Shed genial influence, mild ; and the pale Moon
Repair'd her waning orb.——Next thefe is plac'd
The vile Blafphemer, He, whofe impious Wit
Profan'd the facred Myfteries of Faith,
And 'gainft th' impenetrable walls of Heav'n

H

Planted

Planted his feeble battery.   By thefe ftands
The arch-Apoftate : He with many a wile
Exhorts them ftill to foul revolt.   Alas !
No hope have they from black Defpair, no ray
Shines through the gloom to chear their finking fouls ;
In agonies of grief they curfe the hour
When firft they left Religion's onward way.

    Thefe on the left are rang'd : But on the right
A chofen Band appears, who fought beneath
The Banner of Jehovah, and defy'd
Satan's united Legions.   Some, unmov'd
At the grim tyrant's frown, o'er barb'rous climes
Diffus'd the Gofpel's Light ; fome, long immur'd,
(Sad fervitude !) in chains and dungeons pin'd ;
Or rack'd with all the agonies of pain
Breath'd out their faithful lives.   Thrice happy They
Whom Heaven elected to that glorious ftrife !——
Here are they plac'd, whofe kind munificence
Made heav'n-born Science raife her drooping head ;
And on the labours of a future Race
Entail'd their juft reward.   Thou amongft Thefe,
Good SEATON ! whofe well-judg'd benevolence
Foft'ring fair Genius bade the Poet's hand
Bring annual off'rings to his Maker's fhrine,
Shalt find the generous care was not in vain.——

Here

Here is that fav'rite Band, whom mercy mild
God's beft lov'd Attribute adorn'd ; whofe gate
Stood ever open to the Stranger's call ;
Who fed the Hungry ; to the Thirfty lip
Reach'd out the friendly cup ; whofe care benign
From the rude blaft fecur'd the Pilgrim's fide ;
Who heard the Widow's tender tale ; and fhook
The galling fhackle from the Prifoner's feet ;
Who each endearing tye, each office knew
Of meek-ey'd heav'n-defcended Charity.——
O Charity, thou Nymph divinely fair !
Sweeter than thofe whom ancient Poets bound
In Amity's indiffoluble chain,
The Graces ! How fhall I effay to paint
Thy charms, celeftial Maid ; and in rude verfe
Blazon thofe deeds thyfelf did'ft ne'er reveal ?
For Thee nor rankling Envy can infect,
Nor Rage tranfport, nor high o'erweening Pride
Puff up with vain conceit : ne'er didft thou fmile
To fee the Sinner as a verdant Tree
Spread his luxuriant branches o'er the ftream ;
While like fome blafted Trunk the Righteous fall,
Proftrate, forlorn.   When Prophecies fhall fail,
When Tongues fhall ceafe, when Knowledge is no more,
And this Great Day is come ; Thou by the Throne
Shalt fit triumphant.   Thither, lovely Maid,

Bear

Bear me, O bear me on thy foaring wing,
And through the Adamantine Gates of Heav'n
Conduct my Steps, fafe from the fiery Gulph
And dark Abyfs where Sin and Satan reign !

But can the Mufe, her numbers all too weak,
Tell how that reftlefs Element of Fire
Shall wage with Seas and Earth inteftine war,
And deluge all Creation ? Whether (fo
Some think) the Comet, as through fields of air
Lawlefs he wanders, fhall rufh headlong on,
Thwarting th' Ecliptic where th' unconfcious Earth
Rolls in her wonted courfe ; whether the Sun
With force centripetal into his orb
Attract her long reluctant ; or the Caves,
Thofe dread Vulcanos where engend'ring lye
Sulphureous Minerals, from their dark Abyfs
Pour ftreams of liquid fire ; while from above,
As erft on Sodom, Heav'n's avenging Hand
Rains fierce combuftion.——Where are now the works
Of Art, the Toil of Ages ?——Where are now
Th' Imperial Cities, Sepulchres and Domes,
Trophies and Pillars ?——Where is Egypt's boaft,
Thofe lofty Pyramids which high in air
Rear'd their afpiring Heads, to diftant times
Of Memphian Pride a lafting monument ?——

Tell

'Tell me where Athens rais'd her Towers ?—Where Thebes
Open'd her Hundred Portals ?—Tell me where
Stood fea-girt Albion ?—Where Imperial Rome
Propt by Seven Hills fat like a fceptred Queen,
And aw'd the tributary world to peace ?—
Shew me the Rampart, which o'er many a hill,
Through many a valley ftretch'd its wide extent,
Rais'd by that mighty Monarch, to repel
The roving Tartar, when with infult rude
'Gainft Pekin's tow'rs he bent th' unerring Bow.

But what is mimic Art ? Even Nature's works,
Seas, Meadows, Paftures, the meand'ring Streams,
And everlafting Hills fhall be no more.
No more fhall Teneriff cloud-piercing height
O'er-hang th' Atlantic Surge.—Nor that fam'd Cliff,
Through which the Perfian fteer'd with many a fail,
Throw to the Lemnian Ifle its evening fhade
O'er half the wide Ægæan.—Where are now
The Alps that confin'd with unnumber'd realms,
And from the Black Sea to the Ocean ftream
Stretch'd their extended arms ?—Where's Ararat,
That Hill on which the faithful Patriarch's Ark
Which feven long months had voyag'd o'er its top
Firft refted, when the Earth with all her Sons,
As now by ftreaming cataracts of fire,

H 3

Was

Was whelm'd by mighty waters?——All at once
Are vanish'd and diffolv'd; no trace remains,
No mark of vain diftinction: Heaven itfelf,
That azure vault with all thofe radiant orbs,
Sinks in the univerfal ruin loft.——
No more fhall Planets round their central Sun
Move in harmonious dance; no more the Moon
Hang out her Silver Lamp; and thofe Fix'd Stars
Spangling the golden canopy of night,
Which oft the Tufcan with his optic glafs
Call'd from their wond'rous height, to read their names
And magnitude, fome winged minifter
Shall quench; and (fureft fign that all on earth
Is loft) fhall rend from Heaven the myftic Bow.

Such is that awful, that tremendous Day,
Whofe Coming who fhall tell? For as a Thief
Unheard, unfeen, it fteals with filent pace
Through Night's dark gloom.——Perhaps as here I fit,
And rudely carol thefe incondite Lays,
Soon fhall the Hand be check'd, and dumb the Mouth
That lifps the fault'ring ftrain.——O! may it ne'er
Intrude unwelcome on an ill-fpent hour;
But find me wrapt in meditations high,
Hymning my great Creator!

" Power

                " Power fupreme !
" O everlafting King ! to Thee I kneel,
" To Thee I lift my voice.   With fervent heat
" Melt all ye Elements ! And Thou, high Heav'n,
" Shrink like a fhrivel'd Scroll ! But think, O Lord,
" Think on the beft, the nobleft of thy works ;
" Think on thine own bright Image ! Think on Him,
" Who dy'd to fave us from thy righteous wrath ;
" And 'midft the wreck of Worlds remember Man !"

H 4

THE

THE
PROVIDENCE
OF THE
SUPREME BEING.

BY

GEORGE BALLY, M. A.

M DCC LVIII.

THE

PROVIDENCE

OF THE

SUPREME BEING.

BY

GEORGE ELLIS, M.A.

M.DCC.LXIII.

THE

PROVIDENCE OF THE SUPREME BEING.

SOVEREIGN of Nature, Omniprefent King,
Effential Goodnefs ! Thou, whofe plaftic Word
Call'd from the womb of Darknefs into day
This beauteous Syftem, which, if Thou withdraw'ft
Thy ftaying hand, would inftantly relapfe
Into primeval Nothing ! Who fhall dare
To circumfcribe thy Centre, that extends
Far as Creation's ampleft range ; or fet
Bounds to thy Providence, that clafps at once
In its parental all-incircling arm
The tow'ring Seraph, and the grov'ling Worm ?
Each link, that weaves the univerfal chain
Of Order, and connects th' amazing plan,
Is faften'd to the footftool of thy throne.
All Caufes, in thy Intellect compriz'd,
Obvious as light that fills th' uncrowded eye,
Rank'd in their feries ftand, and wait thy nod

To

To iſſue into action, and atchïeve
Eternal counſels.   Wiſdom infinite
Sits at the helm preſiding, and directs
Each ſev'ral movement to the purpos'd end.
Thou giv'ſt the vegetable tribe to draw
Its kindly nutriment.   Th' inliv'ning ſap,
Obedient to thy Laws, through fitted tubes
Aſcends fermenting, and at length matur'd
Breaks forth in gems, and germinates in leaves.
By Thee each Family of flow'rs is cloth'd
In one unvarying dreſs, and breathes the ſame
Tranſmitted eſſences ; and, though the loom
No virgin fingers ply to ſwell her pride,
The lily ſhines more gorgeouſly array'd
Than monarchs, where the Eaſt with hand profuſe
Show'rs on their pomp barbaric pearl and gold.
O'er all thy works, exuberance of love,
Thy care unweary'd watches.   Hence conſerv'd
Each kind, each being, and each want ſupply'd.
To Thee the tenant of the paſture lifts
His aſking eye : to Thee with ſuppliant voice
The ſhaggy tyrant of the wilderneſs
Roars his petition, as he roams the waſte
Intent on prey.   Thou, common Father, op'ſt
Th' exhauſtleſs treaſures of thy bounty : All
Are fill'd, and ev'ry heart with joy rebounds.

Yet

Yet are there found of Man's imperial race,
So favour'd, and by reafon high advanc'd,
(That ray infus'd to light him to his God)
Who, rebels to their Maker, fpurn his rule,
And impious dare in narrow fpace include
Infinity itfelf.   In Heav'n, fome fay
Blafpheming, fits in majefty fupine
Th' Eternal King, and flumb'ring on his throne,
From Earth, and all its cares alike remov'd,
A liftlefs dull beatitude enjoys.
Conceit abfurd! yet fuited to the foil
Of Epicurus' garden, rank with weeds
That kill Religion's root.   No bufy God
His blind unguided atoms muft controul,
But Chance muft build his World, and govern too.
That fcheme of Happinefs, he frames for Man,
Muft, as he doats, to Deity extend ;
Whofe Blifs would be impair'd, if reftlefs thought,
And Nature's vaft moliminous concerns
Should violate the Sabbath of his reft.
Philofophizing fool, who ne'er couldft fhake
The cumbrous load of matter from thy foul,
And pierce thofe regions, where One fovereign Mind,
One pure diffufive Energy at eafe
By fole volition acts his purpofes
Through the wide realms of Being ! He to all,

Centre

Centre without circumference, is nigh,
Is intimately prefent : nought eludes
His Knowledge ; nought impedes his mighty Pow'r,

   If the World floats by ev'ry cafual blaft
Driv'n to and fro, without a pilot-hand
To regulate its courfe, fay, why do all
Hearken to Laws appropriate to their kind ?
Why never ftray the devious Orbs, but keep
Their ftations, and with fteady pace repeat
Their periodic journies ? Whence to Plants
Peculiar feeds allotted, and a leaf
That marks their lineage ? Or how taught by turns
To flourifh, and diverfify the year ?
Whence is each particle of matter fway'd
Or to attract its neighbour or repel ?
In Brutes to individuals whence affign'd
With rule precife the fame organic make,
As beft the functions of their kind promotes ?
Why prompted all to propagate their breed,
To fhun the noxious, feek the wholefome food ?
This fettled Order through the whole diffus'd,
Thefe Laws invariably purfu'd, proclaim
As with a trumpet's found a Pow'r unfeen,
Who fits not idle on th' empyreal fphere,
Wrapt up in contemplation of Himfelf

Through

Through endlefs ages, but who all furveys
In Space, his boundlefs fenfory, and fills
Earth with his Goodnefs, with his Glory Heaven.

And yet fhall Man, as fhipwreck'd from the womb
On the World's bleak inhofpitable coaft,
As by his Maker carelefsly expos'd,
Bewail his orphan lot, and cry that God
Regardlefs of his welfare flights his pray'rs ?
Shall not a Sparrow fall without his will,
Shall not a Raven croak in vain ; yet Man,
Heir of Eternity, Creation's pride,
Be left to wander in the maze of Life
Without a Guide, a Father, and a Friend ?
How fhall he 'fcape th' embattel'd ills that war
Againft his foul, th' unnumber'd fhafts that fly
Wing'd with deftruction, if no hand unfeen
Invefts him with a fhield, and guards his fteps ?

But Man (ingenious to contrive his woe,
And rob himfelf of all that makes this vale
Of tears bloom comfort) cries, If God forefees
Our future actings, then the objects known
Muft be determin'd, or the knowledge fail :
Thus Liberty's deftroy'd, and all we do
Or fuffer, by a fatal thread is fpun.

Say,

Say, fool, with too much fubtilty mifled,
Who reafon'ft but to err, does Prefcience change
The property of things ? Is aught thou fee'ft
Caus'd by thy vifion, not thy vifion caus'd
By forms that previoufly exift ? To God
This mode of feeing future deeds extend,
And Freedom with Foreknowledge may fubfift.

    Nor think that ev'ry moment Nature's courfe
Muft take a diff'rent bias to comply
With each occafion.   He, to whom are known
The wants and the deportment of each being,
May fuch a Plan original have fram'd
As All adjufted may confpire to make
One compact Syftem ; where the Saint devout,
And fin-polluted Infidel may find
Forecafted, in th' eftablifhment of things,
Effects proportion'd to their varying ftamp
Of moral character.   Look round and fee
Reward and punifhment in part difpens'd
To Man by Nature's gen'ral Laws : fee Health
Fly the luxurious Glutton's rich repaft,
And with the Hermit at his temp'rate board
Sit a pleas'd gueft : fee calm unruffled Joy
With dovelike wing infold the virtuous breaft,
While arm'd with harpy-talon keen Remorfe

Hovers

Hovers o'er Guilt, and poifons ev'ry fweet.
Lo ! (to convert our vices into rods)
Paffions indulg'd beyond a certain bound
Lead to a precipice, and plunge in woe
The heedlefs agent.   Avarice o'erfhoots
Its deftin'd mark, and with abundance curs'd,
In wealth the ills of poverty endures.
Ambition, when the pinnacle is gain'd
With many a toilfome ftep, the pow'r it fought
Wants to fupport itfelf, and fighs to find
The envy'd height but aggravates the fall.
Unbridled Luft inftead of Pleafure's rofe
The prickly thorn oft grafps, with pangs of mind,
And body now tormented, now condemn'd
To bleed a victim on the bed it ftains.

Nor deem this Order broke, thefe Laws infring'd,
As oft as Vice in the warm funny beam
Of Fortune wanton bafks, and Virtue droops
Forlorn, by Penury's chill wintry blaft
Affail'd.   That luxury and pomp perhaps
Is but the fplendid cover of diftrefs
Rankling within ; while confcience ever gay,
And placid refignation to his lot,
Cheer the poor tatter'd Pilgrim, and derive

I

A fla-

A flavour to his cafual homely meal,
The rich man's labour'd dainties cannot yield.

    Dar'ft thou decide where Mercy fhould diftil
Its foft refrefhing dews, where Juftice pour
The vials of its treafur'd wrath, who know'ft
Man in appearance only ? Oft beneath
The faintly veil the Votary of fin
May lurk unfeen, and to that Eye alone,
Which penetrates the inmoft heart, reveal'd.
And He, whom Cenfure fingles from the herd
To brand with infamy, whom Envy loads
With black'ning colours, to th' Omnifcient Judge
(Whom nought can biafs, and whom nought deceíves)
May otherwife appear, and fitly fpread
His fwelling fails before the profp'rous gale.
Befides, that opulence, thou vainly gild'ft
With fpecious name of good, if fcann'd aright,
Is Heav'n's fharp Vifitation to the fool.
See him the giddy round of riot tread,
And madly purchafe at a price immenfe
Want, fhame, difeafe, and heart-corroding grief:
Or fee him brooding o'er the facred heap
Unenvy'd by the Beggar whom he hates:
And then pronounce him happy if you can.

But

But how this equal ſcale upheld, thou cry'ſt,
When, like the ruſhing deep, Adverſity
Pours all its billows o'er the virtuous head ?
Stop thy complaints.   God ever in the ſtorm,
As in the calm, preſides.   The Man, perhaps,
Thou pity'ſt, draws his comforts from diſtreſs.
That Mind ſo poiz'd, and center'd in the good
Supreme, ſo kindled with Devotion's flame,
Might with Proſperity's inchanting cup
Inebriate have forgot th' all-giving Hand,
Might on Earth's vain and tranſitory joys.
Have built its ſole felicity, nor e'er
Wing'd a deſire beyond its ſenſual ſtye,
Grov'ling, impure, and level'd with the Brute.

Thus by th' appointment of that Pow'r who weighs
What with our welfare, not our wiſh, comports,
Our Bliſs may be connected with our Woes.
Hence Graces, wither'd by too warm a beam,
May ſpread and flouriſh in the dreary ſhade :
And Pleaſure, to voluptuous Guilt deny'd,
May bloom ambroſial from Affliction's thorn.

Too ſhort is Reaſon's line to ſound the depths
Of heav'nly wiſdom ; raſh her cenſure too,

When

When she presumes to cavil at His ways,
Who oft obliquely to th' intended goal
His steady but meandring course directs,
Makes Opposites harmoniously combine
His grand eventful counsels to mature,
That Man, by common notices unmov'd,
By Admiration may be taught to fear.
He, who this complex mass of wonders call'd
From Chaos, and from darkness launch'd those lights
That gild the fluid ether, oftimes bids
'Midst the well-temper'd strife of jarring wills
Order from tumult break, from evil good.
He reins the fury of the waves, and bounds
The rage of Man, and makes the friendly storm
Drive when he lifts the vessel into port.
Abasement by his guidance shall exalt,
Disgrace ennoble, and Misfortunes bless.

See base ungen'rous Envy swell the breasts
Of Israel's sons : see Joseph for a dream,
Typic of future greatness, doom'd to feel
The rigours of fraternal hate.   And can
Such venom'd hate in kindred bosoms dwell ?
How shall defenceless innocence escape
Impendent death, when savage Brethren lift

The

The murd'rous fteel ? Prevailing nature melts
Reuben's foft heart, arrefts the bloody deed,
And heav'n-directed Ifhmaelites convey
To diftant climes the purchas'd fpoil, than all
Their fpicy wealth more precious.   Pharian realms
Receive the facred charge, the Patriarch's hope.
Vanifh the clouds, the welkin brightens round,
Illufive profpect ! foon new woes fucceed :
A lovefick Miftrefs fmiles, and Fortune frowns.
To flighted charms and womanifh revenge
Th' innoxious Youth falls an unpity'd prey,
And in a dungeon's gloom his pious foul
Pours to his God in pray'r, nor pours in vain.
For now the myftic web of Providence
Gradual unfolds, fhades foften into light,
And on th' admiring eye coherence dawns.
The rage of Brethren, and th' opprobrious fale
Confpire to realize his dream ; the wife
Of Potiphar unconfcious weaves the meed,
And calumny to honour fmooths the way.
Quick fhifts the fcene : the dungeon for a throne
Is chang'd.   The Hebrew next to Egypt's king,
In all the pride of regal pomp array'd,
Shines through the land of Nile rever'd, and lives
To cherifh Ifrael's drooping age, to pant

I 3

With

With filial tranfport on the Patriarch's breaft
Big with tumultuous joy.   His brethren round,
Sheaves of his dream, in marfhal'd order ftand,
And pay obeifance to his Sheaf, that rears
Its head aloft, and triumphs in its height.

    Great is the Lord JEHOVAH, high above
The loftieft flight of raptur'd praife ; his throne
Is built on Equity's broad bafe ; his Arm
(Though oft invifible to mortal ken)
Is ever ftretch'd to prop the finking good,
Or crufh the wicked.   Not a wheel amongft
Th' infinite orbs, which roll the fates of Man,
And Kingdoms in their rapid whirl, but glows
Diftinct with eyes, and in a meafur'd courfe
Harmonious verges to fome certain goal.

    See ! the fond Mother takes her fad adieu,
And flow-receding cafts a tearful glance
Where floats the rufh-wove ark : to calm her grief,
To give her darling to her throbbing breaft
The Memphian princefs fpeeds, and (Heav'n fo wills)
Nurtures in Wifdom's lore the Youth ordain'd
Ifrael to free, and humble Pharaoh's pride.

                                        When

When Judah totters on the brink of fate,
And guileful Haman meditates the death
Of blamelefs Mordecai, what hand can ward
The threaten'd blow, and give the wiles to fall
Retorted on the Machinator's head?
His Hand alone, who vindicates the Juft,
That plucks from Arrogance the boafted plume,
And plants it on meek Virtue's brow.   In vain
With ev'ry blandifhment the Perfian wooes
Sleep to his wakeful lid.   The Volume's fpread,
Where the Jew's faithful ferviccs inroll'd
Rufh on the monarch's fight.   Go, Haman, now,
And glory in thy ftratagems, condemn'd
To deck the triumphs of the Man thy hate
Mark'd for deftruction.   To the regal feaft
Go, fhort-liv'd gueft.   For know Death goes along
A reveller, and points the hidden fhaft.
Look from the palace; fee Fate's engine rife
Tremendous, and extend its arms for Thee
Its cruel builder, and unpity'd load.

When artful Malice broods o'er dark revenge,
When ftern Oppreffion frowns, and Ills furround,
Let not the Good defpair, but reft fecure
Beneath ADONAI's fhadowing wing.   His Eye

                    Beholds,

Beholds, his out-ftretch'd Arm condu&ts their fteps
Through Death's incircling horrors; and when broke
Each feeble anchor, when the tenth wave rolls
Its gather'd ruin, plucks them from the deep..
Nor let them murmur, though their way be oft
Perplext with briers, and with crags o'erhung,
But onwards prefs unfainting to the goal,
Where, to o'erpay their momentary toil,
Applauding Angels hold th' unwith'ring wreath
Of beatific Joy.   From ardent lips
Let the fweet incenfe of melodious praife
Afcend to Him who vifits all his works,
But chief the fon of Man.
        Pow'r infinite,
Thou Giver, and Prefcrver of my being,
Who rul'ft all Caufes, govern'ft all Events,
O teach me ever to thy will refign'd
To bear my lot with patience, and efteem
That Beft which Thou ordain'ft.   In weal or woe,
In health or ficknefs, let me ne'er forget
Thy Mercies : ev'n in thine affli&tive rod
May I a Father's tendernefs adore,
Who chaftens but to heal, in wrath benign !
Avert thofe ills that hover o'er my head,
And with thy fhield incompafs all my paths.

Of

Of earthly goods that portion Thou affign
Which with my prefent and my future blifs
May beft accord ; and grant this humble ftrain
May be a prelude to that nobler fong,
Which by thy Grace, this dreary vale paft through,
My Soul, with brighter views of Providence
Illum'd, and kindling from a near accefs,
Shall chaunt refponfive to th'Angelic Choir.

DEATH.

D E A T H.

BY

B. PORTEUS, D. D.

M DCC LIX.

D E A T H.

FRIEND to the wretch, whom ev'ry friend forsakes,
I woo thee, DEATH ! In Fancy's fairy paths
Let the gay Songster rove, and gently trill
The strain of empty joy.—Life and its joys
I leave to those that prize them.—At this hour,
This solemn hour, when Silence rules the world,
And wearied Nature makes a gen'ral pause !
Wrapt in Night's sable robe, through cloysters drear
And charnels pale, tenanted by a throng
Of meagre phantoms shooting cross my path
With silent glance, I seek the shadowy vale
Of Death !—Deep in a murky cave's recess
Lav'd by Oblivion's listless stream, and fenc'd
By shelving rocks and intermingled horrors
Of yew' and cypress' shade from all intrusion
Of busy noon-tide beam, the Monarch sits
In unsubstantial Majesty enthron'd.

At

At his right hand, neareft himfelf in place
And frightfulnefs of form, his parent Sin
With fatal induftry and cruel care
Bufies herfelf in pointing all his ftings,
And tipping every fhaft with venom drawn
From her infernal ftore : around him rang'd
In terrible array and ftrange diverfity
Of uncouth fhapes, ftand his dread Minifters :
Foremoft Old Age, his natural ally
And firmeft friend : next him difeafes thick,
A motley train ; Fever with cheek of fire ;
Confumption wan ; Palfy, half warm with life,
And half a clay-cold lump ; joint-torturing Gout,
And ever-gnawing Rheum ; Convulfion wild ;
Swoln Dropfy ; panting Afthma ; Apoplex
Full-gorg'd.—There too the Peftilence that walks
In darknefs, and the Sicknefs that deftroys
At broad noon-day.   Thefe and a thoufand more,
Horrid to tell, attentive wait ; and, when
By Heaven's command Death waves his ebon wand,
Sudden rufh forth to execute his purpofe,
And fcatter defolation o'er the Earth.

   Ill-fated Man, for whom fuch various forms
Of Mifery wait, and mark their future prey !
Ah ! why, All-righteous Father, didft thou make

This

This Creature Man ? Why wake th' unconfcious duft
To life and wretchednefs ? O better far
Still had he flept in uncreated night,
If this the Lot of Being !—Was it for this
Thy Breath divine kindled within his breaft
The vital flame ? For this was thy fair image
Stampt on his foul in godlike lineaments ?
For this dominion given him abfolute
O'er all thy creatures, only that he might reign
Supreme in woe ? From the bleft fource of Good
Could Pain and Death proceed ? Could fuch foul Ills
Fall from fair Mercy's hands ? Far be the thought,
The impious thought ! God never made a Creature
But what was good.   He made a living Man :
The Man of Death was made by Man himfelf.
Forth from his Maker's hands he fprung to life,
Frefh with immortal bloom ; No pain he knew,
No fear of death, no check to his defires
Save one command.   That one command (which ftood
'Twixt him and ruin, the teft of his obedience,)
Urg'd on by wanton curiofity
He broke.—There in one moment was undone
The faireft of God's works.   The fame rafh hand
That pluck'd in evil hour the fatal fruit,
Unbarr'd the gates of Hell, and let loofe Sin
And Death and all the family of Pain

To

To prey upon Mankind.   Young Nature faw
The monftrous crew, and fhook through all her frame.
Then fled her new-born luftre, then began
Heaven's chearful face to low'r, then vapours choak'd
The troubled air, and form'd a veil of clouds
To hide the willing Sun.   The Earth convuls'd
With painful throes threw forth a briftly crop
Of thorns and briars; and Infect, Bird, and Beaft,
That wont before with admiration fond
To gaze at Man, and fearlefs croud around him,
Now fled before his face, fhunning in hafte
Th' infection of his mifery.   He alone,
Who juftly might, th' offended Lord of Man,
Turn'd not away his face ; he full of pity
Forfook not in this uttermoft diftrefs
His beft-lov'd work.   That comfort ftill remain'd,
(That beft, that greateft comfort in affliction)
The countenance of God, and through the gloom
Shot forth fome kindly gleams, to chear and warm
Th' offender's finking foul.   Hope fent from Heaven
Uprais'd his drooping head, and fhew'd afar
A happier fcene of things ; the Promis'd Seed
Trampling upon the Serpent's humbled creft,
Death of his fting difarm'd, and the dank grave
Made pervious to the realms of endlefs day,
No more the limit but the gate of life.

Chear'd

Chear'd with the view, Man went to till the ground
From whence he rofe ; fentenc'd indeed to toil
As to a punifhment, yet (ev'n in wrath
So merciful is Heaven) this toil became
The folace of his woes, the fweet employ
Of many a live-long hour, and fureft guard
Againft Difeafe and Death.——Death though denounc'd
Was yet a diftant Ill, by feeble arm
Of Age, his fole fupport, led flowly on.
Not then, as fince, the fhort-liv'd fons of men
Flock'd to his realms in countlefs multitudes ;
Scarce in the courfe of twice five hundred years
One folitary ghoft went fhivering down
To his unpeopled fhore. In fober ftate,
Through the fequefter'd vale of rural life,
The venerable Patriarch guilelefs held
The tenor of his way ; Labour prepar'd
His fimple fare, and Temperance rul'd his board.
Tir'd with his daily toil, at early eve
He funk to fudden reft ; gentle and pure
As breath of evening Zephyr and as fweet
Were all his flumbers ; with the Sun he rofe,
Alert and vigorous as He, to run
His deftin'd courfe. Thus nerv'd with Giant Strength
He ftem'd the tide of Time, and ftood the fhock
Of ages rolling harmlefs o'er his head.

K

As

At life's meridian point arriv'd, he ſtood,
And looking round ſaw all the vallies fill'd
With nations from his loins ; full well content
To leave his race thus ſcatter'd o'er the Earth,
Along the gentle ſlope of life's decline
He bent his gradual way, till full of years
He dropt like mellow fruit into his grave.

   Such in the infancy of time was Man,
So calm was life, ſo impotent was Death.
O had he but preſerv'd theſe few remains,
Theſe ſhatter'd fragments of loſt happineſs,
Snatch'd by the hand of Heaven from the ſad wreck
Of innocence primæval ; ſtill had he liv'd
Great ev'n in ruin ; though fall'n, yet not forlorn ;
Though mortal, yet not every where beſet
With Death in every ſhape ! But He, impatient
To be compleatly wretched, haſtes to fill up
The meaſure of his woes.   'Twas Man himſelf
Brought Death into the world, and Man himſelf
Gave keenneſs to his darts, quicken'd his pace,
And multiplied deſtruction on mankind.

   Firſt Envy, Eldeſt-Born of Hell, embru'd
Her hands in blood, and taught the Sons of Men
To make a Death which Nature never made,

And

And God abhorr'd, with violence rude to break
The thread of life ere half its length was run,
And rob a wretched brother of his being.
With joy Ambition faw, and foon improv'd
The execrable deed.   'Twas not enough
By fubtle fraud to fnatch a fingle life,
Puny impiety ! whole kingdoms fell
To fate the luft of power ; more horrid ftill,
The fouleft ftain and fcandal of our nature
Became its boaft.——One Murder made a Villain,
Millions a Hero.——Princes were privileg'd
To kill, and numbers fanctified the crime.
Ah ! why will Kings forget that they are Men !
And Men that they are Brethren ? Why delight
In human facrifice ? Why burft the ties
Of Nature, that fhould knit their fouls together
In one foft bond of amity and love ;
Yet ftill they breathe deftruction, ftill go on
Inhumanly ingenious to find out
New pains for life, new terrors for the grave,
Artificers of Death ! Still Monarchs dream
Of univerfal Empire growing up
From univerfal ruin.——Blaft the defign,
Great God of Hofts, nor let thy creatures fall
Unpitied victims at Ambition's fhrine !

K 2

Yet

Yet fay, fhould Tyrants learn at laft to feel,
And the loud din of battle ceafe to roar;
Should dove-ey'd Peace o'er all the earth extend
Her olive branch, and give the world repofe,
Would Death be foil'd ? Would health, and ftrength, and
       youth
Defy his power ? Has he no arts in ftore,
No other fhafts fave thofe of war ?——Alas !
Ev'n in the fmile of Peace, that fmile which fheds
A heavenly funfhine o'er the foul, there bafks
That ferpent Luxury : War its thoufands flays,
Peace its ten thoufands : In th' embattled plain
Though Death exults, and claps his raven wings,
Yet reigns he not ev'n there fo abfolute,
So mercilefs, as in yon frantic fcenes
Of midnight revel and tumultuous mirth,
Where, in th' intoxicating draught conceal'd,
Or couch'd beneath the glance of lawlefs Love,
He fnares the fimple youth, who nought fufpecting
Means to be bleft—But finds himfelf undone.

Down the fmooth ftream of life the Stripling darts
Gay as the morn ; bright glows the vernal fky,
Hope fwells his fails, and Fancy fteers his courfe ;
Safe glides his little bark along the fhore
Where Virtue takes her ftand ; but if too far

                  He

He launches forth beyond Difcretion's mark,
Sudden the tempeft fcowls, the furges roar,
Blot his fair day, and plunge him in the deep.
O fad but fure mifchance ! O happier far
To lie like gallant Howe 'midft Indian wilds
A breathlefs corfe, cut off by favage hands
In earlieft prime, a generous facrifice
To Freedom's holy caufe; than fo to fall
Torn immature from life's meridian joys,
A prey to Vice, Intemperance, and Difeafe.

Yet die ev'n thus, thus rather perifh ftill,
Ye Sons of Pleafure, by th' Almighty ftricken,
Than ever dare (though oft, alas ! ye dare)
To lift againft yourfelves the murderous fteel,
To wreft from God's own hand the fword of Juftice,
And be your own avengers——Hold, rafh Man,
Though with anticipating fpeed thou'ft rang'd
Through every region of delight, nor left
One joy to gild the evening of thy days,
Though life feem one uncomfortable void,
Guilt at thy heels, before thy face defpair,
Yet gay this fcene, and light this load of woe,
Compar'd with thy hereafter. Think, O think,
And ere thou plunge into the vaft abyfs,
Paufe on the verge awhile, look down and fee

Thy future manfion ?——Why that ftart of horror ?
From thy flack hand why drops th' uplifted fteel ?
Didft thou not think fuch vengeance muft await
The wretch, that with his crimes all frefh about him,
Rufhes irreverent, unprepar'd, uncall'd,
Into his Maker's prefence, throwing back
With infolent difdain his choiceft gift ?

    Live then, while Heaven in pity lends thee life,
And think it all too fhort to wafh away
By penitential tears and deep contrition
The fcarlet of thy crimes.   So fhalt thou find
Reft to thy foul, fo unappall'd fhalt meet
Death when he comes, not wantonly invite
His lingering ftroke.   Be it thy fole concern
With innocence to live, with patience wait
Th' appointed hour ; too foon that hour will come,
Though Nature run her courfe ; But Nature's God,
If need require, by thoufand various ways,
Without thy aid, can fhorten that fhort fpan,
And quench the lamp of life.——O when he comes,
Rous'd by the cry of wickednefs extreme
To Heaven afcending from fome guilty land
Now ripe for vengeance ; when he comes array'd
In all the terrors of Almighty wrath ;
Forth from his bofom plucks his lingering Arm,

And on the miscreants pours destruction down !
Who can abide his coming ? Who can bear
His whole displeasure ? In no common form
Death then appears, but starting into Size
Enormous, measures with gigantic stride
Th' astonish'd Earth, and from his looks throws round
Unutterable horror and dismay.
All Nature lends her aid.   Each Element
Arms in his cause.   Ope fly the doors of Heaven,
The fountains of the deep their barriers break,
Above, below, the rival torrents pour,
And drown creation, or in floods of fire
Descends a livid cataract, and consumes
An impious race.——Sometimes, when all seems peace,
Wakes the grim whirlwind, and with rude embrace
Sweeps nations to their grave, or in the deep
Whelms the proud wooden world; full many a youth
Floats on his watery bier, or lies unwept
On some sad defart shore :——At dead of night
In sullen silence stalks forth Pestilence :
Contagion close behind taints all her steps
With poisonous dew ; no smiting Hand is seen,
No found is heard ; but soon her secret path
Is mark'd with defolation ; heaps on heaps
Promiscuous drop : No friend, no refuge near ;

K 4

All

All, all is falfe and treacherous around,
All that they touch, or tafte, or breathe, is Death.

   But ah ! what means that ruinous roar ? Why fail
Thefe tottering feet ?—— Earth to its centre feels
The Godhead's power, and trembling at his touch
Through all its pillars, and in every pore,
Hurls to the ground with one convulfive heave
Precipitating domes, and towns, and towers,
The work of ages.   Crufh'd beneath the weight
Of general devaftation, millions find
One common grave ; not ev'n a widow left
To wail her fons : the houfe, that fhould protect,
Entombs its mafter, and the faithlefs plain,
If there he flies for help, with fudden yawn
Starts from beneath him.—Shield me, gracious Heaven !
O fnatch me from deftruction ! If this Globe,
This folid Globe, which thine own hand hath made
So firm and fure, if this my fteps betray ;
If my own mother Earth from whence I fprung
Rife up with rage unnatural to devour
Her wretched offspring, whither fhall I fly ?
Where look for fuccour ? Where, but up to thee,
Almighty Father ? Save, O fave thy fuppliant
From horrors fuch as thefe !—At thy good time

Let

Let Death approach; I reck not—let him but come
In genuine form, not with thy vengeance arm'd,
Too much for Man to bear.   O rather lend
Thy kindly aid to mitigate his ftroke,
And at that hour when all aghaft I ftand
(A trembling Candidate for thy compaffion)
On this World's brink, and look into the next;
When my foul ftarting from the dark unknown
Cafts back a wifhful look, and fondly clings
To her frail prop, unwilling to be wrench'd
From this fair fcene, from all her cuftom'd joys
And all the lovely relatives of life,
Then fhed thy comforts o'er me; then put on
The gentleft of thy looks.   Let no dark Crimes
In all their hideous forms then ftarting up
Plant themfelves round my couch in grim array,
And ftab my bleeding heart with two-edg'd torture,
Senfe of paft guilt, and dread of future woe.
Far be the ghaftly crew! and in their ftead,
Let chearful Memory from her pureft cells
Lead forth a goodly train of Virtues fair
Cherifh'd in earlieft youth, now paying back
With tenfold ufury the pious care,
And pouring o'er my wounds the heavenly balm
Of confcious innocence.——But chiefly, Thou,
Whom foft-ey'd Pity once led down from Heaven

To bleed for Man, to teach him how to live,
And, oh! ſtill harder Leſſon! how to die,
Diſdain not Thou to ſmooth the reſtleſs bed
Of Sickneſs and of Pain.——Forgive the tear
That feeble Nature drops, calm all her fears,
Wake all her hopes, and animate her faith,
Till my rapt Soul anticipating Heaven
Burſts from the thraldom of incumbering clay,
And on the wing of Extaſy upborn
Springs into Liberty, and Light, and Life.

HEAVEN:

H E A V E N;

A

V I S I O N.

BY

J. SCOTT, M. A.

Ἐγω γαρ ει μην μη ωμην ηξειν πρωτον μεν παρα Θεȣς σοφȣς τε και αγαθȣς, επειτα και παρ' ανθρωπȣς τετελευτηκοτας, αμεινȣς των ενθαδε, ηδικȣν αι, ȣκ αγανακτων τω Θανατω. PLATO.

M DCC LX.

HEAVEN.

I.

FULL many a tedious hour, with care oppreſt,
 Stretcht on my weary bed, I wakeful lay,
Sad troublous thoughts, like hornets, ſtung my breaſt,
 And bruſht the dews of balmy ſleep away.
Ah! what avails, I cry'd with painful toil,
 By Virtue's ſtedfaſt ſtar the bark to guide,
Far from * ACRASIA's wily-wandring Iſle,
 Where eaſe and pleaſure the frail heart divide,
If life's ſhort voyage undiſtinguiſh'd tends
To darkneſs, and the land where all forgotten ends ?

II.

Shall Worth lie hid in Sorrow's baleful ſhade ?
 And no reward ſhall ſuff'ring Goodneſs find,
While VICE triumphant lifts her pamper'd head,
 † Nor hears the ſteps of Vengeance cloſe behind ?—

* *Spenſer's* FAIRY QUEEN, Book II.
 † *Antecedentem ſceleſtum deſeruit Pœna.* HOR.

Thea

Then take me, Pow'r of Beauty, to thy arms,
　　And lull, ah lull to peace my troubled foul!
Difclofe, O God of Wine, thy purple charms,
　　I'll drown reflection in the mantling bowl!
'Gainft wind, and tide, let Stoic dullnefs fail,
Be mine the calmeft fea, and Pleafure's brifkeft gale.

III.

Penfive I mus'd, 'till rofe the blufhing Morn,
　　And fpread her faffron mantle o'er the fkies;
When pitying MORPHEUS fhook his opiate horn,
　　And flumbrous humours drown'd my weary'd eyes;
Yet FANCY ftill awake, to footh my pain,
　　Sweet fcenes of joy in livelieft hue pourtray'd;
She call'd forth all her bright ideal train,
　　And pleafing truths in myftic dreams convey'd:
Oh fail me not, thou fair enchanting Pow'r,
At Sorrow's grim approach, and Care's diftrefsful hour!

IV.

Borne thro' the yielding air, methought I flew
　　To fome more blifsful clime, fequefter'd far
From this frail world, that juft appear'd to view,
　　Like the faint glimm'ring of a diftant ftar.

Deep

Deep in the fea's encircling wave 'twas plac'd,
    As gems in filver; hoary Ocean fmil'd
Chear'd with the pleafing fight; and * from his breaft
    Sent his fweet children, breezes frefh and mild:
No clouds, nor darknefs, veil'd the chearful fcene,
Nor wintry blafts deform'd the ground's eternal green.

V.

Lo to the Weft a large and fpacious plain,
    Where meet in concert, wood, and hill, and dale;
Brighter than all that mufe-led Poets feign
    Of Ida's grove, and Tempe's hallow'd vale:
Tho' Peneus there revolves his † amber ftream,
    And fuppliant Daphne fpreads her branching arms;
Still trembling left the Sun's prolific beam,
    Too fiercely wanton, blaft her virgin charms:
Would'ft thou efcape? Go, coy relentlefs maid,
Go chufe fome worfe retreat, fome lefs luxurious fhade?

VI.

There blooming groves, gay fmiling with delight,
    From her fair womb fpontaneous Nature brings;
Where percht on every bough, all richly dight
    With painted plumes, fome ‡ harmlefs Siren fings:

* Ενθα μακαρων νασαν ωκεανιδες αυραι περιπνεοιν Pind.
† Αλεκτεινον υδωρ. Callim.—*Amnis purior electre.* Virg.
‡ *Nemoris Siren, innoxia Siren.* Strada's Nightin.

Pleas'd with the wild notes Zephyr flits unfeen,
  And on his mufky wings the found conveys;
While trickling foft, each vary'd paufe between,
  The murm'ring riv'lets roll their filver bafe;
Winds, waters, birds in feemly fort agree,
And am'rous Echo blends the liquid melody.

VII.

Nor there alone was charm'd one fcanty fenfe:
  The loaded trees ambrofial fruitage bear;
The * weeping fhrubs their fpicy gums difpenfe,
  Whofe fragrance frefh-imbalms the buxom air;
Thoufands of flow'rs their filken webs unfold,
  Amarants, immortal amarants arife;
Thefe beaming bright with † vegetable gold,
  And thefe with azure, thefe with Tyrian dyes;
There laughing fweetly red the rofes glow,
While from their breathing fouls celeftial odours flow.

VIII.

But hark, a voice foft-warbling ftrikes my ear!—
  " Behold, O man, fair Virtue's ample meed;
" Behold thefe radiant plains, this ftar-girt fphere,
  " By righteous Jove her portion are decreed!

* *Flet tamen, et tepidæ manant ex Arbore Guttæ.* Ovid. Met.
† Ανθιμα δι χρυσυ φλεγει. Pind.

" Mould

" Mould not, ah mould not then in idle cell,
   " But ſtrive theſe rapt'rous Manſions to attain ;
" Here all the wiſe, the brave, the virtuous dwell,
   " Eternal ages * free from care, and pain :
" Here in ELYSIAN ſeats, their calm abodes,
" Live in communion bleſt, † with heroes, and with gods !"

IX.

Eaſtward to this methought a diff'rent ſcene,
   Of equal beauty, charm'd my raptur'd ſight :
Wide ſpacious lawns with ſwelling hills between,
   And groves of bliſs, and gardens of delight.
There lotes, and palms their copious branches twine,
   And over-arching form delicious bow'rs ;
There guſh nectareous rills of dulcet wine,
   And honey'd ſtreams revolve their milky ſtores ;
Freſh-bleeding myrrh, and caſſia ſhed perfume,
Ananas ſwell with ſweets, and wild pomegranates bloom.

X.

Faſt by a fount, whoſe ‡ *ſpicy waters* glide
   In am'rous mazes, on the velvet ground
With bluſhing flow'rs all goodly beautify'd,
   A ſmiling troop of Virgins dance around ;

---

* Ἀδακρυν νεμονται αιωνα. PIND.

† Παρα μεν τιμιοις Θεων. Ibid.

‡ Called by the *Arabic* Writers *Zenzebil*, and promiſed by *Ma-homet* to all the Faithful.

L
                Fairer

Fairer than Delia's silver-bufkin'd train,
    When erft, Ladona, by thy lilied banks,
Or cool * Eurota's laurel-fringed plain,
    To breathing lutes they tript in feemly ranks;
And fairer, Cypris, than thy wanton quire,
That melt the foul to love, and kindle fierce defire.

XI.

Their eyes, † like pearls within the fhells conceal'd,
    Beauteous and black; their lips with rubies vye;
On their fair cheeks, with white and red anneal'd,
    What thoufand dimpling Smiles in ambufh lie!
See, fee they point to yon embow'ring fhade,
    Where cool gales fan their odorif'rous wings,
And Flora's frefheft, fofteft couch is fpread;
    The whiles fome one this lovely ditty fings!
Thro' all my veins what thrilling tranfport flew
To hear the nectar'd words, dropping like honey'd dew!

XII.

" Hafte, gentle youth, for lo, the way is plain!
    " Hafte, gentle youth, and hear the Prophet's call!
" Thefe are the joys that true Believers gain,
    " Immortal joys, that never know to pall.

---

* ———— In Eurotæ Ripis
Exercet Diana Chorós ———— Virg.
† See *Sale's Koran*, Chapter the 56th.

                       " Come

" Come then, ah come, thy weary limbs recline
" On filken beds of rofes fweetly ftrow'd,
" Where to thy touch compliant bows the vine,
" All faint and lab'ring with the lufcious load ;
" Where Nymphs of Paradife their charms reveal,
" And with their am'rous fpoils thy greedy eyes regale !"

XIII.

She ceas'd——And molten with excefs of joy,
Voluptuous Hope was bufy in my breaft :
When lo, fwift-darting from th' extremeft fky,
With Seraph-plumes, an Angel ftood confeft !
A pure immortal Crown adorn'd her head,
Of gold inwove with jewels ; in her hand
The Book of Life, and Mercy was difplay'd,
With ruddy drops of dying Martyrs ftain'd ;
Her eagle-eyes were quick, and paffing bright,
Yet beam'd ferene, and mild, with Heav'n's celeftial light.

XIV.

"And O fond foolifh man," fhe cry'd, " forbear
" Idly to glote on forms fo light, and vain !
" What are thefe jocund fcenes, but empty air,
" The fleeting coinage of a phrenzy'd brain ?—

L 2

" Yet

" Yet ev'n in Thefe, as * darkly thro' a glafs,

　" Some faint, fome glimm'ring view the eye may gain

" Of thofe unmingled joys, that far furpafs

　" Whate'er of blifs the wit of man can feign;

" Thofe pure Delights, that flow in ftreams divine,

" Where thy imperial Tow'rs, O heav'nly SALEM, fhine!

XV.

" For know, my Son, that they whofe worth is try'd,

　" As gold by fire, by great and virtuous deeds,

" Soon as the carnal fetters are unty'd,

　" That chain the foul, and ftript thefe mortal weeds;

" Haply fhall foar, in Robes of Glory clad,

　" To heav'nly Manfions, bright Abodes, prepar'd

" † Ere the foundations of the deep were laid,

　" Or the firm pillars of the earth were rear'd;

" Ere GOD his golden compaffes employ'd,

" And markt this beauteous World on Chaos dark, and

　　　" void.

XVI.

" There fhall they live, O happy, happy fpirits! ·

　" There fhall they live remov'd from all the cares,

" And thoufand ills, that feeble flefh inherits:

　" No greedy Want, nor wayward Luft, that tears

* 1 Corinth. chap. xiii. 12.　　† Prov. viii. 6. 24. 25. 27, &c.

" With

" With vip'rous rage the breaſt from whence it ſprung,
" Their deep-emboſom'd peace ſhall e'er torment ;
" But hymning ſweet, the Angel Troops among, ,
" Their undiſturbed lays of pure content,
" The ſmiling hours immortal ſhall employ,
" In trance of holy eaſe, or extacy of joy.

XVII.

" Then ſhall their eyes, from cloudy films ſecure,
" With lightning-glance unmeaſur'd ſpace behold ;
" And all the thouſand Stars, that pave the floor
" Of Heav'n, with orient pearl, or living gold ;
" Then floating thro' the boundleſs Deep of air,
" An azure ſea, like gems of richeſt hue,
" Myriads of Worlds thick-ſcatter'd ſhall appear,
" With all their bright Inhabitants to view ;
" Their active minds ſhall traverſe, quick as thought,
" Creation's ample fields, the range 'twixt GOD and
" nought.

XVIII.

" And oh what ſtreams of muſic ſweet, and clear,
" Shall drown in deep delight their raptur'd ſouls !—
" Ay me, in vain to Man's unpurged ear
" Their heav'nly Notes each tuneful planet rolls !

L 3

" Ay

" Ay me, in vain with foftly-thrilling voice,
  " * Thro' ev'ry land they hymn their Maker's Praife,
" While Choirs of young-ey'd Cherubims rejoice,
  " And to their golden Harps mellifluous Lays
" Attuning, *Holy, holy, holy,* fing,
" *O Lord, Almighty God, the Saints' eternal King!*

XIX.

" But not in vain the tuneful planets raife
  " To pure etherial fouls their voice divine;
" Nor yet in vain their great Creator's praife
  " Do gladfome choirs of young-ey'd Cherubs join:
" No bleffed Sp'rit but hears the facred fong,
  " And wakes his lyre melodious part to bear
" In the fweet fymphony; while all the throng
  " Of angels, and arch-angels, nay, the ear
" Of God delighted liftens to the ftrains.—
" In Heav'n, and heav'n-born minds fuch rapt'rous
   " concord reigns!

XX.

" But where, ah where can glowing tints be found
  " To paint the charms of † SION's facred place,
" ‡ Where CHRIST the Lamb in radiance fits enthron'd,
  " The || lively Image of his Father's Grace?

* Pfal. xix. 3, 4.   † Heb. xii. 22.   ‡ Pfal. ii. 6. || Heb. i. 3.

" O

" O Flow'r of love! O * glorious Morning ſtar!
  " O † Sun of Righteouſneſs, whoſe healing wings
" Brought life, and peace, and mercy from afar!
  " From Thee the light, thou beaming Fountain,
    " ſprings,
" That guides poor mortals in their weary way,
" Thro' black Affliction's night, to Pleaſure's endleſs day!

XXI.

" Jesus!——and didſt thou leave thy Bow'rs of joy?
  " And didſt thou leave thy Father's dear embrace,
" Content with agonizing pangs to die
  " For man's forlorn, rebellious, ſinful race?
" What bliſs to hear the high myſterious ſtory,
  " By all the Prophets, all th' Apoſtles ſung,
" And noble army' of Martyrs, crown'd with glory;
  " Where bleſt, the ſix-wing'd Seraphins among,
" They drink immortal, from thy rapt'rous ſight,
" Conceiveleſs draughts of Love's ineffable delight!

XXII.

" Hail, ſaints of light! who once the patient train
  " Of ſilent Sorrow, thro' the thorny road
" Of mis'ry toil'd, and unappall'd by pain
  " With Pilgrim-feet the long, long journey trod!

* Rev. xxii. 16.   † Mal. iv. 2.

L 4   " O taught

" O taught by them, thou man of earth, suftain
    " With firm unweary'd arm the dang'rous fight!
" The * Prize of thy High-calling dare to gain,
    " † Victorious Palms, and robes of fpotlefs white;
" So in ‡ the Book of Life thy name fhall fhine,
" And Heav'n's eternal joys, and tranfports all be thine."

XXIII.

Scarce had fhe fpoke, when that || Cherubic car,
    Inftinct with foul, and thofe felf-moving wheels,
That whirl'd the holy Sage, from CHEBAR far,
    Appear'd :—— my breaft the rufhing impulfe feels !
I fee, I fee thy glitt'ring turrets rife,
    Celeftial SALEM, all of § lucid gold,
Inlaid with gems of thoufand, thoufand dyes !
    And lo, the everlafting gates unfold
Their ¶ doors of pearl, and o'er my aching fight
Full tides of glory flow, and ftreams of living light !

XXIV.

Of Light furpaffing far thy glimm'ring ray,
    (More bright, more clear, more glorious, more divine)
Tho' dreft by thee, ** O golden Eye of Day,
    In gaudy robes the fparkling diamonds fhine;

* Phil. iii. 14.   † Rev. vii. 9.   ‡ Rev. iii. 5. || Ezek. i.
§ Rev. xxi. 18, 19.   ¶ Rev. xxi. 21.
** Ω χρυσεας αμερας βλεφαρον.   SOPH.

Tho

Tho' yon fair Moon to thee her luftre owes,
   Gilding with borrow'd light the mountain's brow;
And Iris fteals from thee each tint, that glows
   In the gay forehead of the fhow'ry Bow:
Faint is thy feeble blaze, O beauteous Sun!
Such peerlefs beams appear from Truth's eternal throne.

XXV.

See thro' the ftreets, * like liquid jafper clear,
   The Fount of life in mazy error flows!
Thro' the bright † Cryftal fands of gold appear,
   And heaps of pearly grain; while blooming grows,
On either bank of dainty flow'rs profufe,
   The Tree of Life fuperior o'er the reft,
Whofe teeming branches nectar'd fruits produce:
   ‡ Twelve various fruits of fweetly-vary'd tafte,
From ev'ry leaf || falubrious dews exhale,
And pure elixirs breathe in ev'ry balmy gale.

XXVI.

Lo there, diffus'd along the facred brink,
   Angelic choirs replete with love and joy,
Conceive their God, and from his prefence drink
   Beatitude paft utt'rance!—There they lie
On flow'ring beds of balfam, caffia, nard,
   And myrrh, a wildernefs of rich perfumes;
Embalm'd they lie, like that Arabian bird,
   'Midft od'rous fhrubs, and incenfe-breathing gums,

* Rev. xxi. 11.   † Ibid.   ‡ Rev. xxii. 2. || Ibid.

Whofe life fprings recent from the fun-born fire,
While clouds of fpicy fmoke in bluifh wreaths afpire.

XXVII.

But fpare, O fpare me, Heav'n!—my fainting foul
    Sickens with blifs too great for mortal fenfe!
Come, o'er my limbs thy quick'ning waters roll,
    Life-giving ftream, and all thy balm difpenfe!
And thou, fair Tree, the fource of all our woes,
    (That bloom'd fo fatal erft in EDEN's glade,
Tranfplanted fince to Heav'n) thy friendly boughs
    Extend, and wrap me in thy browneft fhade!
O veil me from the LAMB's too glorious fight,
From Majefty's full blaze, infufferably bright!

XXVIII.

Trembling I wak'd with fweet excefs of joy,
    And on the wings of Sleep, more fwift than wind,
Away the fickle, fond delufions fly;
    Yet leave their Fairy-fteps the trace behind:
Hear then, ye fainted Myriads, from your fpheres,
    And gently beam your kindlieft influence down;
Lift, lift my thoughts above life's groveling cares,
    To Joys fublime, and Virtue's glorious Crown!
O guide my Virgin-Soul the high Abode
To reach, the HEAV'N OF HEAV'NS, where reigns
    th' eternal GOD!

PURITY

PURITY OF HEART.

BY

J. SCOTT, M. A.

Ειδον ϐλιϖι, ειδον η ϖηγη τ8 αγαθ8. ANTONINUS.

*Sic vivendum eft, tanquam in confpectu vivamus; fic cogi-
tandum, tanquam aliquis in Pectus intimum infpicere
poffit, et poteft.* SENECA.

M DCC LXI.

PURITY OF HEART.

IN that rude climate where the Alps arife,
And mountains heap'd on mountains threat the fkies,
From one prolific hill their wat'ry ftores
The Rhone, the Rhine, the Po, the Danube pours:
Thro' diff'rent lands their diff'rent courfe they bend;
Now prone in rapid cataracts defcend,
Boil, foam, and roar, the trees impetuous tear,
And grate hoarfe thunder on the diftant ear;
Now ftealing gently thro' their oozy bed,
O'er fmiling plains their beauteous plenty fpread,
With nect'rous dews the purple vineyards feed,
Bid olives rife, and harvefts crown the mead,
Fair Commerce all her canvafs wings unfold,
And fly to diftant funs, and fhores of gold:

Thus from the Heart, that feat of joy, and woe,
In various ftreams our various Paffions flow:
Now, loud as Ætna's fmouldring torrents roar,
They burft impetuous; tides of reeking gore

Whelm

Whelm in promifcuous ruin heaps of flain,
And dreary defolation fweeps the plain !
Now gentler grown, with current fmooth and mild,
They chear the barren, footh the thirfty wild,
By Reafon guided, checkt, impell'd, produce
In Life's fair plan all Ornament and Ufe.

This fruitful fource, thus rightly underftood,
Of greateft evil, or of greateft good,
Whence all their hues our tinctur'd Paffions draw,
O watch, preferve it pure, with facred awe !
Can ftreams be clear from fountains dark and foul ?
Or Actions good, corrupt, and bafe the Soul ?
No, Lucius, no—fair Virtue trembling flies,
Or fhould fhe ftay, her boafted beauty dies ;
Devotion turns to farce, and fenfe and fpirit
Are—what ?—the venal Statefman's grand demerit.

When dear to Virtue, to his country dear,
Accomplifht Pollio charm'd the public ear,
Firm as a rock 'midft wav'ring fenates ftood,
And boldly ftem'd corruption's venal flood,
What crouds admir'd his wit and manly fenfe !
What crouds ador'd his patriot eloquence !
Tis paft, 'tis gone—and lo the wife, the brave,
The virtuous Pollio is a titled flave.

Blufh,

Blush, Freedom, blush! thy fav'rite Son is fold,
And love for Thee submits to love for gold ;
Dead to all fame, and to his parts unjuft,
He makes God's gift a pander to his luft.

Not fo CAMILLUS, BRITAIN's dear delight,
Firm to his truft, inflexible from right ;
Born to fupport his drooping country's caufe,
Maintain her freedom, and fecure her laws,
To guide the frail machine with ceafelefs care,
Each crazy fpring, and tott'ring wheel repair.
Bleft Statefman, that can Attic wit combine
With Roman ftrength, and Eloquence divine ;
Can Attic wit, and Roman ftrength employ,
To blaft the foes of heav'n-born Liberty !
In vain Ambition fpreads her tinfel charms ;
And Pleafure woos him with extended arms,
Drawn by no Party's devious glare aftray,
Thofe wand'ring fires, that glitter to betray,
Up Virtue's fteep afcent the Patriot toils,
And meets his due reward in BRITAIN's fmiles.

Say what 'twixt POLLIO's and CAMILLUS' part
The diff'rence makes ? I'll tell you, friend—the Heart :
Be This the Patriot's pride, with this uncrown'd
Wit is a jeft, and Eloquence a found :

I   This

This too the Saint's delight — unwarm'd within
Pray'r is mere babbling, fanctity is fin.

   Conftant at Church AVARO prays fo loud,
His noify zeal confounds the gaping croud ;
With hands uprais'd, and heav'n-projected eyes,
Full thrice a day he fmites his breaft and fighs :
Diffembling wretch, with heart fo prone to evil,
A mere machine, a ftopwatch to the Devil ! —
Will Nature's awful GOD fo juft, and wife,
Whofe inftant glance thro' all creation flies,
Pervades each Movement of our inmoft fouls,
Where thought impelling thought continual rolls,
Pleas'd with fuch off'rings view with partial Eye
Thy fpecious form, and well-feign'd fanctity ?
No — he beholds thee, Wretch, tho' wrapt in pray'r,
A Wolf difguis'd, a painted Sepulchre ;
Regards no more thy cant, and godly whine,
Than yon dumb ftatue, on the marble fhrine,
Whofe hands are feen in holy rapture clos'd,
And ftedfaft Eyes to heav'n alone difpos'd,
Pray'r's fenfelefs image, where no foul within
Speaks thro' the form, and animates the mien.
When all the breaft is pure, each warm defire
Sublim'd by holy Love's etherial fire,

On

On winged words our breathing Thoughts may rife,
And foar to heav'n a grateful facrifice;
Not fo, my Friend, when carnal Paffions reign,
And groffer acts of fin the Heart diftain;
Our fouls all clotted by contagion grow,
And brood, and grovel in the duft below:
Like ling'ring Ghofts, that loath, as fables fay,
To leave the body, haunt their kindred clay.

But ah how few a firm, and faithful band,
Th' affaults of warring Paffions can withftand!
With whirlwind-force they now the Heart affail,
Now with furprize, and crafty feints prevail,
Betray the fort, thro' Friendfhip's fair difguife,
Till half-confenting vanquifh'd Virtue dies.
For ev'ry Vice to Virtue is ally'd,
And thin partitions their weak bounds divide:
To the pale Mifer, bent with fordid pain,
And brooding, harpye like, o'er ill-got gain,
His fav'rite Vice the garb of Virtue wears,
And dreft by paffion honeft Thrift appears:
'Tis Nature's law, voluptuous CLODIO cries,
Steaming from ftews, and brothel revelries;
'Tis Nature's law, decrepid HIRCUS fwears,
Love-fick, and lewd, at more than feventy Years:

M

What

What, PUBLIUS, made thy gentle foul defpife
The ftricteft bonds, and deareft charities ?
Rous'd thy young blood to more than civic ftrife,
And arm'd thy hand againft thy Sov'reign's Life ?
The Dæmon Difcord rofe in CATO's form,
And blew the trump to freedom's falfe alarm ;
He caught the found, and, mad with patriot pride,
In faction's curfed caufe the rebel dy'd.

    Thus the fond heart, by fome dear paffion fway'd,
Frail and corrupt is foon to fin betray'd ;
Vice by degrees a firm poffeffion gains,
And o'er the willing Soul defpotic reigns :
Dreadful no more the meagre hag appears,
Purfu'd by doubts, and harrow'd up with fears.
Trickt out in lavifh ornaments fhe fmiles
A dang'rous Circe fraught with charmful wiles.
When fome lone Traveller, from Ontario's fhore,
Hears Niagara's rufhing Cat'racts roar,
Appall'd he ftands, with chilling horrour pale,
Or flies impetuous to fome diftant Vale,
Where prone beneath the Myrtle's od'rous fhade
Peaceful and calm may reft his aching head ;
Not fo the native hind by cuftom brave,
Carelefs he hears the foaming Surges rave,

Views

Views the wild Scene with firm and fteady brow,
And cleaves in fport the madding Waves below;
Thus when at firft from Virtue's path we ftray,
How fhrinks the feeble heart with fad difmay!
More bold at length, by pow'rful habit led,
Callous and fear'd the dreary Wilds we tread,
Behold the gaping Gulph of fin with fcorn,
And plunging deep to endlefs death are born.
O fad eftate, defilement bafe and foul,
When Vice lethargic fpreads o'er all the Soul;
When Confcience, that impartial judge affign'd
By Heav'n to check, approve, condemn the mind,
Like Bufo fleeps, and leaves poor Virtue's caufe
To a brib'd Jury, and to tyrant laws,
To lufts corrupt and vile, that wrong to right
Prefer, and, blind with rage, call darknefs light.

How bleft are they, my Friend, whofe Hearts are free
From Vice, and Paffion's grofs Impurity!
Whofe mental Eyes ideal truths behold;
And purg'd from films and tinctures of earth's mold,
Pervade with lightning-force that bleft abode, .
Where veil'd in brightnefs reigns th' eternal GOD.
So * Lowther lives—No taint of modifh fin
Defiles the Image of his God within;

* Sir William Lowther, of Swillington, in Yorkfhire, Bart.

Far

Far from the fpotlefs temple of his mind
Each bafe affection flies, and leaves behind
Religion, and a love for all mankind :
Of manners gentle and of truth fevere,
Tho' plain not ruftic, courtly yet fincere ;
Benevolent like heav'n, when all around
It drops down fatnefs on the weary ground :
No coftly dainties on his board are fpread,
'Tis luxury to him the poor to feed ;
Superior far to all the pomp of drefs,
He cloaths the fhiv'ring Beggar's nakednefs !
A friend to every want, and every Woe,
Nor fcarce to Vice when in diftrefs a foe ;
So LOWTHER lives—Oh may he long remain
The pleafing fubject of my moral Strain !
And when at length he quits the well trod ftage,
Retire the joy, and glory of his age ;
As fome fam'd Actor from the Scene withdraws,
While crouds tumultuous thunder out applaufe,
Or Grecian Victor, when the race was done,
The Crown of glory claim'd, by Virtue won.

Oh could I live like him, and thus depart,
What fober home-felt joy would fwell my heart !
No love of fame fhould then difturb my breaft,
Nor this, nor that Man's cenfures break my reft :

Malice

Malice in vain a cloud of duſt ſhould raiſe,
And Envy nip the tender buds of praiſe:
Pleas'd would I view the placid Scene within,
(Thro' a clear Medium, undiſturb'd by ſin)
Where all the Virtues to perfection riſe,
And bear their bluſhing glories to the ſkies;
Bleſt in Oblivion leave the World behind,
And till with care the garden of my mind,

AN

AN

H Y M N

TO

REPENTANCE.

BY

J. SCOTT, M. A.

Ειδε ευχαις λυσιν των αμαρτηματων ευρισκομεν, και της θευς θερα‑
πευομεν, και μεταβαλλομεν, δια της προς το θειον επιστροφης
την ημετεραν κακιαν ιωμενοι, παλιν της των θεων αγαθοτητος
απολαυομεν. FRAGM. PYTH.

M DCC LXII.

AN

A N

HYMN TO REPENTANCE.

BASE World, begone!—Thy falfe delufive Joys
　　No more fhall lead my feet aftray—
　　Hence to the young, the vain, the gay,
And proudly deck them with thy tinfel toys!
　　Nor flatt'ring Hope, nor flavifh Fear,
　　* Thofe Nails that to this mortal Frame
　　Fix the fond Soul, my Breaft fhall tear;
　　No thirft for Pleafure, Wealth, or Fame,
Tempt me to quaff thy charmed Cup, whofe tafte
Unmolds the Form divine, and turns the Man to beaft.

　　Bafe World, begone!—Caft on a friendly Shore
　　　　No more I dread thy defart deep,
　　　　Where fwift the rufhing Tempefts fweep,
　　And mad Winds rave, and boiling Billows roar:

* Ὁ γαρ ηδοντς και αλγηδονος ηλος, ος προς το σωμα την ψυ-
χην προσηλοι. PLUT.

Behold

Behold no more, with wild Affright,
The Rocks clofe-lurking for their prey,
The black Clouds burfting on my Sight,
While round the livid Lightnings play;
O fave us, fave us!——Hark the doleful Cry,
All mortal Strength is vain, they faint, they fink, they die!

Betimes efcap'd, while yet breathe Summer-gales,
While yet on Ocean's tranquil breaft
The little Halcyon builds her neft,
I fhorten all my Oars, and furl my Sails;
O Wretch profane, fure triple Brafs
Girds thy proud heart, O Wretch profane,
To let the doubtful Autumn pafs,
Yet tempt the Dangers of the Main;
Carelefs of Home the blifsful Port defpife,
Tho' fcowl the low'ring Heav'ns, & Storms of Winter rife!

For me, I hang the votive Tablet high,
And to this lone fequefter'd Vale,
With Care, and weary Watches pale,
Retire, and mufe upon Eternity.——
Come, Goddefs of the tearful Eye,
With folemn Step, demure, and flow,
Thy full heart heaving many a Sigh,
And Clouds of Sadnefs on thy brow;

Oh

Oh come with Aſhes ſprent, in Sackcloth dreſt,
And wring thy piteous hands, and beat thy plaintive
      breaſt.

Such was thy form, O heav'n-deſcended Maid,
   When at her deareſt Saviour's feet,
   Bedew'd with tears, and Odours ſweet,
Poor Magdalene repentant wept, and pray'd :
   She wept, and ſwiftly to the Sky
   The Steam like hallow'd Incenſe roſe ;
   When lo her Sins of Scarlet dye
   Grew white as Wool, or Mountain-ſnows :
The Morning Stars with Joy triumphant rang,
And all the Sons of God their loud Hoſannas ſang !

Come then, my Magdalene, thy Aid impart,
   O'er all my Soul thy balm diffuſe,
   And ſoften with the fleecy dews
Of penitential Tears my ſtubborn heart ;
   Teach me to ſearch with honeſt ſkill
   The Wounds that rankle in my breaſt,
   To curb my Luſts, correct my Will,
   And chuſe, and cleave to what is beſt ;
Teach me to urge, with never-ceaſing care,
The force of holy Vows, and Violence of Pray'r.

Oh

Oh come, my Magdalene, but leave behind,
　　Leave far behind thy frightful Train;
　　Grim Penance, with an iron chain
Wont his gall'd Legs at ftated hours to bind:
　　A barefoot Monk the fiend appears,
　　With Scourge in hand, and beads, and book,
　　His Cheeks are furrow-worn with tears,
　　Sunk are his Eyes, and lean his Look:
O wretched Fools, beguiling and beguil'd,
Can God be pleas'd to fee his Image thus defil'd? ——

Drive too away that wild diftracted fprite
　　Enthufiafm, and that foul fiend
　　Remorfe, that loves his Heart to rend,
And fting himfelf to Death with fcorpion fpite:
　　But chief that Tyrant of the Soul,
　　That curfed Man of Hell, Defpair;
　　See, fee his livid Eye-balls roll!
　　What canker'd Teeth, what grifly Hair!
Anguifh, and trembling Fear his Confcience quail,
And all Hell's damned Ghofts the fhrieking Wretch affail!

O fly with fuch terrific Forms as thefe,
　　And feek the weary wakeful Bed,
　　Where the pale Murderer is laid
A ghaftly Prey to Horror and Difeafe:

Or

Or where th' Oppreffor voids his breath,
  Deaf to the Widow's bleeding Cries ;
  Or from a bofom black as Death,
  The Plunderer of his Country fighs ;
Where Libertines expire, and Atheifts lie
Harrow'd with doubts and fears, and curfe their God, and die !

See worn with Pain LORENZO, once fo gay !——
  The Pow'rs of Nature are at ftrife,
  And the dim wafted Lamp of Life
Juft feebly lifts an intermittent ray.
  Oh mad, oh worfe than mad to leave
  To the fhort Mercies of an hour
  Eternal Joys !—What would he give,
  What thoufand Worlds, if in his pow'r,
For time mifpent, to watch, to faft, to pray,
And wafh with contrite tears his fhameful Sins away ? ——

Poor Wretch, in vain !—Before his frantic Eyes
  Th' inexorable Tyrant ftands,
  And arm'd with Scorpions in their Hands,
The fury-Terrours of his confcience rife !
  What agonizing Pangs he feels !
  What Tortures !—What convulfive Throes !
  O fall, ye Mountains, fall, ye Hills,
  Preferve and hide him from his Woes !

Have

Have Mercy, Heav'n !——Thy Succours, Jesu, bring,
Retriumph o'er the Grave, and draw Death's poignant
      fting.

Save me, what Shrieks !——And is there no faint Ray,
    No glimm'ring from that light ferene,
    That gilds Death's melancholy fcene,
And guides the Soul on her eternal Way ?
    Hark the laft Pang ! He faints !——He dies !
    His Spirit burfts forth, and fhiv'ring pale
    To fome black horrible Manfion flies,
    There to defpond, and howl, and wail,
Till Nature's wreck, till from the fhrivel'd Skies
The laft dread Trump fhall call, " Ye Dead, awake,
    " arife !"

O come betimes, fweet Penitential Pow'r,
    And from fuch Soul-diftracting care,
    Such chilling Horrours of Defpair,
Preferve me, fhield me, at Death's trying Hour !
    From Guilt of black enormous Dye
    My breaft is free ; I ne'er betray'd
    A Virgin's eafy Faith ; no murd'rous Lie
    In fecret Whifpers have convey'd,
Nor with the Mufe's everliving ftore
Embalm'd the carrion corpfe of Wealth, or Pride, or Pow'r.

From

From Truth's ſtraight Path, and Virtue's thorny Way,
   Have wandring Meteors falſe, and vain,
   The Glare of Honour or of Gain,
'Thro' Dirt, and Danger drawn my ſteps aſtray ?
   Have I rejeᴄted Reaſon's Aid,
   And giv'n to headlong Luſts the Rein ?
   Or prone beneath the myrtle Shade
   Of Indolence and Pleaſure lain ?
Have I the tribute of a Tear deny'd,
When Want unheard hath wept, and injur'd Orphans cry'd ?

Good Heav'n forbid !——Yet ſtill within my Soul
   Some leprous Spots of Guilt remain :
   Oh could I cleanſe each groſſer Stain
In Jordan's Tide, or Siloa's healing Pool !
   Fond Thought !——More ſalutary Pow'rs
   In Sorrow's ſwelling ſtream reſide,
   Than Siloa's Pool at ſtated Hours
   Could boaſt, or Jordan's cleanſing Tide ;
This from the Soul ſharp Humours can repel,
Cure ev'ry feſtring Wound, and Death's dread Torments
     quell.

Here many a beauteous Pearl of coſtly Price,
   And many a Gem of purer ray
   Than all Golconda's Mines diſplay,
Lie hid in Darkneſs far from vulgar Eyes :

For

For Thefe the cloifter'd Virgin pines,
Torn from each pleafing tender care;
For Thefe her placid Breaft refigns
To midnight Grief, and midnight Pray'r;
Poor, haplefs Maid!—May Heav'n her Vows regard,
And all her wakeful Pains with endlefs blifs reward!

Go fly, ye filken fons of Pleafure, fly,
And barter for fantaftic Joys,
Spurn'd by the Great, the Good, the Wife,
What Afia's Monarchs have not Worth to buy!
Chace ev'ry cloudy Thought away,
Whofe ferious Gloom o'ercafts the Soul;
To Rapture give Life's little day,
And bid full Tides of Pleafure roll;
Go where the loofe-rob'd Forms of wild Defire
Expand their Wanton Charms, and prefs the buxom Choir!

'Tis Madnefs all!—Be mine unknown to Sin,
And Paffions bafe, fome lone Retreat,
Some hoary Hermit's mofs-grown Seat,
Far from the guilty World's tumultuous Din,
Whether in HAGLEY's facred Shades,
Where Infpiration breathes around,
And by the much-lov'd Thefpian Maids
Their LUCY's plaintive Bard is crown'd;

Or

Or Hackfall's Bow'rs, and woodland Walks invite,
Where Nature's various Charms, all rude of Art, delight.

O Lawns!—O Hills!—And O thou pleafant Vale,
  Where Ure's meandring Waters roll!
  What penfive Pleafures foothe my Soul,
What tender melancholy Thoughts prevail
  At thy Approach?—While am'rous Jove
  On Flora's bofom deigns to play,
  Still let me haunt thy blifsful Grove,
  Where all the rural Graces ftray;
There bid the folly-fetter'd World adieu,
And Wifdom's filent Steps with holy Zeal purfue,

There Contemplation dwells, that hoary Sire,
  And points the way that leadeth right
  To thofe moft glorious Manfions, bright
With burning Stars, and everliving fire:
  There, on her filver Anchor ftaid,
  Sweet Hope to Heav'n directs her Eyes;
While Faith, that eagle-fighted Maid,
  Her far forefeeing Tube applies,
Whofe mighty pow'r reveals the bleft Abode,
In beatific Trance, where Saints enjoy their God.

N

THE

THE
REDEMPTION.

BY

JOHN HEY, M. A.

M DCC LXIII.

N 2 CONTENTS.

CONTENTS.

IN order to form a well-grounded judgment concerning any mysterious doctrine which is said to have been reveal'd by God, the first natural step seems to be, to examine whether the Body of Laws and Doctrines of which it is a part, is really of divine original, or only of human invention; if the concurrence of external and internal testimony makes it more probable that it is the former than the latter, the next step is to examine with all possible caution and candour, what is clearly said in the books so reveal'd concerning such doctrine. This being done, the only necessary enquiry which now remains is, whether any objections can be offer'd of such strength as to invalidate the former testimony: if not, the whole is to be receiv'd for truth. This then is the general plan of the following exercise; and in pursuance of it, the Author, after hinting at the modesty, plainness, moderation and openness to conviction with which subjects of this nature ought to be contemplated and difcufs'd, (line 20—29) by way of introduction, first points out the external evidence of Revelation (30), then the internal (43), with the improbability of its coming only from intelligent creatures superior to Man (85).——The prejudice from its appearing strange is next shewn to be a groundless one (97); and the consistency of the whole story both with itself and the known circumstances of Mankind, a presumption in its favour (105).

The rest of the Contents are as follow. The History of the Fall (115), — its consequences; natural evil (150), moral (200), — the reasonable fears consequent upon the latter (213), — the gradual preparation of the world for the coming of the Meffiah (224), — his life, sufferings,

N 3

exaltation,

THE

THE
REDEMPTION.

WHOM shall the bard that dares of themes to sing
Such as th' Angelic Choir in wonder mute
Vainly * revolve, whom shall the bard invoke?
He trembles while he dares.   Eternal Spirit!
Whom shall he call but thee? Thou think'st not scorn
To make thyself a lowly habitant
In the mean cottage of the human breast,
When Purity has been thy Harbinger:
Come then, and lead the Virtues in thy train;
Allot to each her office; ceafelefs guard
Still let them hold around this earth-born heart,
And watch with closest glance its languid pulse,
And purge the bursting humors as they flow,
Lest Vice or Ignorance should prompt a lay .
To stain with foul disgrace the ways of Heav'n.

* 1 Pet. i. 12.

But

But above all do thou, Humility,
Come from thy chofen place remote ; thine eye
Downcaft advance, quicken thy loit'ring ftep;
And myftic dew of Caution fprinkle round :
The empty word myfterious erafe ;   20
The curious pride that rufhes with bold ftep
Into the awful counfels of Heav'n's King,
Check ;—nor allow the gairifh paint of Art.
O may the ftrains glide even, uniform,
Far diff'rent courfe from Fancy's light cafcade ;
Unruffled by the ftorms of Cruelty
Gender'd in Perfecution's gloomy cave :
Free may they flow, tranfparent, uncongeal'd
By th' icy breeze of Infidelity.   29

Heard ye that voice ? Sure 'twas the voice of Heav'n :
In mild, majeftic ftrains it pierc'd my ear,
While Nature trembled at th' exalted found
Ev'n from her inmoft frame ; what ailed thee
That thou didft tremble ? That ev'n thou, proud Sea,
Retiredft back with flight precipitate,
Heap'd into monftrous mountains Chaos-like ?
Why from the thirfty breaft of flinty rock
Gufh'd the refrefhing Stream ? Why, fell Difeafe,
Thy dreary habitations didft thou quit ?
And thou, O Grave, ope thy voracious Jaw,

Yielding

Yielding thy firm-feiz'd prey (unwonted gift)
At the dread found?—'Twas fure the voice of Heav'n.

    And now on adamantine tablet fee   **43**
Engrav'd in charaƈters indelible
Th' important embaffy; ye Learned, read,
And tell us——did the vaft, ftupendous chain,
Deliver'd by the great Creator erft
Into the hands of Nature, and fince held
By her with grafp unfhaken, burft its hold
Obedient to fome noxious Spirit of air,
(If true, how paffing ftrange!) only to caft
Still thicker darknefs round our filmy eyes?
Or is the meffage of a kindlier fort?
Difplays it fcenes fuch as from human eye
Malice would hide for ever?——Say, ye Learn'd,
Its Laws how fram'd? Steal they with wily art
Fair-promifing into th' unwary breaft,
And there diffufe their pois'nous juices round,
Firft pleafing, then deftroying? Or proclaim they
Firft trial, then reward? Tend they to blefs
The brutal appetite, or purer mind?
Whom do they claim their Author? Him who made
And will'd us happy? Speak, O ye that gaze
Intent upon the dazzling adamant!
—— Behold they fmile propitious! and lo, now

                           With

With nod benign they prompt our timid steps
To join their labours, and with studious eye,
Trace out the treasures of the sacred page.

    Here may I stand infix'd! in rapt'rous awe
Collecting the bright rays of truth that beam
From ev'ry point resistless: narrow orb!
O that thou didst avail thyself t' expand,
And catch the blaze of each illustrious beam!
That thy refracting powers could quench this glare,
And give to ev'ry image that thou form'st,
Grace of distinctness! But it may not be.
——Yet much is clear: yes, num'rous are the rays
That dart instruction on this weakly sight,
And mark the truths to Man of chief import,
And light him on to *human* happiness.
——Here may I stand infix'd! until this mind
Is satiate with pure wisdom from above;
And till this heart imbibes the gen'rous warmth
That brooks no limit of benevolence.

    'Tis Heav'nly all! no spirit of *human* mould,
Gross and impure, could dare such lofty flights
Ev'n on Imagination's waxen wings.
Come then such tidings from the spirits of *air?*
Vain thought! the *good* obey their Maker's will;

                                    Far

Far diff'rent tafk from fpreading to the eye
Of wand'ring mortals, meteors of deceit;
And never did *malignant* Dæmon joy
To fhew all worlds the fount of human blifs,
And wave the enfigns of his own defeat.
Ah no! 'tis Heav'nly all!

Here read we then the ftory of our race;
Strange—wond'rous tale!—yet is it therefore falfe?   97.
Surmife of narrow mind! ev'n truth is ftrange
If now it firft appear to human view,
Or if 'tis but illumin'd partially,
Here bright and there obfcure; did now this hand
Firft move, the Sun firft rife, that plant firft grow,
Wou'd not all view them with aftonifhment?
—— But is the fignet of Heav'n's gracious King
Imprefs'd on error? Truth and Falfehood's dregs   105
Can they Incorporate in one friendly mafs?
Ah no! fcarce ere can Falfehood with itfelf
 Form a confiftence; and 'twixt that and truth
There is a ftrong repulfive faculty,
That fpurns th' attempt of mixture fo impure,
— Here read we then the Story of our Race:
But read with cautious fear; left Falfehood fly
 Cloath'd in Conjecture's captivating guife,
 Win us unwary to her foul embrace.

Form'd

Form'd from the duſt the Parent of mankind   115
Poſſeſs'd each faculty by Heav'n decreed
For uſe or ornament of *Man:* no want
He knew; no imperfection he perceiv'd;
Save what all things endued with conſcious ſenſe
Muſt ever feel; dependence on their Lord,
The firſt eternal Being: wholeſome food
Was his repaſt; not chos'n, as by his Sons,
After experiment where Danger lurks
And frequent Death; but vegetating free
Within that ſpace where his unarmed foot
Trod with ſecurity the harmleſs turf,
And gather'd as the voice of Heav'n enjoin'd.
Far, ſure, muſt be Diſeaſe from this bleſt ſcene,
And Wearineſs and wan Infirmity:
Yet was the human body moulded erſt
Of Matter, ſtill diviſible; whoſe parts,
Knowing nor ſenſe nor ſelf-connecting pow'r,
Time ſoon had moulder'd into native duſt,
Had not the word of the Creator bid
That Tree ariſe, whoſe ſalutary fruit
Convey'd Refreſhment with perfection big,
Preſerving pow'rs obnoxious to decay,
In the full vigour of immortal youth.
—Diff'rence of good and ill for man to know
Was needleſs ſure, while with the fearleſs eye

Of

Of an obedient fon, he might look up
To the Almighty Father of his race,
And claim his guidance; to that Heav'nly Friend
He might appeal, whofe all-perceiving ken
Diftance deceiv'd not, number ne'er confus'd,
Who faw all qualities of all things: Whence
To Man fo favour'd, cou'd there e'er arife
Temptation to do evil? Whence a caufe
Why one fenfation he fhou'd e'er conceal,
Why caution or protection he fhou'd ufe?
No; 'twas in naked purity he rov'd,
Needing nor Art's concealment nor defence.
Led by the filken cords of Heav'nly Love,
He trod the paths of Safety; yet not bound
In iron chain of dire Neceffity;
For confcious Liberty ftill fmil'd within,
And rais'd the heart-felt glow of felf-applaufe
At each obedient act: 'twas Liberty,
Not as of late time, harraffing the foul
With everlafting doubt; impelling oft
In various paths; paths terminating all
In thickeft clouds of drear obfcurity;
But to one only doubt 'twas all confin'd;
Whether the rank of mortals new-create
To God their guide fhou'd conftantly appeal,
Or Man himfelf fhou'd be the guide of Man.

O fatal

O fatal Curiofity and Pride,
(Fatal tho' rais'd by fuch bewitching arts
That Candour pities, while ftern Juftice blames,)
Ye made the hazardous, th' important Choice !
Yet had the ear of Man imbib'd this threat
In unfufpected force : (for knows the heart
Sufpicion, unexperienc'd in deceit ?)
" The fruit of Life fhall ne'er bedew thy lips
" If fuch thy choice"—'twas Mercy, gracious Heav'n,
Pronounc'd this fentence 'gainft Man's firft revolt :
Mild was the Law that will'd but to recall
A voluntary gift; no other ill
Enfuing, fave what from the choice itfelf   180
Flow'd of neceffity.—Yet, O juft God !
In what o'erwhelming torrents does it flow !
The beams of Heav'nly light ftrike not his eye ;
He wanders loft in Danger's thickeft maze,
His only guide a faint and glimmering lamp :
At ev'ry turn fee Mifchief fudden ftart,
While oft her Remedy in deepeft fhade
Shuns ev'n th' exploring eye of Diligence.
How frequent are his falls ! th' unnotic'd ftep
Scarce ever fafe ; th' experience ev'n of Age
Of weak avail, to tread the maze unhurt.
Now fee this Lord of earth protect his head
From elements created for his good ;

And

And now the impulfe of his nature check,
Till Time informs him, whether, on the whole,
It tends to Mis'ry or to Happinefs.
Behold him, or envelop'd in Diftruft,
Or running into ever-prefent ill,
Productive foon of endlefs diffidence.

But the grand fource of Mis'ry ftill remains   200
Unnotic'd : When the all-creative Pow'r
Into exiftence call'd the race of Man,
Relations beautiful were form'd 'twixt him
And certain modes of action ; proper, meet
To make him happy, and to be the teft
Of his obedience ; confonant to thefe
He ftill had acted under God his guide ;
But fince Ambition fnatch'd the dang'rous rein,
Eager to drive o'er arduous paths unknown,
What Sun has feen thefe Laws inviolate ?
What Man can ftrike the pure unconfcious breaft ?

And yet, prefumptuous reas'ner, wilt thou fay   213
No ill fhall follow ? Wherefore then thefe Laws ?
Or can that ill be adequately paid
To men yet fubject to perpetual falls ?
Incredible ! Hence fee a length of woe
To which no bounds appear ; ftretch ere fo far

O

The

The aking eye of Fancy, ftill there frowns
The threat'ning ftorm of mifery beyond;
Its gloom ftill heighten'd by the awful truth,
Th' indifputable truth, that *God is juft*.
—But read again the Story of our race.—

Scarce had this revolution of our fate   224
Left us in horror of the thickeft night,
When Mercy 'gan to dart a twilight beam,
And gave to Man a faint and diftant hope,
That the bright Sun of righteoufnefs would rife,
And diffipate this gloom of black Defpair.
---And now the rays of confolation glance
With growing luftre through th' illumin'd air;
Till ev'ry eye, caught by the orient beams,
Expectant turns towards the refplendent Eaft,
To view the glorious brightnefs of his rifing.

The Son of God is born; in form of Man   235
He paffes through the changes of our life,
And fpotlefs, bears th' infirmities of guilt;
Republifhes that ancient law of Heav'n
Which Man was firft ordained to obey;
And though difguis'd, impair'd, disfigur'd, clog'd,
Difplays it in its genuine purity,
And all its native comelinefs of form.

His

His fteps are prompted by Benevolence,
His glare of greatnefs foften'd by the fhade
Of mild deportment; from his modeft lips
Expires th' incenfe bland of Heav'nly Truth.
—But, O great Lord of all! what piercing fcenes
Now fnatch my eye impetuous o'er the page!
Mis'ry at ev'ry glance! O quicker far
Than cold Expreffion's pace it darts along ¢
O Treachery! Ingratitude! blind Scorn!
What havock do ye make!——Bleft innocence!
How doft thou groan beneath thofe dreadful pangs
Which Guilt that only caus'd, fhould only feel!
—But foft! ev'n Mis'ry, fo eventful, wills
To be recorded, nay, and ponder'd o'er
With thought deliberate. Shall Aftonifhment,
Or Gratitude or Pity fway the breaft,
While we again perufe the tragic tale?

The Son of God, a voluntary Victim,
Spotlefs himfelf, to buy devoted Man,
To reinftate him in his loft domain,
To give for prefent, future pow'r o'er Death,
To ope the friendly portal of Repentance,
And guide the tott'ring ftep of Piety
Through her long pilgrimage, to certain blifs,
—Dies!—In confufion fhrink each tow'ring thought,

O 2

Each

Each luftful appetite, each wild defire!
Affliction, thou may'ft raife thy drooping head,
Thou, Mis'ry, fmile! unmoving is your moan
While Man's Redeemer hangs upon the Crofs.

But let not grief, though from the tender heart
It burft refiftlefs, ftop th' important tafk;
Perufe we ftill the ftory of our race.
—Such are the virtues of this Victim flain:
Yet virtues not promifcuoufly beftow'd;
On thofe alone deriv'd in full extent
Whofe fteady truft can fpurn the prefent good,
And wait the meed of dim Futurity;
Whofe humble mind, carelefs of felf-defert,
On him can fix its perfevering hopes:
Hopes, not vain Fancy's fabric, light as air,
Burfting, like bubbles, on a near approach;
But founded on firm Reafon's folid rock:
For lo, the fon of Man from the cold grave
Triumphant rifes; haft thou now a doubt
Whether this great, ftupendous facrifice
Avails to draw the pois'nous fting of Death?
He rifes; not to drag a tedious life
'Midft mortal frailties, but ere long to fpring
From this grofs earth, and claim a purer air:
At the right hand of Majefty on high

To

To fit, with never-fading glory crown'd;
His name, throughout Creation's ample range,
Far above ev'ry other name extoll'd,
Of Being that exifts on Earth's domain,
Or through the fathomlefs abyfs of Heav'n.
Touch'd with a feeling of infirmities,
Such as deprav'd Humanity laments,
With ceafelefs interceffion there he pleads;
Perfects our wretched facrifice of pray'r
And frail obedience; 'fore the throne of God
Off'ring them up with the accepted claim
Of his prevailing Merits: gives our tears
The wond'rous efficacy to blot out
The ftains of Guilt, indelible before;
And waits the round of Time to judge the World,
And introduce the honeft Penitent
Into the ceafelefs glory of his Lord.

" But fure in Eden's grove God was the guide   310
" Of wand'ring Man; and fhall th' anointed Son
" Only in part reftore the charter loft
" By difobedient choice of our firft Sire ?"

To ftrike thee dumb, read here—the Spirit of God
From Heav'n defcending, dwells in dome of clay;
In mode far paffing human thought, he guides,

O 3

Impells,

Impells, inftructs : intenfe purfuit of Good
And cautious flight of Evil he fuggefts,
But in fuch gentle murmurs, that to know
His Heav'nly voice, we muft have done his will :
Such dictates only *Liberty* obeys ;
Th' *undoubted* voice of Heav'n a guide unapt
For beings now experienc'd in ill,
And doom'd to walk the wild, perplexing paths
Of conftant Trial and Uncertainty.

Such is the wond'rous ftory of our Race :   326
—Proftrate thyfelf, O Man ! With lowly heart
And wonder-clofed lips—paufe—think—revolve !
Think what thou art, and that the great Supreme
Has deign'd to vifit thine infirmities.
Think of that tie which binds thy Nature's laws ;
What facred magic muft pervade each link,
When all the pow'rs of Heav'n and Earth are mov'd
At its difunion ! O with horror think
Of each rebellious action or intent :
For now thou know'ft how evil unforefeen,
May flow in changelefs tenor, ev'n from Laws
Promulg'd by Wifdom and Benevolence.
— But thanks be to the Father of mankind,
Who op'd this avenue to real blifs,
Remov'd each gloomy fhade of nat'ral fear,

And

And on a folid bafe eftablifh'd Hope,
Pointing the way to Immortality ! ·   343
Is there the Man, who hefitates to join
This fong of gratitude ? Exifts there one,
Blindly prefumptuous, who dares to claim
From Juftice his *deferved* happinefs ?   347
Is there, that with a fenfelefs difregard
Cafts the cold eye of Indolence along
This facred Tablet ? carelefs if he draw
The living water from this purer fource,
Or from the troubled wells of his Forefathers ?
If thou, my friend, art fuch, O hear the voice   353
That fhouts to wake thee from thy fatal dream :
Think with what cries the partner of thy Soul
Would rend the air, if on the narrow brink
Of yon tremendous rock, he faw thee dance
With heedlefs mirth : O think thou hear'ft them now !
Would it reftore thy fhatter'd limbs to plead
Thy difregard of danger ?—But from whence
This carelefs eafe ? Does the great Lord of Heav'n   361
Reveal the nice Relations of thy State,
Regardlefs of the Duties which enfue ?
Are thy Redeemer and thy Heav'nly Guide
Made known, to be neglected or defpis'd ?
Sooner fhall Sophiftry pervert my mind
To think that harden'd wretch of Heav'n approv'd,

O 4

Who

Who leaves his Parent, aged and infirm,
To crawl through life in unfupported woe;
Or yields the helplefs Orphan, or the Poor
To the Oppreffor's unrelenting fangs.
—Thou fay'ft that forrow will draw down the eye   372
Of Mercy from above: that future care
Will foon extenuate the paft offence:
But from what region do the magic pow'rs
Of Fancy conjure up this airy Hope?
Go to the Senfual; do his bittereft tears   377
Avail to bring back Plenty to his board?
Or can they from his wafting limbs remove
The peftilential gnawing of Difeafe?
Go to the dread tribunal of the Law,
And hear the Murd'rer plead the num'rous Suns
That faw no repetition of his crime:
Say, does he thus ward off the blow?
Juftice is deaf to the unmeaning plea.

But ftill methinks the frown of Difcontent   386
Sits low'ring on thy brow: thou would'ft be taught,
" What Virtue is in voluntary Death
" To reconcile offenders to their Judge."
But fay, fhould filence give thy needlefs doubts   390
To fpend themfelves in air; dar'ft thou conclude
The voice we heard was not the voice of Heav'n?

What

What province in the guidance of the world
Doft thou uphold, that all the fecret fprings
Of Government muft be difplay'd to thee?
Prefumptuous reptile! it is thine to know
What it is thine to practife: all the reft,
To thee obfcure, to God is clear as Day.
—Remember too—" the Univerfal Caufe 399
" Acts not by partial, but by gen'ral Laws:"
Remember that of thefe, tho' fome thou fee'ft,
Myriads are hid from thine all-curious eye;
While Nature's prodigies before thee move,
Convincing thee of ignorance profound.
Tell me the Law whereby the Earthquake's rage
Inftant o'erwhelms in ruin unforefeen
The boafted monuments of human pride:
Why the Volcano pours his liquid fire;
Why Peftilence and Famine ftalk the earth,
And ravage uncontroll'd: th' unnumber'd laws
Unfold to which thou giv'ft one empty name
Of Chance. Shall thefe, vain man! elude thy fearch,
Enacted for the ordinary courfe
Of Nature's operations; and fhalt thou
Murmur at the obfcurity of thofe
Deriv'd from Exigency's latent fprings?

 Once more that Adamantine Tablet view; 417
The grand Redemption of degen'rate Man

Is not a fingle, independent act,
But one great Syftem; that perchance involv'd
In the one only greater, God's high Law
Pervading and fupporting ev'ry part
Of the ftupendous Univerfe: to thee
Dark are this Syftem's limits; nay, the whole
To thee unknown, fave fome minuter fpots
Difplay'd to fhew the part thou haft to act
In the alarming Scene.   But know that he
Who of a Syftem fees but part, fees none.
Behold yon ftately Edifice; where Art
And Nature lavifh all their richeft ftores,
To charm thine eye with Majefty and Grace:
—Let all, fave that fmall fragment, now be veil'd:—
Say, do it's beauties ftrike without impair?
Where is the Symmetry that fmil'd around,
The Greatnefs that fo dazzled? Where the Ufe
That warm'd the Judgment into Admiration?
Alas, the veil was drawn, and they are fled.
—Think'ft thou the Indian, tho' before the Sun
He bend the knee of worfhip, can conceive
Aught of thofe Glories which ev'n thou conceiv'ft,
Who fee'ft him roll around his ponderous Mafs,
Enliv'ning ev'ry Planet in his train;
And in their rapid courfes while they fing,
With godlike firmnefs curbing their bold flight,
And poizing them in heav'nly harmony?   He

He who on Syſtems oft with ſerious care   446
Has fix'd Attention's eye, muſt oft have ſeen
The tendency of parts to work their ends,
Diff'ring from his opinion preconceiv'd.
Who of ye all, that murmur at the means
By the Supreme for Man's Redemption choſe,
(Forgetting all that ſage *Experience* taught,)
Shall ſee yon Peaſant hide within the ground,
Far from his anxious view, the precious grain,
His great ſupport and friend, in ſtedfaſt hope
Soon to behold it yield a glad increaſe;
And ſhall not ſtrait put forth the friendly hand
To check the progreſs of his wild deſign?
—Aſk we, in ſhort, where 'tis ye find the chain,
Which here ye want, connecting *means* with *end?*
Shall ye not ſay, " *Experience* is our guide?"
Where then your guide is blind, how weak the hope
To find the latent object of your ſearch!

But tell me, can thy mem'ry range thro' time,   464
Ev'n from the firſt Creation of our Race,
And ſee the ſcatter'd tribes of varying men
Recurring to the feeble victim's aid
To expiate the guilt of paſt offence;
Both where the light of Revelation ſhone,
And where dim Reaſon ſhed a fainter ray;

Can'ſt

Can'st thou such Uniformity behold,
Nor yet prefume there is a Law of God,
Whereby the facrifice of his dread Son
Avails to purchafe immortality ?
—If ftill Impatience or Sufpicion haunt   475
Thy mind, where Knowledge will not deign to dwell;
Ponder that holy Tablet's precious lore ;
Perchance, to recompence thy modeft fearch,
New light may beam from the great Fount of light,
And pathways, hitherto untrod, appear.
But fure we may with confidence unblam'd
Dare to pronounce, that while the low'ring mifts
Of human ignorance fo deep involve
The mis'ry we efcape, and blifs we gain ;
No eye fo clearly fhall perceive the means
Of gaining or efcaping, as to judge,
With Reafon's fuffrage, *how* they work their end.

  " Ign'rance the narrow mind of man may brook : 488
" But fhall Infenfibility's cold hand
" Allay all ferment betwixt Right and Wrong,
" Wife and Unwife ? That were to leave no praife
" Due ev'n to God.   Perfift we then to fay,
" That to *prevent* more fuits the Good and Wife,
" Than to *permit*, what muft anon be heal'd."

           Be

Be not deceiv'd : we feek not *here* to find
A felf-exiftent Being good and wife;
Or fuch thou own'ft, or groundlefs all debate
Of the unfolding his myfterious will :
This wou'd we know; whether the fame great Lord,
Who over Nature's powers fublime prefides,
Did doubtlefs utter this alarming Voice,
And bid this holy Tablet be engrav'd.

Arife then, thou that wou'd'ft *prevent* our Fall,
Arife, and let us fee thee rule the world
After thy darling principle : from thence
Judge we, if to the fame one point converge
Thy fchemes, and the decrees of Nature's God,
——Behold yon circle of domeftic friends,
Each to his nightly couch ferene retire,
Unconfcious of the fatal Spark which, fhed
From Indifcretion's brandifh'd torch, now pants
And labours to diffufe it's baleful pow'rs.
Heav'ns! with what horror do the burfting flames
Diffolve the feal of Sleep ! Amazement ftarts,
And wild Confufion bounds with frantic ftep
Throughout the tott'ring manfion : How to fly,
The firft, great care.   O defperate refource !
Behold that tender Youth fpring from on high
And truft himfelf to Air : Alas! too fure

Some

Some feeble Limb is shatter'd by the fall :
But see Compassion's friendly hand stretch'd out
To mitigate the anguish of his *Soul*;
And Med'cine's balm soothing the *Body's* pain,
Able, ere long, Health's firmness to restore.

Had thy superior wisdom govern'd here,
This scene had been *prevented*; then what need
To clog the mind with dull Discretion's bonds,
Or goad it with Compassion's pungent spur,
Or give to nat'ral bodies healing pow'rs ?
—Thy scheme no doubt is wise : but yet methinks
Boasts not a freedom from these slight defects ;
—Man first of human nature it despoils ;
Then bids the Lord of Heav'n reverse that plan
His Wisdom form'd before the birth of Time.

" Be then this Ill permitted ; and it's cure   535
" Reserv'd in Mercy's inexhausted stores ;
" But can that remedy proceed from Heav'n
" Which wills us to conceive th' Almighty Pow'r
" Lab'ring thro' years, with cumb'rous instruments,
" Imploring too a Mediator's aid,
" Ere he his gracious purpose can effect ?
" —Better befits his pow'r to speak the word
" And heal."—But say, dost thou expect a change

Sudden

Sudden and self-effected to arise
From the great God of Nature? Shew us then
Some upstart being perfect at it's birth,
Or instant perishing without decay.
Shew us the hand of Providence unarm'd
With instrument, or senseless, or inform'd:
How did thy mind, thy body, all thy pow'rs
Attain that fulness of Maturity?
And whence the Good and Evil of thy state,
But from the creatures of thy Sov'reign Lord?
His Scourge the Tyrant, his Reward the Friend,
His Gift the Fruits of earth, his Messengers
The Winds, his Minister the flaming Fire.

" Grant then that thus to remedy is wise;
" Yet does the God of Justice disregard
" If Guilt or Innocence be doom'd to pain?"
Hence with the impious thought! But dost thou deem
That voice was not the voice of Nature's God,
Because it publish'd our deliv'rance wrought
By suff'rance meek of voluntary woe?
Alas! full little dost thou mark the scenes
Of Providence, which flit before thine eye,
How oft in them is wretchedness of Guilt
Alleviated by suff'ring Innocence!
—Mark that impetuous Youth: the fev'rish fire

Of

Of Paſſion ſeizes all his nobler pow'rs:
The Phantom Pleaſure trips with airy ſwim
Before his dazzled eye: mark the purſuit
How eager, how intenſe?—and now he hopes
To graſp her in his arms—and now ſhe flies—
Ever at diſtance, ſeeming ever near.
At length behold her vaniſh from his view,
When lo, a griſly band of pallid Fiends,
The meager train of Want, ſurround and ſeize
Him languid with purſuit; now ſee him bound
In ſqualid fetters by Profuſion knit,
Stranger to Liberty, and the pure breath
Of wholeſome air. Deſpair mean while aloof,
Hovers expectant of her deſtin'd prey.
—But whence that hoary ſage who enters there,
The meek tears ſtealing down his furrow'd cheeks,
And Virtue's footſteps printed on his brow?
His ſtaff a weak ſupport for Age and Grief!
—Sure 'tis Paternal Love: mark with what care
He gazes on the guilty Youth! how mild
Are his reproaches, and his Soul how bent
To reſcue him from Slavery and Woe,
Regardleſs of the ill himſelf muſt bear!
Can'ſt thou ſee this, nor own thy Nature's Law
Decrees ſuch friendly interchange of pain,
While we are paſſing thro' this vale of tears?

—And from whence is it, that the Son of God
Shall not, if fuch his gracious will, affift
In the grand progrefs tow'rds eternal blifs,
And fuffer for the guilty race of Men ?

But let Contention ceafe : wait we the Hour,   598
When all things fhall arrive to that one point
Whereto they have converg'd ere fince the World
Was firft awak'd from Chaos into Life.
When all the parts of this unfinifh'd Scheme
Shall be compacted in one perfect Whole ;
And what was deem'd unfit, fhall ftrike the eye
With all it's genuine Symmetry and Grace ;
Then fhall the Juftice and Benevolence
Of our Eternal Lord unclouded fhine ;
Seen by Reflection's broken rays no more ;
Themfelves the naked objects of our view :
Then fhall the great Redeemer of Mankind,
Nay ev'ry meaner Sufferer, receive
The meed, tho' long-referv'd, of ten-fold Blifs :
And Mercy hide in her maternal Breaft
The fhame of him, who trembles to look up
To the Tribunal of the Righteous Judge.

P

T H E

THE

CONVERSION

OF

ST. PAUL.

BY

JOHN LETTICE, M. A.

MDCCLXIV.

THE

CONVERSION

OF

St. PAUL.

" YES—gentle Shade (Heav'n on thy bounty fmile!),
" The lib'ral purpofe of thy glowing Heart
" Breaths nought fave Peace, Religion, and the Love
" Of facred Verfe. Thou woo'ft the myftic Pow'rs
" That frame fweet Numbers to the golden Lyre,
" To fly thofe turbid Regions, where, contemn'd
" The chafter Honours of poetic Lore,
" Loft all the Dignity of antient Song,
" Long have they chanted to the frantic Voice
" Of civil Difcord, and fraternal Rage
" Refponfive. May thy gen'rous urgent Call
" Allure the Wand'rers to CAM's hallow'd Groves,
" Once more to fill thefe much-neglected fhades
" With fweeteft Minftrelfy of magic Sound:."

P 3

Such

Such Anſwer from the Voice of Fancy flow'd,
As late, methought, ſome Viſion's airy Charm
Call'd to my View the venerable Shade
Of SEATON, much lamenting that the Muſe
Regardleſs of th' exalted Province, erſt
Aſſerted with ſuch jealous Care, ſhould yield
Her Lyre divine, her high-enchanting Strains
To Spleen, Revenge and unrelenting Hate,
The baleful Offspring of diſaſtrous Times.

Come then, ſweet Chantreſs of celeſtial Airs!
Inſpire thy ſuppliant Vot'ry, whilſt he ſings
The Man of Tarſus, from Gamaliel's Feet
Rais'd to the Converſe of the living God.

How thick that Cloud! that Darkneſs how profound!
Which o'er the mental Sight blind Prejudice
Suſpends, impervious to the brighteſt Rays
Of moral Evidence.   Ah zealous Saint!
Had Heav'n to Thee vouchſaf'd no ſtronger Light
To guide thy devious Foot-ſteps through the Gloom
Of Error's Maze, long as the vital Stream
Had warm'd thy dauntleſs Heart, the ſwelling Pride
That Nature gave, th' unconquerable Rage
Of Jewiſh Bigotry, the callous Senſe
Deaf to the Charmer Reaſon's Call, ſo long

Had

Had chain'd to Earth thy captivated Soul.
But—Gracious Pow'rs! what Burst of blazing Light!
Lo! where th' effulgent Streams of purer Day,
Surpassing far the Radiance of the Morn
First rising o'er the Bow'rs of Paradise,
Spring from Heav'n's azure Canopy! And hark!
Some Voice tremendous, like the fearful Roar
Of rushing Cataracts, pervades the Air—
" Saul! Saul! what Madness lifts thine impious Arm
" To brave th' Omnipotence of Heav'n? Forbear,
" Rash Mortal! Check thine unavailing Rage,
" Nor longer with eternal Adamant *
" Wage fruitless War.   What? Can an Insect's Sting
" Rift the firm Oak? Or shall the Lion fall
" A recreant Victim to the timid Lamb?—
" With Rev'rence wait the high Behests of Heav'n;
" And know, proud Reptile! 'tis that Sov'reign Pow'r,
" Th' immortal God thy Fury braves, whose Voice
" Arrests thine Ear."   Soon as the first Alarm,
That lock'd each Sense in dumb Astonishment,
Had ceas'd, the prostrate Seer, with trembling Tongue,
The heav'nly Vision fearfully addrefs'd—

* Ἀδάμαντα πάσχειν——carried with it, among the Antients, the same proverbial Import as—πρὸς τά κέντρα λακτίζειν.

          " O !

" O ! Source divine of Love and Goodnefs ! loft
" In the wild Tranfports of th' impaffion'd Soul,
" Terror, Remorfe, Hope, Gratitude and Joy
" By turns triumphant o'er each captive Thought,
" What fhall I fpeak, or how be filent ? Deign,
" Eternal Spirit ! to declare thy Will :
" Say, why vouchfaf'd thy Prefence, why difplay'd
" Thy Glories to a Reptile of the Duft ?"
He ceas'd.—The Voice celeftial thus reply'd—
" Arife ! to fair Damafcus' Walls purfue
" Thy deftin'd Courfe ; there fhall the deep Decrees
" Of Heav'n, ere long, to thine illumin'd Senfe
" Unclouded fhine." Obedient rofe the Seer
Of God high-favour'd ; but behold ! his Eyes
Plung'd in the Torrent of th' empyreal Blaze
To dreary Night confign'd.   Th' obfequious Train,
The Partners of his fell vindictive Zeal,
Speechlefs with Horror, guide his painful Steps
To the fam'd City.   Three long tedious Days
An Exile from the chearful Sun, no Food,
No Draught refrefhing to his Wants fupply'd,
There did he ponder, in his chearlefs Breaft,
The Mazes of th' Almighty's Will.   Three Days
Expir'd, by Heav'n's propitious Guidance led,
Arriv'd the Minifter of Light.   He fpoke
The magic Word of Faith ; and inftant fell

The

The Veil of Darkneſs from the Zealot's Eye.
Once more the vivid Splendor of the Sun
He ſaw, and thus pour'd forth th' extatic Joy:
" Hail, bleſſed Orb! ætherial Brightneſs, hail!
" Welcome! the genial Luxury of Light;
" Thrice welcome it's Return! But Oh! what words
" Shall hail the Day-ſpring of immortal Truth!
" What Words can paint the Radiance of her Beams
" Firſt darting on the Soul! Purg'd the thick Film
" Of Jewiſh Ignorance from Reaſon's Eye,
" Now ſtand reveal'd the wiſe, the wond'rous Schemes
" Of Providence.   I ſee, confeſs, adore
" The Miracle of Mercy, Grace and Love,
" Vouchſaf'd Man's guilty Race, vouchſaf'd e'en Me!

Th' enraptur'd Convert ceas'd.   The ſacred Lymph,
Myſterious Prelude of regenerate Life!
Confirm'd th' auſpicious Change.   Faith, Fortitude,
Light-winged Hope, and the cherubic Throng,
That with the ductile Spirit of the Soul
Congenial, ſtill attend on Virtue's Paths,
Hov'ring around Heav'n's fav'rite Proſelyte,
Fix on his Breaſt their adamantine Seal.

Each holy Rite perform'd, the zealous Saint
Pour'd from his Tongue ſpontaneous the Stream

Of

Of Eloquence and Infpiration.   Lo !
The gazing Synagogue, in wonder wrapt,
Devour his pregnant Speech.   Th' inftructive Sage
With fimple Stile, deliberate Addrefs
And nervous Argument, now vindicates
The great Meffiah.   Now with Words that live,
With Thoughts that burn, the laft tremendous Day,
Expiring Nature and the Doom of Man,
He thunders on the Soul.   Sin's ghaftly Front,
Her Shape deform'd, the Poifon of her Touch,
Behind Her Vengeance with eternal Fire,
He next defcribes.   Affrighted Confcience 'wakes ;
The Murd'rer ftarts aghaft ! th' Oppreffor groans ;
Th' Adulterer trembles, and the Harlot weeps.
What Heart fo pure, fo innocent of Vice,
But fhudder'd there ?——Now with mellifluous Tongue,
He fooths the Scorpion-fting of confcious Guilt.
Behold ! each faded Countenance relum'd
With Hope and Gladnefs, whilft the chofen Saint
Unfolds the Myft'ries of redeeming Love,
Of Grace and Mercy infinite, difplays
The high Rewards of Penitence and Life
Reform'd, the Freedom of the Chriftian Yoke
Avers, and teftifies th' eternal League
'Twixt Happinefs and Virtue.   Now to crown
The Preacher's Tafk, with fweet perfuafive Phrafe,

He

He wins th' enchanted Auditors to Peace,
Long-fuff'ring, Gentlenefs and focial Love,
The godlike Spirit of his Mafter's Laws!

Was this the hot vindictive Pharifee?
O ftrange Converfion! This th' impetuous Saul,
That late dire Menaces and Slaughter breath'd?
Was this, fage * Prieft, the Minifter of Wrath
Fix'd by the dreaded Sanction of thy Power
To hurl Perdition on the rifing Church?
What? Were thofe Hands, now lifted up to Heav'n
To blefs Man's great Redeemer, once imbrued †
In the pure Blood of his devoted Saints,
And confecrated Martyrs? Wondrous Change!
But what can check that all-controuling Power,
Who turns the Courfe of Nature at his Will;
Whofe Word was Med'cine to the Sick, whofe Call
Awoke the Grave's cold Tenants, whofe firm Step
Trod the foft Surface of the Ocean, whilft
His potent Voice bad the curl'd Waves fubfide,
And hufh'd the Wind's wild Uproar into Peace?

Behold! th' illuftrious Convert now invades
The Reign of Gentile Darknefs.   See! appall'd

* The high Prieft of *Jerufalem*.

† ῝Ος ταύτην τὴν ὁδὸν ἐδίωξα ἄχρι θανάτου, &c. Acts xxii. v. 4.

Black

Black Superſtition, with her baleful Throng
Of ſelf-bred Fears, and unembodied Forms
That haunt Deſpair; the foul unholy Train
Of molten Idols and fantaſtic Gods
Shrink at his Preſence, like the fleeting Shades
Of ſullen Night, when firſt Hyperion's Orb
Scatters it's purple Radiance o'er the Skies.
Nor long the Majeſty of Jove ſupreme
Withſtood the Thunder of the Preacher's Tongue.
Totter'd his Throne, his golden Sceptre fell;
Nor more Olympus trembled at his Nod.
No longer ſmoak'd his odoriferous Shrines
With Frankincenſe and Myrrh, the fragrant Breath
Of Araby; nor bleeding Hecatomb
Diſtain'd his bluſhing Altars.   Solemn Praiſe
And Pray'rs devoutly breath'd, the Tears, the Sighs
Of penitential Grief, the broken Heart
Now form'd the Gentile's purer Sacrifice
To the true God.——The philoſophic Lore
Of learned Athens ſunk e'er long, eclips'd
By Truth's reſiſtleſs Blaze.   The vain Parade
Of empty Jargon and unmeaning Forms
No longer won the proſtituted Praiſe
Of wond'ring Greece.   The Stoic's fond Pretence
Was urg'd no more; the boaſted Apathiſt
Confeſs'd the Strength of Nature, own'd the Power,

The

The Ufe of Paffion, deign'd to feel himfelf,
And fympathize the Miferies of Man.
Nor long the Dictates of thy fenfual Mind
Allur'd th' unwary Step of Youth to Sin,
Lafcivious * Sophift! Thy Difciple erft
That quaff'd the lufcious Sweets of Circe's Cup,
Hung on the Siren's fafcinating Tongue,
And thrill'd with Tranfport at the Harlot's Smile,
Now fighs for Pleafures which no Eye hath feen,
No Ear hath heard, nor mortal Heart conceiv'd.
No more he babbles of thy foolifh Dreams
Of felf-concurring Atoms, and blind Chance
Omnipotent: where'er he turns his Eyes,
Amaz'd he traces, thro' each wondrous Scene,
The Hand of Providence. Each Attribute
That points th' Almighty Parent of the World
To Man's Conceptions, legibly portray'd
On Nature's Page, th' enlighten'd Convert fees;
And as he views, his elevated Breaft,
With inextinguifhable Ardor, burns
For Truth, for Life and Immortality.
Where'er the Preacher roll'd the powerful Tide
Of Infpiration, from each fabled Haunt
Foul Error fled, whether the Roman School,
Or Attic Portico her Prefence held;

* Epicurus.

Or

Or the dark Inmate of the Pagan Shrine,
She heap'd vain Incenfe to fome Idol-God.
O ! may thofe living Oracles of Light,
That boaft the Sanction of thine hallow'd Pen,
Illuftrious Convert ! o'er each gloomy Land,
Where ftill pale Fear and Superftition reign,
Spread the rich Treafures of immortal Truth.
May the lewd Prophet's Brothel-Paradife,
Bafe Hope of wretched Ignorance and Luft,
Allure no more the Pilgrim's weary Step
To Mecca's Walls : no longer Fohi's Name
Ufurp the proftrate Adoration, due
To God alone : nor more th' unconfcious Sun
Provoke the trembling Indian's fruitlefs Vow.
But may one Mind, one Faith, one Hope, one God
Unite the fcatter'd Progeny of Man.

THE

CRUCIFIXION.

BY

THOMAS ZOUCH, M. A.

M DCC LXV.

THE

THE

CRUCIFIXION.

ENOUGH has fiction's fairy scene deceiv'd
My dreaming hours of youth : with penfive ftep
Mufing along the cloyfter's filent gloom
Thee, Holy Truth, I woo : thy graceful charms
Far lovelier than the damafk rofe that glows
On beauty's cheek, the poet's moral ftrain
Excite.—Ye fabled fongs, adieu ! adieu,
Imagination, to the dazzled eye
Shooting thy gorgeous phantoms ! hence, ye dreams
Of fublunary glare, the gem of wealth,
The plume of honour ! To her awful fhrine
Devotion wafts me, where the white-rob'd prieft
With heart-felt tranfport on the wing of prayer
Extatic rifes, or with waving hand
And all the decent elegance of eafe
Myfterious truth unfolds, whilft on his tongue
Attention hangs enraptur'd.   At that altar

<table><tr><td>Q</td><td>Peace</td></tr></table>

Peace sheds her balmy influence, far from Guilt
And all his hideous offspring: Envy wan
With jaundic'd eye: Ambition's bluftering voice
Brawling for titles: hollow-hearted fmile
Of cringing Adulation: dog-ey'd Luft
Rifling the bofom of chafte innocence.

    For fay, can fancy, fond to weave the tale
Of blifs ideal, feign more genuine joy
Than thine, PHILANDER, when the Man of God
Gives to thy hand the confecrated cup,
Bleffed memorial of a Saviour's love!
Glowing with zeal the humble Penitent
Approacheth: Faith her foftering radiance points
Full on his contrite heart: Hope cheers his fteps,
And Charity, the faireft in the train
Of chriftian virtues, fwells his heaving breaft
With love unbounded. Feaft of blifs fupreme
To eat the bread of life, to drink the cup
Of benediction!—Memory bids the fcene,
Th' important fcene, arife, when dread difmay
Alarm'd the nations. Melt, thou heart of brafs:
Death triumph'd o'er its victor. Wild amaze
Seiz'd all the hoft of heaven, moaning their God
In agony transfixt, his every fenfe
A window to affliction: forrow fill'd

Their

Their tide of tragic woe, and chang'd the note
From fervent rapture to the gloomy strain
Of deepest lamentation.   O how pure
Th' effulgence of his bounty, that completes
Redemption's mighty work, the source of joy!

Hail heavenly Love, that with eternal sway
Pervades creation's amplest bounds! 'Twas Love
That bade existence spring to life: the sun,
Inspher'd in radiancy, began his course,
And vegetation from the earth's warm lap
Call'd forth her genial powers.   'Twas Love that form'd
Redemption's glorious plan.   Ye white-wing'd hosts,
Cherubs and seraphs, that enrob'd in light
Drink the pure stream of ever-during day,
In hallelujahs chaunt the grateful hymn
Of adoration: from your sapphire seats
Hail the glad tidings, that to Man is giv'n
A Saviour merciful.   But chiefly ye,
Daughters and sons of Adam, raise the song
Of gratulation meet.—Ye young, ye gay,
Listen with patient ear the strains of truth:
Ye who in dissipation waste your days,
From Pleasure's giddy train O steal an hour,
With sage reflexion nor disdain to gaze
The solemn scene on CALV'RY's guilty mount,

Q 2

Where

Where frighted nature shakes her trembling frame,
And shudders at the complicated crime
Of deicide.—The thorn-encircled head
All pale and languid on the bleeding cross,
The nail-empierced hand, the mangled feet,
The perforated side, the heaving sigh
Of gushing anguish, the deep groan of death,
The day of darkness, terror and distress :
Ah! shall not these awake one serious thought ?

Sin, I detest thee : murd'rous child of night,
Hence to thy native hell! in Eden's vale
Rov'd our first parents, bosom'd in content,
Gay as the spring, and innocent as gay.
Thou dash'd their draught of bliss, their sweets of joy
Mingling with gall. Misfortune's haggard crew
Hence o'er the wide creation ruthless prowl'd,
And rioted on man. Can aught arrest
Th' Almighty's anger ?—Yes : the victim bleeds,
His own dear Son, from bondage to exalt
A ransom'd world, to blast the damning power
Of Satan, Sin, and Death. How chang'd from him,
Whose Majesty in native lustre shone
Sevenfold, when on th' eternal throne he smil'd,
Long ere yon planets in their measur'd Orbs
Revolv'd : or walking on the whirl-wind's wing

He

He rais'd his arm, and drove the rebel brood
Down to their black abyfs : beneath his feet
The flames flafh'd horrible : before him fled
The ghaftly train of peftilence and woe.

On Revelation's facred page intent
The eye of faith furveys the mighty deed
Shadow'd in myftic type, when Abram urg'd
By heaven's all-wife beheft, with eager zeal
Snatch'd from a mother's weeping care * the child
Of laughter, on Moriah's fecret top
Binding the fpotlefs hands of innocence.

How vain the breath, how empty all the boaft
Of popular applaufe ? To day we foar
The fons of fortune, favour'd by the croud,
Their idol and their God.   The morrow blights
Our bud of fame.   The rabble change their notes
From hoarfeft acclamation to the hifs
Of harfh contempt : the many-headed beaft
Hark how he fhouts for blood and impious carnage !
See Ifrael's humble King, mild as the lamb
Beneath the murdering knife, amidft the fneer
The taunt of mad reproach, led to the crofs,

* יצחק Ifaac a rifu dictus eft. Gen. xxi. 3. Buxtorf.

To shame and bitter death.   Him late they rais'd
To fame's bright summit, when they sung his name
With loud hosannas, or with silent ardor
Dwelt on his tongue, list'ning the happy lore
Of evangelic joy.   Ye ruffian tribe,
Ah ! check the ruthless Rage, that drowns the voice,
The faithful voice of reason, to your God
Prefers sedition's son, whom foul with crimes
Ripe vengeance waits, and awful justice calls.

  Ye men of Judah, let one languid spark
Of soft compassion melt your iron hearts !
O stay the cruel stroke, the blood-stain'd scourge
Forbear : O spare, for pity spare that wound :
Support his falt'ring steps : he faints, he dies :
Your King, your meek Messiah faints : he sinks
Beneath th' oppressive load ; up the steep mount
He toils panting, and harrass'd with fatigue.

  But shall oblivion's raven wing o'ershade
The ever-blooming fame of Salem's daughters ?
Then weep, ye fair, and with prophetic tears
Swell the full stream of Grief, sincere as erst
When Herod's vengeful arm in infant blood
Drench'd his wide-wasting sword : with rueful shriek
The childless parent wander'd Rama's streets.

Your

Your gentler breasts to sympathetic sigh,
Indulgent nature melts.   Remorseless Man
With heart of roughest mold sheds not one tear,
Nor wails a Saviour's death.   To you the Muse
Shall twine her wreath of praise: ye felt his pangs,
Ye moan'd his agonizing grief of Soul.

How calm the Sufferer! not one rageful word
Of wild impatience: no resentment shakes
His harrow'd breast.   Chearful and mild he meets
The savage king of terrors.   Lo! to Heaven
On mental wing his zealous prayer ascends.
But ah! for whom?—For you, ye sons of pride
That led him to th' accursed tree of shame.
" Father, forgive them."—Hence, far hence the fury
Of wrath and vengeful hatred! Christian Love,
With universal Charity inspire
My breast: extinguish every latent spark
Of low revenge.   Give me to breathe the flame
Of tenderest affection, to sustain
Unruffled and serene the mean attacks
Of enmity and slander.   Thus to tread
A Master's heavenly steps, like him, to bear
With patient mind insult and rash abuse,
Be this my boasted glory, this my pride!

Q 4

Great

Great God of Truth, ſhall equal terrors fall
On innocence and guilt ? The noon-tide ray
Mix with the midnight gloom ? The Son of Man,
The great High Prieſt, harmleſs and undefil'd,
With impious ruffians numb'red, dies the death
Of unrelenting juſtice ? Fierce as Hell
Yon harden'd murd'rer breathes out his angry ſoul
In blaſphemous defiance.   Foul reproach
Flows from his venom tongue : avenging death
With tenfold darkneſs brooding, opes to view
Scenes of eternal pangs, where penal wrath
With unextinguiſhable fury burns.
Some chearful beam of Hope, ſome gleam of Heaven,
Burſts on the brother of his crimes.   He weeps :
Repentance darts into his convict heart
A ray of Peace.   The riſing arm of wrath
Drops the impending Thunder ; mercy ſmiles
Benign.   E'en tho' the blaze of guilt outglare
The ſcarlet's crimſon hue, fair mercy ſheds
Her hoard of joy, and whitens every ſtain.

Come then, Repentance, with thy piercing ken
The dark receſſes of my heart pervade :
Fill me with real ſorrow : nought avails
The ſable ſackcloth, or the vain grimace
Of hypocritic pomp.   When ghaſtly death

Hovers

Hovers around my couch, it nought avails
To break the curtain'd flumber of the night
Counting the figur'd beads, to wear the hour
With repetition's empty Hymn, to grafp
The gilded Crucifix. — Fantaftic rites
Of papal ignorance!—All wrapt in grief,
Whilft youth with manhood's vigor nerves my limbs,
The young blood circling in it's channel'd path,
I bend the fuppliant knee :—"Father of Heaven,
" Father of mercies, fnatch from ruin's gulph,
" Snatch me from fin."—Temptation fpreads her lure
With meretricious art. Wanton defire,
Fierce as the waken'd fury of the deep,
Riots : O for a faithful friendly hand
With pious art to guide the light-wing'd fkiff,
And waft it from the tempeft's boift'rous rage !

See 'midft the croud, that thronging round the hill
With mad difcordant roar of barb'rous joy
Gape on the Crofs, a felf-convicted wretch
Shivering. Damp horror fills his guilty breaft
With pungent throes. On his wide-rolling eye
Diftraction frantic fits and black defpair.
Accurfed luft of gain, that fteels the heart
'Gainft pity's foft emotions, breaks the tye
Of dear affection, plunges all the foul

In fin and woe ! What for fo poor a price,
Th' Affaffin's hireling wages, to betray
A Saviour and a God ! and with the kifs
Of friendfhip too !—Thou fpecious Man of blood,
Fly from thyfelf, thy bittereft deadlieft foe.
Confcience with never-dying worm corrodes
Thy tortur'd bofom.—'Tis the Lamb of God,
The bleffed Jefus, whom thy treach'rous hand
Configns to death : Heard'ft thou that figh of grief
That fhook earth's tottering bafe ? Saw'ft thou thofe Limbs
Writhed with pain ? 'Twas he that taught the word
Of Peace and Love, that ftopp'd the horrid rage
Of dire difeafe, and from their gloomy cell
Call'd out the filent dead.   Th' expiring figh
Again he heaves.   Heard'ft thou that cutting pang,
Ifcariot ! Go, whilft dumb amazement holds
The frozen multitude : cavern thy pelf,
Perfidious traitor.   Vengeance, clad in blood,
Burning with rage, unfheathes her wafteful fword,
Purfues thy fteps, and hunts thee down to death.

Whilft ruin burfts the Temple's inmoft veil,
And 'midft furrounding fcenes of horror roam
The grifly fpectres, as at midnight hour ;
Far from the pomp and pageantry of pride
Pilate fequefter'd fits the venal judge,

Corruption's flave, that gloated on the fpoils
Of innocence oppreffed.   What avails
Or trophy'd blaze of power or glofs of wealth
To footh the fever'd phrenzy of his foul ?
He burns, as with a raging calenture,
'Tortur'd by jarring paffions.—Why that Look ?
Thofe broken accents ? Thou dark, dufky Man,
Say can his fpotted fkin the leopard change ?
In vain thou feek'ft the pillow of repofe.
The noon-tide fun, velop'd in darknefs dim,
His golden glory fhrouds : But ah ! what night
With darknefs dim fhall fhroud thee from the eye,
The piercing eye of guilt ? With impious hand
Profane not thus the limpid ftream : not all
The ocean's wave can wafh off that foul fpot
Of murder.   Heaven's vindictive juftice reigns
Unbrib'd by wealth.   E'en now thy anxious mind
Anticipates its fate.   Deftruction waits
Thy fteps : the tyrant of imperial Rome
Drives thee to exile : in the defart Ifle
Breathe to the taunting air thy doleful plaints.
Engender'd erft on pride and coward fhame,
The monfter Suicide his influence dire
Sheds o'er thy melancholy-tinctur'd foul
Baleful.   Go dafh thee down the rocky fteep,
Or plunge into thy breaft the thirfty fword

That

That pants for blood.—But lo! a different scene!
What tho' th' autumnal ficknefs ftalks around,
What tho' the rage of noon-day peftilence
Slays her ten thoufands; yet beneath the fhade
Of Providence the good Man fmiles fecure
And undifmay'd.   As refolution firm
The lov'd Difciple ftands, in manly grief
Silent.—Illuftrious Saint! endear'd to him
Who knows the hidden fecret thoughts of Man,
Friendfhip on thee her choiceft treafures pour'd.
What heavenly tranfport to mix foul with foul
In liberal converfe ; to imbibe the words
Of bleffed truth, from wifdom's mouth to catch
Inftruction's fweeteft leffons !—See thy King,
Thy Friend from his triumphant infamy
Looks down with condefcenfion ; deigns to crown
Thy holy fortitude.   With filial care
His tender pledges guard : When age with fnow
Shall fow thy temples, then fhall vifions blefs
Thy nights ; nor fhall the envied wreath thy brow
Entwine, ere ruin raze thefe haughty walls ;
Ere the proud Roman eagle clap her wing
Hovering o'er Salem's defolated towers.

    What pencil's glowing colours know to paint
A mother's deep diftrefs ? Faft by the crofs

With

With eyes and hands uplifted, wrap'd in woe
All motionless and mute, she views her Son,
Her God beneath the weight of others sins
Bow his afflicted head.   Thus Eve, absorpt
In sorrow's trance, her darling offspring ey'd
Welt'ring in blood : expressive silence spoke
Her pangs of agony : the big-swoln tear
Burst down her cheek : around her beauteous form
The golden tresses flow'd in rude disorder,
Whilst Adam at her side in vain assay'd
Bland consolation.   Secret grief o'erwhelms
MARIA's throbbing breast.   Now languor wan
Unnerves each sense : tender remembrance soon
Wakes in her soften'd heart the fond, fond scenes,
When sweet domestic peace confirm'd her bliss,
Shelter'd beneath a husband's faithful arm
From humbling infamy.   Thrice happy pair !
They gently trod the flowery path of Life :
They ate the bread of temperance, round their board
Contentment laugh'd, blithe as a blooming bride.
Lull'd on her lap the infant God-head oft
Repos'd him weary.   Tho' no trumpet's sound,
No host of cherubim his praise attun'd,
Maternal rapture on his lovely name
With fondness dwelt : ponder'd each pleasing sign
Of future splendor.—Oh ! what an awful change !

The

The rude wind tempefts the bright dawn of hope.
Mute is the tongue of eloquence that aw'd
A lift'ning multitude : languid the lips
That fmil'd complacence round, and every grace
Gently diffus'd.   Dim in its ghaftly orb
The beaming eye of Majefty is funk.

But tho' with adverfe wind the gray ftorm lours,
Shall fullen difcontent awake the voice
Of querulous defpair ? Thou fecond Eve,
O ftop the falling tear ; the figh reftrain.
And ye, felected flock, that fcatter'd late
Fled from your Shepherd, from defpondence raife
Your drooping hearts : refume the fmile of joy.
Burft are the gates of Death : blunted the fting
Of Sin : Meffiah mounts th' exalted car
Of triumph.   As Elijah rapt of old
To Heaven, victorious o'er the murky grave,
He rifes to the realms of endlefs day.

Thus when the infant Moon her circling fphere
Wheels o'er the Sun's broad difk ; her fhadow falls
On Earth's fair bofom : darknefs chills the fields,
And dreary night invefts the face of Heaven.
Reflected from the lake full many a ftar
Glimmers with feeble languor.   India's fons

Affrighted

Affrighted in wild tumult rend the air.
Before his idol god with barb'rous shriek
The Brachman falls : when soon the eye of day
Darts his all-cheering radiance, from the gloom
Emerging.   Joy invades the wondering croud,
And acclamation rushes from the tongue
Of thousands that around their blazing pile
Riot in antic dance and diffonant song.

Far from this earthly ball th' advent'rous Muse
Uplifted, dares to foar her aëry way
To where in immortality enthron'd
The great Redeemer fits at God's right hand.
No fond illusion cheats me ; from this shell
Of clay, the foul to brighter climes afpires,
Nor feeks imagination's waxen wings
To fpeed her courfe.   Almighty, infinite
The filial Godhead reigns : old Ocean flies
Affrighted at his awful nod, whilft Heaven
Bows trembling.   Mercy's gentle attribute
Tempers his juftice : he protects the poor
In needful hour of dearth, and from the duft
Raifes the weeping penitent : his wrath
The blood of goats averts not, or the fat
Of coftly hecatombs, or altar wreath'd
With clouds of incenfe, tho' in Phrygian mood

The

The laurel-nurtur'd priefts their Pythic hymn
Attemper to the virgin choir, that chant
'Their Doric harmony.   Nor deigns he not
With pity's eye the contrite heart to view
And troubled fpirit : pureft facrifice
By him accepted.   O emblazon wide.
His Name, ye creatures that in Heaven, in Earth
Or in the wide fea breathe.

       " Dread Judge of all!
" Anointed King ! Saviour of fallen Man !
" All praife to Thee be given ! ere time began
" Thou art, in thy unfathom'd effence vail'd
" Immenfe.   But ftill Perfection deign'd to bear
" Th' infirmities of Man : th' Eternal dyed,
" Th' Almighty fuffer'd woe.   All Heaven beheld,
" And hymn'd in admiration's loudeft notes
" Thee crucify'd.   Can aught of mortal fong
" Equal thy glory whilft on Earth ? What tongue
" The congregated wonders of thy life
" Can fpeak ? To Thee fhall Wifdom yield her palm
" Of fame : in vain fhe boafts the letter'd art,
" And all the mazy folly of the fchools,
" Socratic knowledge, or the Stag'rite's pomp
" Of idle fpeculation.   King of kings,
" O let thy bright example roufe the foul
" To meek humility ! great Interceffor,

            " Pour

" Pour on thy meaneſt ſupplicant the boon
" Of pardon and remiſſion.   Wean his mind
" From earth-bred care.   When the grim hand of Death
" Shall ſnatch me weary to the darkſome grave,
" When the laſt trumpet's ſound ſhall ſhake this globe,
" And deſolation urn yon diſorb'd worlds,
" Oh ſmile forgiveneſs.   At that awful hour
" Propitious chaſe away the fears that fright
" The fluttering ſoul, nor let thy blood in vain
" Drop from the croſs! the while may reaſon guide
" My every wiſh! may true religion ſtrew
" Life's varied path! 'Tis her's to wipe the tear
" From ſorrow's eye, to light the lamp of Hope,
" From Revelation's copious fount to pour
" The ſtreams of Comfort, Peace, and holy Love."

R

THE

THE

GIFT OF TONGUES.

BY

CHARLES JENNER, M. A.

M DCC LXVII,

R 2   THE

THE

GIFT OF TONGUES.

GOD's wond'rous pow'r, on That great day reveal'd
When from on high the Sacred Influence fell
Knowledge and light furpaffing human lore
Diffufing in its courfe, vent'rous I fing.
O for one tranfient gleam from that pure fount
Of light celeftial, whofe all-pow'rful rays
Inftant difpell'd the mifts of Ignorance,
Inform'd the mind, and urg'd the willing tongue !
O for one fpark of that tranfcendant Fire,
Which fhed its rapid influence through the Soul,
Kindling at once in the aftonifh'd mind
The facred flame of heav'n-directed Zeal,
In ftrains pour'd forth of Wifdom heaven-taught,
Which in conception, to perfection fprang,
Mocking the tedious fteps of human Wit !
Too vain that wifh.—But thou O Spirit pure
Who deign'ft to guide the wayward heart of man,

R 3

When

When confcious weaknefs claims thy aid benign,
Thou from whofe eyes the palpable obfcure
Nought hides, who mark'ft my inmoft Soul,
And check'ft with care paternal ev'ry ill,
Suggefting kindly pure and holy thoughts,
Frame thou my mind ; Difpofe my humble heart
To feel thy goodnefs and adore thy might ;
Grant me, with faith to read thy wond'rous works,
To hear with joy, to tell with gratitude ;
Grant me, at humble diftance, to revere
Thofe acts of pow'r, I know not how to fcan ;
Grant me, with fcorn to view the Sceptic's pride
Who dares to tread the dark, meand'ring maze,
And ftrive with mortal ken, (how fhort ! how dim !)
To trace the fteps of dread Omnipotence ;
Grant me, with humble yet exulting mind,
In all thy wond'rous works to mark the end,
Nor rafhly ftrive to comprehend the means ;
To view, with rev'rent awe, the mighty Caufe,
And feel with gratitude the bleft Effect ;
Grant me, in this meek, fober frame of mind,
To view thy goodnefs, and to fing thy praife ;
So fhall my lays, though rude, attention claim,
Nor ufelefs fink in cold oblivion's wave ;
Warm from the heart they bear intrinfic worth,
And confcience fhall bear witnefs to their truth.

'Twas

'Twas on that day, that memorable day
When erſt the Prophet of the favour'd ſeed
From Iſrael ſprung, high-honour'd Moſes held
With trembling awe, converſe with God himſelf;
'Twas on that day, when round the ſacred mount
The rapid lightnings ſhot their livid glance,
Flaſhing a larger and a larger curve,
Whilſt the dread Thunder, mutt'ring from afar,
With ſullen murmur deep'ning in its courſe,
Burſt ratt'ling all around in diſcord wild,
When, 'midſt the horror of the awful ſcene,
The holy Prophet learn'd thoſe high beheſts
By which to lead his ſacred flock, and ſhew
Types of a purer plan in days to come;
On that ſame day, the ſtill more ſacred flock
Of Chriſt, who only mourn'd his recent loſs,
Stol'n from the clamours of the impious croud
In thought purſu'd his ſteps to Heav'n, and cheer'd
Each other's griefs with thoughts of bliſs to come.

Not hopeleſs did they grieve; for o'er the Soul
His laſt bequeſt had ſhed a gleam of Joy;
" A comforter to come" reſtrain'd their tears,
A ſtedfaſt faith ſuppreſs'd the riſing ſigh,
And Expectation rais'd their downcaſt Eyes.
Nor vain their hope; for now with ſudden burſt

R 4

A ruſhing

A rufhing Noife through all the facred Band
Silence profound and fix'd attention claim'd,
A chilling terror crept through ev'ry heart,
Mute was each tongue, and pale was ev'ry face:
The rough roar ceas'd ; when, borne on fiery wings,
The dazzling Emanation from above
In brighteft vifion round each facred head
Diffus'd its vivid beams ; myfterious light !
That rufh'd impetuous through th' awaking mind,
Whilft new Ideas fill'd the paffive Soul,
Faft crouding in with fweeteft violence.
'Twas then amaz'd they caught the glorious flame,
Spontaneous flow'd their all-perfuafive words,
Warm from the heart, and to the heart addrefs'd
Deep funk their force in ev'ry captiv'd ear.

O fee the crowd, preffing with eager fteps
To catch the flowing periods as they fall ;
See how, with wond'ring rapture, they devour
The pleafing accents of their native tongue ;
See how, with eyes uplifted, they advance,
With out-ftretch'd hands and fmiles of focial love
To greet the partners of their native Soil ;
O catch the varying tranfports in their looks,
In awful wonder fee each paffion loft,
When ev'ry Nation urg'd an equal claim.

Fond

Fond men, forbear; and know, the voice of Truth
By weak reſtraints of Language unconfin'd
Flows, independent, from that radiant ſhrine
From whence the day-ſpring draws her glitt'ring ſtore
'To ſhine on all with undiſtinguiſh'd ray,
And ſcatter dazzling light on ev'ry clime.

Immortal Truth! by Inſpiration taught,
Thou ſpurn'ſt the ſervile chains of human art;
In native majeſty array'd, thou ſhed'ſt
Thy radiant beams through all this vale below;
Thy piercing voice reſounds through diſtant clines,
By all diſtinguiſh'd, and by all ador'd.
Thou ſat'ſt enthron'd above yon azure vault,
And mock'ſt the tedious toil of human wit,
What time at Babel's hapleſs tow'r they ſtrove
To reſcue meaning from the load of ſounds,
And give preciſion to the voice confus'd,
Reſtoring Heav'n's moſt pleaſing gift to Man.

Thee neither wind nor wave can circumſcribe.
Wide o'er where Ocean ſpreads his ample bed
Thou flieſt at large, to viſit ev'ry ſhore,
And pour thy ſacred voice in ev'ry heart
In language univerſal. What avail
To thy all-piercing eye, and tongue heav'n-taught,

The

The nice diſtinctions of the critic art,
The fooliſh pride of letter'd pedantry,
Riſing, by ſlow degrees and labour'd care,
From the firſt liſp, which on the infant tongue
Hangs with uncertain cadence, to the height
Of Learning's utmoſt pow'r ? With ſcorn thou view'ſt
The erring paths of Science, falſly call'd ;
Tracing her ſlow ſteps from her Eaſtern home
Whence firſt, in clouded majeſty, ſhe beam'd
A tranſient glance, and tempted the purſuit,
Thou mark'ſt her progreſs from the rapid Nile,
Where Thebes receiv'd her at her hundred gates,
And ſeeſt her roll her ever-wand'ring way
To milder climes, when Greece with open arms
Receiv'd her credulous ; Old Orpheus then
And Linus ſung their fabled lays, and ſpread
A lengthen'd train of philoſophic lies.
Mocking thou view'ſt the pride of human wit,
Whilſt Athens ſelf, fair Science, fav'rite ſeat,
And Rome Imperial, vers'd in ev'ry lore,
Succeſsleſs toil to bring thee forth to view.
Thou ſeeſt unnumber'd Syſtems riſe and fall,
And ev'ry learned age bring new deceits ;
Whilſt tow'ring Pride ſtill lifts her ready hand
To cruſh the fond deluſion of the day,
And inſtant rear a ſtronger in it's place.

But

But O! this blindnefs may not ever be,
And vague Opinion, with ufurping hand,
Bright Wifdom's fceptre may not ever wield;
Thou fpeak'ft Immortal Truth! beneath each pole
The trembling Earth acknowledges thy voice;
Pride catches quick the mortifying found,
Far, far aloof flies ev'ry golden dream,
And all is blindfold Error and diftrefs.
O! 'twas That potent voice, whofe magic pow'r
Burft through the organs of the facred Band,
What time O Salem midft thy hallow'd walls
The mingled crowd from many a diftant realm
In fix'd attention hung upon their words,
Which, with conviction fraught, flow'd unreftrain'd,
Though, fkill'd alone in Virtue's facred lore,
They never had employ'd life's precious hours
In learning's paths; without proud Science wife.

By weakeft minifters th' Almighty thus
Makes known his facred will, and fhews his pow'r:
By Him infpir'd they fpeak with urgent tongue
Authoritative, whilft th' illumin'd breaft
Heaves with unwonted ftrength; High as their theme
Their great conceptions rife in rapt'rous flow,
As quick the ready organs catch the thought,
And, in fuch ftrains as Science could not teach,

Bear

Bear it, in all it's radiance, to the Heart;
The lift'ning throng there feel it's blefs'd effect,
And deep conviction glows in ev'ry breaft.

   See ev'ry crime which ftains the human mind
At their ftrong bidding take it's rapid flight:
Delufion's dreams no more infect the Soul,
High-boafting Pride, fierce Wrath, impetuous Luft,
And Avarice fwelling with hydropic thirft,
Fade, like unwholefome dews before the Sun;
They fade to rife no more; for fee a band
Of radiant Virtues feize their late abode,
And ftamp the manfion with the feal of Truth.
There heav'nly Knowledge fhines in glitt'ring pride,
And Patience fits, with meek fubmiffive fmile
Difarming ftern Oppreffion; Juftice there
Erects her rigid teft of right and wrong;
And there, with God's own armour all-begirt,
Stands Fortitude, erect in Chriftian ftrength;
There Temp'rance ftands, with ever-watchful Eye,
To curb the Paffions with a fteady rein;
And Candour there her golden rule difplays
To act by others as thy heart muft wifh
They, in like circumftance, fhould act by thee;
But chiefly there, in ever-fixed feat,
Sits heav'n-born Charity; her eagle Eye

Thrown

Thrown o'er the wide expanfe of Nature's works,
Where, nobly fcorning ev'ry meaner tye,
She deems all human ills her own, and fighs
If aught of mis'ry dwell beneath the Sun.
With fuch bright guefts the Chriftian mind is ftor'd,
Pledges of trueft Knowledge, Joy, and Peace:
Thefe to make known became the facred tafk
By Heav'n impos'd upon the chofen band;
Thrice happy they to fuch high office call'd,
The bleffed minifters of God's high will!
For them the fulnefs of his might is fhewn,
O'erleaping the ftrong bounds of Nature's law;
Grim Death for them contracts his hafty ftride,
And checks his Dart ev'n in the act to ftrike;
His horrid meffengers Difeafe and Pain
Loofe their remorfelefs grafp unwillingly,
And leave their prey to eafe and thankfulnefs;
For them bright Wifdom opens all her ftores,
Her golden treafures fpreading to their view,
Whilft Infpiration's all-enliv'ning light
Hangs hov'ring o'er their heads in glitt'ring blaze;
Warm'd by the ray they pour the facred ftrain
In Eloquence feraphic; Truths divine,
For ever regifter'd in Heav'n's high page,
Flow from their lips, and glow within their breafts;
Amaz'd they feel the facred extacy,

With

With heav'nly rapture, thrill in ev'ry nerve;
Whilſt in their flowing words, with Wiſdom fraught
Celeſtial, ſhines the heav'nly Spirit pure.
This is no fancy'd pow'r, no idle dream,
No flatt'ring ſcheme by heated Fancy form'd,
The genuine Influence fills each raptur'd Soul,
And beams in ev'ry eye conſpicuous.

Far other flame the vain Enthuſiaſt feels
When, Reaſon by deluſive Fancy led
In ſad captivity, the Thoughts confus'd
Ruſh on his mind in dark and doubtful ſenſe,
His mind a chaos of blind zeal, that ſpurns
Th' unerring clue which mild Diſcretion lends,
Perchance the claſhing images ſtrike out
Some languid ray of caſual light; how ſoon
The weak and momentary glance is loſt
Beneath a load of wild obſcurity.
Much does he labour with ſome weighty thought,
Of Faith, of Grace, of Heav'n, perchance of Hell,
But all in vain he draws the thread confus'd
To tedious length, the end eludes his ſearch,
And leaves him wrapt in wild perplexity
Recoiling ſtill on the ſame beaten track.
Thus wayward Fancy with her vagrant blaze
Miſleads the eye of Ignorance; mean while

In

In vain the steady lamp of Reason burns,
The sure and sober guide to Truth's retreat,
But ah ! consider well ye self-inspir'd,
Ere Fancy, drooping on the bed of Death,
Leaves ye forlorn to seek for Reason's aid,
Consider well, are these the genuine marks
Of heav'nly Inspiration ? Was it thus
In wild extatic rants and dubious phrase,
In doctrines intricate and terms perplex'd
The simple messengers of Jesus spake ?
O search and see, were not their doctrines pure,
And in such plain and modest phrase express'd
As best befits Instruction's wholesome plan ?
Mighty to save, they sought no other pow'r,
No meed, but that which conscious Virtue feels
When she conducts some haplefs wand'rer back
To paths, without her aid, for ever lost.
If such your heav'nly aim, your lives unblam'd
Will give, like theirs, an earnest of your truth ;
If, daily train'd to ev'ry virtuous act,
You tread the steps the blessed Jesus trod
Through the streight path, the way of holiness,
Then may ye lead your flocks to his abode ;
But O beware ! think not the heav'nly guest
Can fix his residence with aught impure ;
Think not the heart which Pride or Int'rest guides

Can

Can ever be the feat of heav'nly grace ;
If yet the holy Spirit deigns to dwell
In earthly domes, 'tis not in thofe defil'd
With Pride, with Fraud, with Rapine, or with Luft ;
Midft the rough foliage of the thorny brake
The cluft'ring Grape not blufhes, and the Fig
Decks not the prickly 'Thiftle's barren ftalk,
Ev'n thus fhall all be meafur'd by their fruits ;
So fpake the living Oracle of truth :
O never, never lofe this facred guide,
By ev'ry blaft of doctrine borne away,
But gazing ever on the Gofpel light,
That endlefs fource of evidence and truth,
Prove ev'ry doctrine by that golden rule,
And " try the Spirits if they be of God."

THE

THE

DESTRUCTION

OF

NINIVEH.

BY

CHARLES JENNER, M. A.

M DCC LXVIII.

S

THE

T H E

DESTRÚCTION

O F

N I N I V E H.

GOD's mercy long abus'd, and heav'nly wrath
Succeeding flow with firm and dreadful ftep
And arm uplifted high, be now my Theme.
Horror ! be thou my Mufe.—And lift ye proud,
Ye rich, ye vain, for 'tis to you I fing,
Lift from your downy beds of Tyrian dye
Where funk in carelefs eafe and worthlefs floth,
In dreams of pleafures paft or joys to come
Batt'ning ye lie ; Lift from your marble Halls
Whence, drowning ev'ry wife and ferious thought,
The wanton voice of Luxury refounds,
Whilft Mirth, uncheck'd by fair Difcretion's law,
Pours from the golden goblet's ample round
The lufcious poifon of mifufed wine,

S 2

And

And hid beneath the garb of Happiness
Steals to your eafy hearts with pleafing guile,
With fweet, but certain death.   O turn awhile
The eye too long on Pleafure's fmiles intent,
On your own breafts turn once it's wand'ring fight:
See ye God's image there ? O rather fay,
See ye not there, what erft the Poets feign'd
The dire effect of Circe's mad'ning draught,
God's holy image all defac'd, and chang'd
To the loath'd form of filthy goats or fwine,
The vital fpark from Heav'n extinct, and funk
By bafe contagion to the abject ftate
Of that blind inftinct which informs the brute ;
Whilft ye, fo perfect in your mifery,
Feel not the mortifying change, but boaft
Your manly fenfe and reafon unimpair'd.

True, ye are rich and great : The orient fun
Which gilds your ftately turrets with his rays
Sees not a clime but whence your riches fpeed ;
No wind that blows but o'er the oozy flood
Wafts your rich barks from fome far diftant fhore :
True, ye have rule o'er all the fea-girt Ifles
Which people the vaft bofom of the deep,
Whilft at your nod their tributary Lords
Wield but your fceptres and difpenfe your laws :

In

In ſtrength well tried that mocks the pow'r of war
Aloft in threat'ning pride your city ſtands,
Scoffing the boaſted works of Memphian Kings
When Egypt with the proud Aſſyria ſtrove
In wealth and luxury; Far off 'tis known
By many a tow'ring ſtruſture high, which lifts
It's proud head to the ſky, glitt'ring with gold;
Within Eaſe, Pomp, and Luxury contend
Throughout each ſpacious ſtreet for maſtery,
Whilſt midnight revels and gay noontide feaſts
Speak joy and mirth and full ſecurity.
Are ye ſo ſafe? Such once was Niniveh!
As yours her pow'r and wealth, as yours her crimes:
Where lies ſhe now? Go ſend your wiſemen forth,
And let them ſearch where rapid Tigris rolls
If there her place be found; or let them try
If chance the banks by fair Euphrates waſh'd *
Boaſt not the poor remains of ſo much pride;
They faulter long nor fix the truth at length.
She who in thraldom led God's choſen flock
And wav'd her banners o'er the ſubjeſt Eaſt,
She who for ages fix'd her ſtately height
In ſuch proud ſort as brav'd the frowns of Fate,

* Though moſt authors are of opinion that Niniveh was ſituated on
the river Tigris, yet no leſs perſons than Cteſias and Diodorus Siculus
repreſent it as ſituated on the Euphrates. Vide note †, p. 271.

S 3

Shone

Shone but a meteor for a moment's gaze
To fall at once nor leave one spark behind,
Not one faint glimpse to say 'twas here, 'twas there,
  Hear then her doom, and tremble for your own.

  Now had th' Almighty Judge of Heav'n and Earth,
Within whose hand the proud Assyria serv'd
But as a scourge to punish Israel's sin,
With indignation view'd the Victor's pride,
Who flush'd with conquest and debauch'd by wealth
Spurn'd at high Heav'n, and midst their gorgeous feasts
Gave honour to themselves, nor thought on God,
Save to blaspheme his name, who impious trod
Beneath irrev'rent feet his high behests
Indulging ev'ry sense ; th' impetuous youth
Following with eager steps and dauntless front
Wherever passion or lewd rapine call'd,
Whilst aged Sires, on tott'ring crutches prop'd,
Look'd smiling on, and with a guilty sigh
Envied their sons the joys they could not share.

  He saw, and turn'd him loth to his revenge ;
Nor struck at once, but with a parent's care
Whose arms are ever open to receive
The humbled prodigal who turns, though late,
To seek his face, sent forth his holy word

Of

Of his moft juft though moft fevere intent
Warning to give.   The word to Jonah came;
Who all unus'd to bear fuch high commands
Save to God's own elect, * with doubtful mind
Paus'd wond'ring.   Ill, full ill fuch paufe became
Him who ere then had heard that mighty voice,
Who knew that found to thofe who difobey
Terrific as the thunder's crafh, but mild
As the foft wind which fann'd Eve's rofeate bow'r
Ere Sin had footing there, to thofe who hear
And fly with duteous heart to execute.
Why did he paufe? Ah why! unlefs to fhew
To after times that he whofe fault'ring mind
But one fhort moment wavers in fufpence
When Duty calls, gives the Arch-tempter time
To gain firm footing in his Soul, and urge
Some well-devifed plea to ftop his courfe.
Why did he hefitate, why inly fhew
Reluctance againft God, or by a thought
Diftruft his firmnefs, or fufpect his truth!
Swift to betray and ever on the watch,
The fubtle Tempter that fhort moment feiz'd

* Jonas *ne fut pas feulement* appellé comme les autres Prophetes, à
reprendre les dix tribus de leur Idolatries, Dieu lui donna *auffi* la com-
miffion d'aller denoncer aux Ninivites la ruine de leur Ville et leur
perte totale. L'Hiftoire de la Bible par Martin, pag. 254.

S 4

To

To raife a mift before the Prophet's fight,
Which fhew'd it poffible to flee from God.

O where was that all-facred fpirit flown
Which erft had glow'd within his fervent breaft,
That fire prophetic, fitted and impell'd
To nobleft purpofes by God's own hand,
Which unappall'd by guilt, uncheck'd by fear,
Should fcatter terror through an impious world,
And tell the dreadful tale of wrath to come!
'Twas gone, and in it's place wild frantic fear
And bafe diftruft and impious doubt fprang up
Sinking the Prophet in the Man.   He flies,
O miferable change! the victim now
No longer the dread harbinger alone
Of heav'nly wrath: he flies, nor turns to think
'Till fcenes of horror ftrike his confcious heart,
And quick deftruction thunders to his foul.
Wide o'er the raging billows of the deep
Wild Horror ftalks with afpect terrible,
Whilft plunging deep full many a fathom down
He learns by fad experience to declare
How heavy 'tis to feel the wrath of Heav'n,
And bear the vengeance of an angry God.
Nor yet untried he tells the happier tale
Of mercy, when with pitying hand outftretch'd

To

To refcue from the very grafp of Death,
That Pow'r fupreme by whom the ftorm is rais'd,
Provides unhop'd-for fafety in the deep.
In vain the lightnings fhoot their ghaftly gleam,
Wild thunders roar, and Ocean groaning deep
Lifts it's o'erwhelming billows to the fky,
Unhurt he iffues from his living tomb,
His glad eye op'ning on the light of heav'n,
And wrapt in wonder, joy and gratitude,
With eager ftep purfues his deftin'd way,
Type of that plan fupreme not yet fulfill'd *,
Which reconcil'd the vengeance due to guilt
With " that dear might" which loos'd the bands of Death.

'Twas morn, and o'er the glitt'ring tow'rs the Sun
Shed wide his kindling beams ; illum'd with gold
Aloft the fpiry turrets fhone, and wav'd
Their filken banners ftreaming in the wind
With gay difplay ; bedeck'd with martial fpoils,
From haplefs Ifrael won, rich trophies rofe,
And frequent grac'd the walls.   With confcious pride
His wide domain the victor Monarch view'd,
Whilft, fitting high amid a gaudy herd
Of Sycophants, he gave a loofe to joy,

* There fhall no fign be given it but the fign of the prophet Jonas.
S. Matt. xvi. 4.

Rais'd

Rais'd a whole nation's voice in feſtive ſongs,
And taught his ready ſlaves, too prone to learn,
That luxury alone is happineſs.

    Slow and unnotic'd through the ſpacious ſtreets
The holy prophet walk'd and mark'd their pride.
He mark'd their pow'r, he mark'd their wealth, and now
A heaving ſigh he ſtole, whilſt all around
The growing multitudes he view'd, who throng'd
Thick as the inſect race which quiv'ring float
With hum inceſſant on the evening breeze.
Sorrowing he mark'd the jocund air which ſhone
In ev'ry face and brighten'd ev'ry eye,
Whilſt all was joy and mirth and careleſs eaſe ;
Sad contraſt to the proſpect in his ſoul !
He ſigh'd, and one mild look of pity caſt,
" Juſt Heav'n—but forty days !—thy will be done !"
Then op'ning ſlow the book of Fate, he turn'd
And " O" he cried " Vain, heedleſs race attend,
" Ye who with giant pride a courſe full long
" Of old, unfeeling vice have run, and ye
" Whom Luxury with ſoft ſeducing ſmile
" Allures, and binds in ſilken chains, attend ;
" Leave, leave, for ever leave your gay delights,
" Your wonted triumphs and your ceaſeleſs mirth,
" For O ſad change ! a long long train of woes,

                                        " Like

" Like a fwart ftorm which gathers in the wind,
" Hangs hov'ring o'er your deftin'd heads, and waits
" But the fcant hour appointed ere it burfts
" And crumbles you to duft.   Unhappy ftate!
" Quick quick the moment comes when all thy ftrength
" Which triumph'd far and wide with greedy pow'r
". Shall fink to lefs than woman's weaknefs, fall'n
" Beneath the hopelefs abject ftate of thofe
" Who felt the keen edge of thy Tyranny.
" I fee thy ftrong tow'rs nod, thy bulwarks rock,
" Thy ftately fabricks from their center heave,
" Whilft Defolation like a whirlwind flies
" In one fad ruin overwhelming all.
" Go feek your King amidft his pageant ftate,
" Nor tremble at his look, but bid him fear;
" And boldly tell him one unwelcome truth,
" That now, ev'n now the hand of Heav'n is rear'd,
" Or ere the fortieth Sun fhall rife and fet,
" To blaft the blooming laurels on his brow,
" And hurl him from his car of triumph down,
" No more to rife, but with his meaneft flaves
" To lie confounded in one gen'ral doom."

All pow'rful is the voice of Truth: Aghaft
The trembling people ftand, nor doubt his words,
Whilft coward Confcience whifpers to their foul

How

How lefs than nothing is the aid which wealth
Or pow'r can lend againft the wrath of Heav'n.
By fenfe of danger rous'd, they bow the knee
And proftrate turn to God, remember'd fcarce
Nor ever fought in moments happier deem'd :
Themfelves fufficient to themfelves, they fcorn'd
To court his fmile, but dar'd not brave his frown.
Fear taught them firft to kneel and firft to pray,
Whilft memory officious to their view
Held the black regifter of their mifdeeds.
Defpair firft taught their harden'd hearts to melt,
And turn'd the flint-ftone to a fpringing-well,
Whence flow'd in copious ftreams thofe contrite tears
Which fail not in the eye of Heav'n to purge
The foul from guilt, and wafh out ev'ry ftain.

Nor vain their pray'rs, their tears; for Heav'n who form'd
Knows well the frailty of the fons of earth,
Nor feeks perfection there, but kindly deigns
To raife the humbled finner from the duft,
And give to penitence the promis'd meed
Of virtue undefil'd.   A nation's tears
Abfolv'd a nation's guilt; and gracious Heav'n
With mild relenting eye and arm reftrain'd
Receiv'd their proffer'd vows.—But ah! how vain,

How

How weak is Man ! how frail his beſt reſolves !
But fraileſt thoſe which owe their haſty birth
To fear ; how ſhort, how tranſient is their life.
Hardly obtain'd, they ſhine but like the ſparks
Struck from the flint, which ſcarce outlive the blow.
Ev'n thus, or ere the fortieth Sun had ſat,
The dreaded ſentence ſeem'd an idle dream,
And the full tide of Sin, awhile reſtrain'd,
Ruſh'd madly forward with redoubled force,
Precluding ev'ry hope of future grace.
That Heav'n ſhould find it eaſier to forgive
Than wayward man alas to be forgiv'n !
But O unhappy ſtate ! O deſp'rate race !
A ſterner prophet, ISRAEL'S COMPORTER *,
Hath dipp'd his pen in blood to write thy doom.
Too deep the reeking ſword ſhall ſtrike, too near
To trifle with its edge ; again 'tis drawn,
And never never ſhall be ſheath'd, 'till wide
It ſpreads deſtruction o'er thy plains, nor leaves
A hand to bury or an eye to weep.

* Naum qui interpretatur Conſolator. Jam enim decem tribus ab
Aſſyriis deductæ fuerant in captivitatem ſub Ezechia Rege Juda, ſub
quo etiam nunc in conſolationem populi tranſmigrati, adverſum Nini-
ven viſio cernitur. Hieron. in Naum.

Hark

Hark where the conqu'ring Mede with furious voice
Calls loud for help ; Stern Babylon replies * ;
Together roll their rattling chariots on,
Their blended Armies gather as they run,
And brandifhing their eager faulchions high
Impetuous rufh like Lions on their prey.
They come, they come, lo where thy weak hofts fly,
Nor fly in fafety ; fee they fink, they fall,
Fall like ripe fruit, or yellow autumn leaves,
And ftrew the victor's path.   Loft in amaze
Thy hardy vet'rans ftand to fee fuch feats
As turn their bloodieft wars to childifh frays ;
And ever and anon with anguifh pierc'd
" Stand, ftand," they faintly cry, but none regards †,
" Turn, daftard flaves," but no one will look back.
Frantic with fear they lofe the pow'r to raife
One warding fhield to break the Victor's ftroke :
Th' enfanguin'd field alone with carnage ftrew'd
Awhile impedes their eager way : But now,
Through fcenes of Horror burfting, at thy walls

* This point, I think, is generally agreed upon, That Niniveh
was taken and deftroyed by the Medes and Babylonians ; thefe two re-
belling and uniting together, fubverted the Affyrian empire. Bp.
Newton on the Prophecies, vol. III. pag. 261.

† Nahum ii. 8.

A thou-

A thoufand banners wave, and purple fpears
Unnumber'd prefs ; vainly thy ports are barr'd,
Thy ftrong tow'rs man'd with many a hardy chief,
Vain thy ftrong holds, vain all thy ancient might,
For lo the rapid flood impetuous fwells *,
And Defolation borne upon its waves
In dreadful pomp, invades thy tott'ring wall,
And rides in horrid triumph through the breach.
Remembrance now calls forth the fiatt'ring tale
Prophetic, which thy fage Forefathers told †,
Your wife men fighing fhake their hoary heads,
Foreboding now th' unlook'd-for time is come
When the proud ftream fhall. lift her rebel waves
Againft thofe facred walls which grace her fhore.

And now thy bulwarks nod, they bow, they fall,
Low, low on earth thy proftrate glory lies.

* Nahum i. 8.

† This alludes to the following paffage in Diodorus Siculus. Hν δ'αυτω λογιον, &c. Atqui vaticinium a majoribus traditum habebat, a nullo capi Ninum poffe nifi fluvius urbi prius hoftis evaderet. Tertio demum anno accidit, ut *Euphrates* continuis imbrium graviffimorum tempeftatibus excrefceus, urbis partem inundaret et murum ad ftadia viginti dejiceret. Tum vero finem habere oraculum, amnemque manifefte urbi hoftem effe Rex judicans, fpem falutis abjecit. Diodorus Siculus, lib. 2.

Now rooted from their bafe the fculptur'd dome,
The ftately column and the ftoried arch,
In awful ruin lie: Whilft ruthlefs War,
The keen Scythe fnatching from the hand of Time,
With fpeedier rage to deal deftruction round,
Levels the work of ages at a blow ;
Nor one proud track of ancient glory leaves,
Save what the rolls of mem'ry may fupply
Uncertain, or the eye inquifitive
Trace from the mould'ring heaps of fcatter'd pride,
As through thy grafs-grown ftreets with fearful tread
The trav'ler ftrays, cafting a wary look,
Left bafking in the fculptur'd cornice lurk
The flimy adder or the mottled fnake,
And ftarting hears the horrid night-bird's fcream
From off the gilded chapiter refound
With lonely eccho through the mofs-grown walls.

Thus blafted in its very noon of pride
Falls the weak State whofe tott'ring bafe is laid
Unftable in the fand of human pow'r.
And mark her fall, ye gen'rous band, who claim
The honour'd name of Patriot, mark it well,
And let it grave this leffon on your heart,
" They raife a Nation's ftrength alone, who raife
" A Nation's virtue ;" think how weak, how vain

Proves

Proves ev'ry State which boafts not her fupport,
Like the myfterious Gourd, beneath whofe fhade
The Prophet fat, it bloffoms for a day;
But deep within its canker'd root conceal'd
The worm of Sin with ever rankling tooth
Preys on its vital part: unmark'd, unfeen
The inbred venom works, 'till drooping faft,
Its blufhing honours finking to the duft,
It fades forgot, nor leaves to after times
The precious odour of a good report.

THE

THE
DEDICATION
OF THE
TEMPLE OF SOLOMON.

BY

WILLIAM HODSON, M. A.

M DCC LXX.

THE

DEDICATION

OF THE

TEMPLE OF SOLOMON.

THE pious act of Ifrael's peaceful King,
Whofe praife re-eccho'd by the trump of Fame
Beyond the confines of remoteft lands,
From Sheba, and from Araby the bleft,
From Afric's deferts, and the Eaftern fhores
Where rapid Indus rolls his golden waves,
To Solyma allur'd unnumber'd crowds,
To hear the wifdom falling from his tongue,
And catch the honey'd accents of his mouth,
I fing.—From that refplendent throne, where rob'd
In majefty ineffable thou fitt'ft,
Defcend, celeftial Mufe! Urania! Thee
I call; defcend, and breathe into my verfe
Thy folemn founds, thy foul-commanding pow'r,
Until it pour its thund'ring tide along,
In numbers equal to its fwelling theme.—

T 3

Fell

Fell Difcord now, her robes befmear'd with blood,
Her breath more fatal than the deadly plague,
Whofe humid wings, furcharg'd with foul difeafe,
Deftroy the blufhes of the rofy fpring,
And blaft fair Nature's pride ; no more laid wafte
The verdant beauty of Judea's plains.
No more the trumpet's fhrill-ton'd clangor pierc'd
The wide-extended vault of Heav'n, and call'd
The warrior forth, where louder than the burft,
When mingled thunders fhake the lab'ring pole,
The din of battle roar'd.   The matron now
And hoary fire, no more, their cheeks bedew'd
With tears, their hands uplifted to the throne
Of Heav'n, befought their fathers God to clofe
Their aged eyes, and give their forrows reft.
For War's deftroying fword had ceas'd to fpread
Its horrors thro' the land, and meek-ey'd Peace,
With Plenty in her train, from her full lap
Shower'd down rich bleffings on the famifh'd earth,
'Till hill and valley fmil'd, and every fcene
Was chang'd from woe, to extafy and joy. ——

Thrice happy nation ! favorites of Heaven !
Selected from the kingdoms of the earth
To be his chofen race, ordain'd to fpread
His glory thro' remoteft realms, and teach

The

The gentile world Jehovah's awful name.
Oh had ye known the bleffings ye enjoy'd !
Ye could not have indulg'd that impious rage,
Which fcrupled not to leave your God, and bow
The knee to Moloch, horrid king ! which dar'd
Defile his holy place, with impious carnage,
And fear'd not to infult his Majefty,
Whofe awful word could crumble into duft
Your idol gods, and you.   At whofe command
Th' affrighted waves retir'd, and ftood on heaps
As tho' an adamantine mound had ftopt
Their rapid courfe, and to the fun,——(a fight,
Whate'er the bards of old fabling relate,
Unkown before ;)——the chambers of the deep
Difclos'd.   But when his chofen race had pafs'd,
At his dread call with mighty noife they rufh'd,
More furious than the rolling blaft of night,
Which inftant from its knotted center tears

The mountain oak, whofe tow'ring head, unmov'd
For ages brav'd the winds of heaven ; or than
The horrid burft which fhakes the cavern'd earth,
When Ætna vomits forth her livid fires ;
And 'mid the fwelling torrent overwhelm'd
The haughty tyrant, and his wretched crew,
Who durft prefume to tread that path, which God
Had made for Ifrael alone.   Oh more

T 4

Than

Than mortal blindnefs! to rejeɗ his kind
Paternal care, whofe bounteous hand, amid
The barren wildernefs for forty years,
Had fed your fathers with the bread of heaven :
Who made you ride upon the vanquifh'd necks
Of mighty kings, and rais'd you up a prince
To blefs Judea's happy land ; a prince
With ev'ry gift adorn'd, and fram'd alike
To dare the horrors of the tented field
While battle roll'd againft his fide, or grace
The gentle arts of peace. — But who, great King!
Can worthily exprefs thy praife ? Thy lyre,
Thy living lyre alone, whofe dulcet founds
In gentleft murmurs floating on the air,
Could calm the fury of the woe-ftruck king,
And footh the agony which pierc'd his heart ;
Or when thou fwept'ft the mafter ftrings and roll'dft
The deep impetuous tide along, with more
Than mortal found, could'ft raife his raptur'd foul
To extafy ; or from the tortur'd ftrings
Harfh difcord fhaking, fink him in the gulph
Of dire defpair, while horror chill'd his blood,
And from each pore the agonizing fweat
Diftill'd ; that deep-ton'd lyre alone, can fing
Thy fervent piety, thy glowing zeal,
Whofe righteous foul, aggriev'd to fee the ark,

That

That holy fanctuary which contain'd
The facred tranfcript of the will of God,
From place, to place, by hands prophane conducted,
And oft, oh facrilege ! become the prey
Of impious Philiftines, refolv'd to build
An holy temple to the God of Hofts,
An habitation to contain this pledge
Of heav'nly love, thofe laws, which from Mount Sinai
Jehovah cloath'd with terrors, while thick clouds,
And darknefs wrapt him round, pronounc'd in founds
Which chill'd the hearts of thofe who heard, and froze
Their vital blood.   Beneath whofe awful feet
Earth trembled, and the lofty mountain fhook,
Hoarfe thunder growl'd, and livid lightnings flafh'd,
While founds of horror and diftrefs, amid
The howling wildernefs were heard. — Approach,
Ye boafted fages of proud Greece ! and Rome !
Approach this facred fcene ! and blufh.   Attend,
Oh vain Philofophy ! thou wand'ring light !
Which haft fo oft mifled our fteps, attend !
And proftrate at this heav'nly fhrine, lament
Thy blindnefs, and forego thy pride ; here caft
Thy trophies down, undeck thyfelf of all
Thy borrow'd plumes, and own the fountain whence
Thy hoary fons receiv'd the living fire,
Which animates the glowing page they penn'd.

Oh

Oh happy David ! whofe exalted foul
Such heav'nly ardour breath'd ; thrice happy thou !
To frame the blefs'd defign, altho' deny'd
The full completion of thy fervent wifh.
That holy care the God of peace referv'd
For thy lov'd Son, whofe hands the bloody fword
Of ruthlefs war had ne'er defil'd, whom Heav'n
Had crown'd with every gift his heart could frame,
His fond ideas paint. ——Yes, favour'd prince !
That envied happinefs was thine ; 'twas thee
Th' Almighty chofe among the fons of men,
To dedicate a temple to his name,
Where he, whofe awful prefence fills the vaft
Immenfity of fpace, who makes the clouds
His chariot, rides fublime the whirlwind's wing,
And guides the raging ftorm, would deign to dwell,
And make his prefence known. ——Th' exalted tafk
Thy princely wifdom worthily perform'd ;
The pride of every region, every clime,
Thy pious care felected for the work,
And brought to Solyma ; whofe magazines
Th' united produce of the world contain'd.
Here might be feen the treafures of the Eaft,
The boafted wealth of Taprobana's * fhores,
With varied fplendour ftruck the dazzled eye,

* Bochart's Chanaan, B. I. Ch. 46.

And

And fham'd thy radiant light, oh Sun ! —— Beneath
Thy foft'ring hand, the glorious ftructure rofe,
Whofe haughty front on maffy pillars built,
Contemn'd the earth, and menaced the ftars.
Whofe roofs, and walls, 'for which old Lebanon
Gave up the pride of years, with precious gems,
And gold were overlaid ; whofe lofty gates
On golden hinges hung, unfolding wide
With folemn found, which thro' the fretted vaults
In pealing ecchoes ran, difplay'd the vaft
Magnificence which ftruck th' aftonifh'd view,
Where every grace, and beauty, art could frame,
Or human fkill invent, blaz'd on the fight. ——
But chief the inner houfe, the holy feat
Defign'd to guard the bleffed covenant
Which Heav'n with man had made, employ'd thy care.
The em'rald's vivid hue, the diamond's glow,
Whofe lucid rays the abfence of the fun
Supplied, compos'd its facred walls.   Here ftood
The confecrated veffels, highly wrought
Of bright Parvaïm gold, where branching palms,
And Cherubs myftic forms, the fculptor's pow'r
And wondrous art difplay'd.   Here too was plac'd
The holy altar, where the great high Prieft
Each year prefented to the throne of Heav'n
The blood of victims, and invok'd the God

Of

Of facrifice, to hear a nation's pray'r.
Two lofty Cherubins with wings of gold,
Of gold from Ophir brought, extended wide
The entrance kept, and fpread a folemn fhade;
And left unhallow'd hands fhould dare defile
The facred utenfils, or curious pry
Into the holy myfteries, a veil
Conceal'd them from the view, through which the Prieft
Alone prefum'd to pafs.——But ftop, my Mufe!
Where is the adamantine pen, whofe courfe
Unwearied as the Sun, has ftrength to paint
Thofe endlefs wonders, where the ravifh'd eye,
From beauty, rang'd to beauty, without end.
Oh glorious Temple! worthy of the God
Whofe fplendid fhrine thou waft! what can compare
With Thee?——Ye wonders of the Heathen world!
Ye boafted wonders! where is now your pride?
Ye pyramids! whofe tow'ring heads arofe
Into the fky, and darkned Egypt's land;
Ye walls of Babylon! the far-fam'd work
Of her, who with a woman's form poffefs'd
The noble firmnefs of a manly foul;
Where is your grandeur now?——Your honour's loft,
Your glory is eclips'd.——Ye works of vanity!
Unworthy incenfe to the pride of Man!
Ye trophies of deftroying Time! Your fame

One

One day shall fail without a vestige left
To shew you once have been,——Not so shalt Thou,
Thrice hallow'd Pile ! whose Heav'n-infpir'd defign,
Seraphic love, and pious ardour breath'd.
For tho' an impious Tyrant's daring hand,
Shall cast thy bulwarks to the ground, and tread
Thy glory in the dust, thy memory
Shall last, pure as th' unfullied light of Heav'n,
Recorded in that hallow'd page, whose truths,
Whose facred truths shall live, when years shall roll
No more, and every period which has mark'd
The furrow'd cheek of Time, amid the vast,
Unfathom'd ocean of Eternity
Be loft.——

       * The golden feafon of the year
Now haft'ned on, when yellow-haired Autumn,
His head with fwelling fheaves, and purple fruits
Encircled, pours his choiceft treafures forth.
Fair Nature's glowing pencil, dipt amid
The blufhing tints which deck the bow of Heav'n,
With rip'ned beauty paints the waving fcene.
The Sun now darts no more that burning rage,
Whose fierce effulgence drives the fainting world,
To feek the cooling ftream, or fhady bow'r ;
His fweeteft beams he fheds, attemper'd foft

---

* It was in the month Ethanim that the people were affembled.

Thro'

Thro' fleecy clouds, whofe animating warmth
With wild luxuriance ftrews the lap of earth,
And crowns the fmiling fields with gen'rous plenty.——
'Twas then Judea's pious King, beneath
Whofe foft'ring care the coftly edifice,
The labour'd work of many a year, receiv'd
That folemn grandeur which became the pride,
And wonder of fucceeding times ; proclaim'd
A folemn feaft, and call'd to Salem's tow'rs
The fons of Judah, fcatter'd wide around
Her diftant hills, from Hermon, to the mount
Of Horeb, down whofe rock-encumber'd fide,
In plenteous torrents roll'd the chryftal ftream,
Struck by that potent Rod, which once ftretch'd forth,
Upon the fedgy waters of old Nile,
To putrid gore his circling waves congeal'd.——
As when the fountains of the roaring deep,
No longer burfting o'er their cavern'd bed,
Had ceas'd to pour their fwelling billows forth,
Nor one unbounded fea this earthly ball
O'erwhelm'd ; th' unnumber'd fpecies who efcap'd
The wild uproar, and univerfal wreck,
Defcended from the cloud-envellop'd top
Of Ararat, to plant the defart wafte,
And animate the lifelefs globe ;—fo rufh'd
The num'rous race of Jacob, to behold

The

The ſacred pomp, and join the general joy.
Scarce could her ample palaces contain
The countleſs hoſt, which crowded to her gates.
No clouded brow was ſeen, but pleaſure fill'd
Each bounding heart, and ſparkled in each eye.
Pale Melancholy, with her murky train,
And Envy's haggard cheek, accurſed brood
Of Sin and Death, far from the happy ſcene
Where decent Mirth, and pious Gladneſs bleſs'd
The circling hours, amid the dreary realms
Of ſable-hooded Night, their native clime,
Where black-brow'd Darkneſs flaps his raven wings,
Their horrid ſhapes, and ſqualid looks conceal'd.
The bounteous King each care ſupplied, and grac'd
The feſtive board, where joyous Plenty ſmil'd,
And generous goblets crown'd the rich repaſt. ———
At length the morn which brought the hallow'd day,
Deſign'd to ſolemnize the myſteries,
And conſecrate to Heav'n's eternal King
The glorious fabric to his honour rais'd,
With roſy ſteps advanc'd, purpling the Eaſt.
Soon as the flaming car of light had left
Old Ocean's bed, and bounding up Heav'n's vault
Upon the gloomy world had pour'd the flood
Of day; the trumpet's lofty ſound the rites
Proclaim'd, and to the royal palace call'd

The

The Priefts, the Elders, and th' unnumber'd crowd,
Which fill'd the walls of Solyma.   The grand
Proceffion thence began.—Firft march'd the guards
In burnifh'd arms refplendent to the fun.
The victims next, more num'rous than the flocks,
And lowing herds, upon a thoufand hills,
An offering of peace approach'd.—To thefe
The great high Prieft, in facred veftments rob'd,
Succeeded, holding in his aged hands
The knife of Sacrifice.   His filver locks
A mitre, rich inlaid with pearls, adorn'd,
Upon whofe front thefe characters were grav'd
In words of gold, HOLINESS TO THE LORD.
Around his trembling limbs, which bent beneath
The weight, was wrapt a purple ephod deck'd
With coftly gems, and gold; and on his breaft
The myftic Urim, and the Thummim fhone.
Behind were feen the Priefts, and Levites, cloath'd
In linen garments white as mountain fnow,
Bearing the holy ark, with reverence,
And awe.   Around in order march'd the fingers,
Hymning Jehovah's name in fongs of praife.
With every ftrain the filver trumpets breath'd
Their fwelling notes, and pierc'd the ambient air;
At which th' attendant throng enraptur'd join'd
The num'rous choir in fhouts of heart-felt joy,

And

And fang Hofannahs to the King of Kings,
Who was, and is, and is to come, 'till Heav'n's
Capacious dome re-eccho'd to the found.
Next came the king array'd in crimfou robes,
And feated on a car of folid gold,
Around him walk'd the nobles of his court,
In purple cloath'd of richeft hue, the work
Of Tyre, for fkill, and cunning fam'd.——Behind
Appear'd the guards, who clos'd the pompous fcene ;
Which round the city's wide-ftretch'd circuit march'd
With flow and folemn pace, until they reach'd
The Temple's lofty gates, whofe ample round
The num'rous train admitted ; where arriv'd,
Within the fanctuary's hallow'd fpace
They plac'd the Ark, and while the great High Prieft
With due luftrations fanctify'd the courts,
And folemniz'd the myfteries, again
They ftruck the chorded fhell, and caroll'd fweet
Th' impaffion'd hymn of praife.——The deftin'd victims
Upon the altar bound, he now approach'd,
To plunge into their breafts the facred knife,
When Solomon defcending from his feat,
Where underneath a canopy of gold
Sublime he fat, and bending low, addrefs'd
The throne of Heav'n.—No more the choral fong
Was heard, their golden lyres no more breath'd forth

U

The

The melting rapture, every voice was hufh'd,
A death-like filence reign'd around, and mute
Attention dwelt upon each tongue.—Oh Thou
Who erft didft open Zacharias' lips,
Eternal Spirit! fearcher of all hearts!
Breathe thro' my inmoft foul that light divine,
Whofe pure unclouded fountains once infpir'd
Thy prophets myftic pens; that I may catch
Th' extatic fervour which inflam'd his breaft,
While raptur'd at the altar's hallow'd foot
Thefe facred accents glow'd upon his tongue:

" FATHER omnipotent! Eternal God!
" Thrice holy! felf-exiftent! Pow'r fupreme!
" Whofe mighty word yon maffy fpheres attun'd,
" And call'd the wonders of creation forth.
" Thou whom the fun in his eternal courfe,
" And morning ftars infpher'd, together quire;
" Jehovah, incommunicable name!
" Before whofe awful prefence, angels veil'd,
" With mighty Seraphim, inceffant hymn
" Their God, in extafy of ceafelefs praife.
" Shalt Thou, unchangeable, eternal King!
" Before whofe ever burning throne, in chains
" Of adamant, Eternity, and Fate
" Lie bound.   Who with the lightning's beam, in words

" Of

" Of fire, engrav'ft thy everlafting laws,
" Upon the front of Heav'n's unbounded fphere.
" Beneath whofe mighty nod, when Thou art wroth,
" The folid mountain from its center fhakes,
" And Earth's ingulph'd foundations ftand reveal'd;
" While Vengeance rifing from his bed of woe,
" To crufh a guilty world, his crefted fnakes
" Erects, and lances from his red right arm
" The flaming thunderbolt.——Shalt Thou refide
" In houfes hands have fafhion'd ? No; beyond
" Creation's ample circuit, where the car
" Of day, pure fount of empyrèal light!
" Ne'er fhed his all-enliv'ning beam, thy pow'r
" Pervades, and fills th' unfathomable void
" Of Chaos, and of Night. —— Yet deign t' accept
" This Temple facred to thy holy name,
" And tho' thou dwell'ft on high, receive our pray'rs.
" Forgive our paft backflidings, may we grieve
" No more that holy Spirit, which has work'd
" Unnumber'd miracles for Ifrael's fons.
" Protect thy chofen race from murd'rous fnares
" Of proud deceitful men, who hunt for blood,
" As roams the famifh'd lion for his prey.
" Arife, oh King of Kings! and difappoint
" Their malice, who unmindful of their God,
" Thy awful Majefty, thy pow'r defy,

U 2

" And

" And bow the knee to Dagon. Who amid
" Their nightly orgies, chant in mad'ning choirs
" His might divine, and give to fculptur'd ftones
" Thy glory, and thy name. Turn from thefe walls
" Their facrilegious hands, whofe impious rage
" Burns to defile thefe hallow'd inftruments,
" Thefe veffels to thy fervice confecrate.
" Oh let no blood to idols offer'd ftain
" This holy altar, nor within thefe roofs,
" To other Gods than thee, let incenfe fmoke.
" Defcend celeftial fpirits ! Ye who wait
" Around the throne of God ! defcend, and guard
" This heav'n-devoted fhrine. Come, holy Love !
" Meek angel ! daughter mild of Innocence,
" And Truth ! leave, leave thy bright enthron'd abode
" On high, and with Religion, fainted maid !
" Propitious guide amid life's darkfome vale
" Our wand'ring fteps. Oh fend thy cherub, Hope,
" To chafe from every contrite heart, the fiend
" Defpair ; and let thy mercy's gentleft ray,
" Refrefhing as the filver dew of heav'n
" Upon the drooping flow'rs, defcend to footh
" The weeping penitent. Breathe thro' our fouls
" Thy heav'nly ardour, teach us to implore
" His tender mercies, whofe paternal love
" Forgave our difobedience. May our hearts

" In

" In duty firm, obfequious to his will
" His laws obey, and to his name alone
" Our adorations give, 'till wrapt beyond
" That ftarry canopy, where Seraphs fweep
" Their living lyres, and fing in notes divine
" The endlefs wonders of creative pow'r,
" We join th' immortal choir, and tune our harps
" To endlefs raptures, and eternal praife."——

He ceas'd.   When lo! a mighty noife was heard
Of rufhing winds, and fire from heav'n confum'd
The facrifice.   Upon the holy feat
The Shechinah defcended, and illum'd
The temple's fpacious walls with radiant glory.
A burning cloud it feem'd, like that which erft
Attended Judah's fons, when to avoid
The galling load of Pharaoh's iron fway,
From Egypt's land they fled.   The unnumber'd Hoft
Amazed at the fight, with holy awe
Their faces veil'd, and proftrate on the ground
In hallelujahs hymn'd Jehovah's name,
To him alone afcribing majefty,
And pow'r.   Jehovah's name the vaulted roofs
Rebound; their acclamations pierce the fkies,
And with the fmoke of facrifice afcend
A grateful incenfe to the throne of God. ——

U 3

THE

THE

DAY OF JUDGMENT.

BY

GEORGE BALLY, M. A.

WRITTEN FOR MR. SEATON's PRIZE, BUT REJECTED.

M DCC LVII.

THE

THE

DAY OF JUDGMENT.

FOE to each strain, which sooths th' unhallow'd ear,
And violates the dignity of song,
The Christian Muse exults to catch her flame
From altars of the living God, to drink
Her inspiration from the fount of Truth.
Glorious her theme and solemn! fit to swell
The raptures of a Seraph, when with hymn
Ecstatic, to his golden harp attun'd,
He makes the throne of Deity resound.

Deign, Holy Spirit, in thy SIBYL's breast,
If pure the shrine, and for th' illapse prepar'd,
To plant a ray of thy celestial light,
That so the visionary maid, enlarg'd
Her tone and feature, may with awful sound
Utter immortal mysteries, may sing
The glories of thy kingdom: how, transfixt

With

With his own arrows, Death shall yield his prey,
And groan in sullen agonies his last :
How Time shall join Eternity's abyss,
And mingling sink ingulf'd : how Earth shall tremble
With fruitful throes, and heave with quicken'd dust,
Man bursting from the prison of his tomb
(By shocks without, by fears within appall'd)
To meet the dread award ; to see his God,
In all the splendors of judicial pomp
Array'd, descending from the empyreal skies.

When siren Pleasure spreads her guilty charms,
And summons all her blandishments to melt
Thy manhood into softness, and debase
The Heav'n-stamp'd image to a grov'ling brute ;
Or when Ambition waves her plumy crest,
And with the gaudy pageant fires thy blood ;
Prompts to break moral ties, as chains that bind
Heroic worth, and check fair Fame's career ;
Heir of eternal life, reflect, O Man,
What to thyself thou ow'st, whose endless doom
Hangs on this squander'd moment, or the next.
To specious phantoms, by thy passions drest
In pleasing glofs, let Fancy's magic glance
Oppose the final and tremendous scene :
Think that thou see'st the veil etherial rent

                                Th' Om-

Th' Omniscient Judge disclos'd, begirt with pow'r
Paternal : shudder at th' imagin'd sound
Of the loud-pealing trump, which Nature hears
Shook from her pristin functions, and convuls'd :
Rapt in sad trance behold the teeming graves
Yawn and unhouse their tenants, trooping all
Where the bright standard of th' ensanguin'd Cross
Waves o'er the throne imperial, in mid air :
Image thyself from subterranean cell
Thrust into light, and summon'd to the bar,
Pallid, aghast, and trembling for thy doom,
Heav'n op'ning all her joys, her torments Hell.
If to thy mind this picture were display'd
In all its heighten'd colourings of awe,
Deep wou'd th' impression sink : no worldly lure
Wou'd tempt the risque of an immortal soul.
Superior to the glitter of a crown,
To INDIA's wealth, or Beauty's roseate smile,
Touch'd by Religion's ray, thy kindling spirit
Wou'd soar on Adoration's eagle wing
To the Triune all-glorious Sun : there drink
Large draughts insatiate from the blissful fount,
In ecstasies ineffable dissolv'd.

In that portentous hour, when ev'ry heart
Shall groan, and sympathize with Nature's pang,

When

When the world, unfubftantial as its joys,
Shall like a fleeting fhadow melt away,
What fhall fuftain the foul ? What fhoot a beam
Of confolation thro' the folid gloom ?
What ? but a retrofpection of the paft,
If, brighten'd with good deeds, the profpect fhew
No darker fpots than errors of furprize :
If, lifted in the fervice of thy God,
Tenacious of thine oath thou ftood'ft the fiege
Of Satan, unfubdu'd, tho' all his wiles
Combin'd with direful enginery affail'd
The more than ftoic fortrefs of thy heart :
Or if, feduc'd, and yielding to his fnares,
Thy foul, with deep contrition fmit, bewail'd
Her bafe defection, and with fervent pray'r,
And vow'd amendment to the throne of grace
Suppliant return'd, and ftruggled for the boon.
Then Confcience, flame implanted from above
To guide thro' life's dark wild our devious fteps,
(That fmiles an angel, or a dæmon frowns)
Will fing her foothing requiem to thy breaft.
Much will it chear thee, if amidft the crowd
An orphan or a widow meet thine eye,
Whofe lighten'd woes confefs'd thy foft'ring hand :
If mild forgivenefs in thy bofom glow'd,
Thy friends embracing, nor excluding foes.

This

This thy bleſt Saviour, unexhauſted ſource
Of love and mercy! when He deign'd to ſhroud
The Godhead in Mortality's frail robe,
Enjoin'd and practis'd.   Heaven is bound to pay
What man's benevolence expends on man.
Than Charity no fairer ſweeter flow'r
The Chriſtian chaplet weaves.   All other virtues
Their end attain'd ſhall ceaſe for ever.   Hope
Shall in Fruition's ocean be abſorpt,
And Faith in Certainty's meridian blaze.
But this ſweet bud, tranſplanted from the bleak
Ungenial nurſery below, ſhall bloom
Immortal in ambroſial EDEN's bow'rs,
And with diffuſive odours glad all heaven.

Thus taught to ſhun the perils of that ſtorm,
Which ſhall the Wicked wreck, but waft the Good,
Propitious, to calm ports of endleſs joy;
The Muſe embolden'd will her taſk purſue,
And all the dread amazing ſcene unfold:
Reckleſs, tho' man condemn her frigid ſtrain,
If Heav'n her modulated life applaud,
The better ſong! and in that ſolemn day,
Which trembling now ſhe meditates to ſing,
Deign to beſtow the bright unwith'ring wreath.

Time's

Time's moſt ſtupendous birth, by glaring types
Prefigur'd, by the dark myſterious voice
Of holy ſeers announc'd, by God himſelf
(Empty'd of glory, and in fleſh reveal'd)
Foreſhewn in noontide luſtre, now diſclos'd
Frowns horrible on Earth's awaken'd ſons.
Yet (ſo inſenſate, and obdur'd his guilt).
Tho' the moſt awful enſigns of diſmay,
Dark'ning the face of Nature, had proclaim'd
The world's approaching obſequies, yet Man
Graſps ſublunary ſhadows, pictur'd clouds,
And anchors on the toſſing wave his hope.
So in the days of NOAH, tho' forewarn'd,
Ere the flood burſt, and whelm'd their impious Heads,
The playful votaries of BELIAL gorg'd
Their rav'ning palate, and in all the luxe
Of lawleſs joys, and wild intemp'rance rag'd.
But now, like centinels aſleep by thoſe
They dread ſurpriz'd, they ſtart, they ſtare, they groan,
And read their woeful ſentence in their fears.

For lo ! the Judge, with Myriads in his train,
Angelic cohorts, hierarchal pow'rs,
And all the thron'd dominions of the ſky,
Proud to adorn the triumphs of this day,
From the bright Empyrean bends to earth

                                                His

His radiant progrefs.   Earth to th' inmoft center
Shakes to and fro aftounded.   Hark ! the trump
Ætherial pours the fleep-difpelling blaft,
And bellows in the cóncave of her womb
Parturient of life, and big with man.
Nature reverft her Lord's beheft obeys,
Her Dead with breath infpir'd, her Quick transform'd.
The vaulted tombs, the cloud-capt pyramids,
Hear the loud-echo'd fummons, and refund
The treafur'd reliques, faithful to their truft.
Nor only labóurs monumental Earth
With human births.   Each element throughout
Glows in this work ; and feels the feeds of man
Unravel from its complicated mafs.
From the four winds, by voice divine compell'd,
Thick fwarming atoms thro' the clouded air
Precipitate their flight, to build anew
The moulder'd frame ; no more to be diffolv'd !
And now its priftin tenement renew'd,
The foul long exil'd, which perhaps had roam'd,
A reftlefs fugitive, the blue expanfe,
Or, wheeling nearer to lov'd earth her flight
Hover'd impatient o'er th' imprifon'd corfe ;
Or, couching on the confines of her doom,
Had wifh'd, or fear'd the grand decifive day ;

True

True to its nuptial tie, this foul returns,
And weds a partner, which shall live for ever.

O rapture to the juft ! to think that they,
When ev'ry planet, ftricken from its orb,
Shall fade, and o'er a ruin'd univerfe
Darknefs incumbent fpread her raven wing,
That they, emerging from the wreck, fhall fhine,
Like cluft'ring ftars around the fun of glory,
In firmaments unconfcious of decay !
See ! how their brighten'd cheek with tranfport glows,
As, rifing from their dank and wormy bed,
They moult corruption ! All on wing they dart
Their wifhes, and anticipate the fkies.
Ah ! how unlike the wicked ! The fcar'd Mufe
Starts at the conjur'd fpectres.   Grant, O Lord,
The Poet may not in that group be feen ;
But fhun thofe terrors, which in fancy chill
His blood, and with a Stygian vapour blot
Each fair idea dawning on his mind !
Slow and reluctant from their dungeon's gloom
They rife unjoyous.   Happier, if they ne'er
Had rifen from Death's dark oblivious vale !
On their dim faded brow fits pale Difmay,
And from their haggard eyes, fhockt with each fight,

Each

Each found that meets their ear, wild Horror glares;
And Defperation, that internal Hell,
Their mien with Sorrow's darkeft fhade imbrowns.

But, hark! again the trumpet's direful clang,
Mixt with triumphal fhouts of banner'd hofts
Rufhing from high, th' affrighted welkin rends,
And to a congregated world proclaims
The Deity's approach.   On radiant clouds
From pureft æther fpun, as on a car,
Borne thro' the yielding air he comes, and Earth,
Unable to fuftain th' effulgent beam
Of Godhead, with her adamantine hills
Shrinks at his prefence, and like wax diffolves.
Lo! thro' the vaft extenfive cope of Heaven
Swells an immeafurable arch, with all
The gay diverfities of light diftinct,
The dread tribunal of our Judge.   Imblaz'd
With Glory's richeft vefture, there he fits
Obvious to ev'ry eye.   Stars confluent crowd
Into a wreath imperial for their King.
His glance outfhines the fun; and, when he waves
Th' ambrofial beamy treffes of his head,
Tremble the fkies, and all creation fhakes.

Tranfcendent majefty of CHRIST! fublim'd
To fplendor from contempt, to higheft blifs

X

From

From depths of woe for us fuſtain'd! how chang'd
From him, whoſe ſacred temples bled beneath
Th' inſulting preſſure of a thorny crown!
From him, who judg'd, condemn'd by vaſſal Man,
Death's deadlieſt pang endur'd; and, to the Sun
Expos'd, who fled the ſpectacle abhorr'd,
Shook CALVARY's dire top, and SALEM's tow'rs
With groans of agonizing Deity!
Look up, affrighted ISRAEL, and confeſs,
Amazingly convinc'd, thy ſad miſtake.
See there th' anointed Lord; the ſame who preſs'd
Thee with endearing call beneath the wings
Of healing mercy to repoſe, when erſt
He ſojourn'd in thy tents; a GOD unown'd;
Tho' Nature thunder'd to each ſenſe the truth,
Suſpended at his beck her pow'rs, or chang'd!
How this his glorious advent, grac'd with pomp
Brighter than that thy carnal hope preſag'd
Of the firſt advent, fatally o'erlook'd,
Harrows thy ſoul! how all thy Elders mourn!
How droops thy Sanhedrim, abaſht to view
The flaming Banner, and the ſentenc'd Judge!

Yet Mercy in that boſom ſits enthron'd,
E'en for his foes an advocate, and melts
The wrathful flaſhes of that awful brow

Into foft beams of tendernefs.   The bleft
Redeemer mitigates the Judge's frown.
Elfe who fo pure, and incorrupt of heart,
As with unfhaken hope to fix his eye
On Majefty's infufferable blaze,
In terrors dreadfulleft array reveal'd?

And now th' Archangel's trumpet thro' the vaft
Expanfe of univerfe, which trembling fwells
The lengthen'd peal, the dire citation founds.
High, o'er the Judgment-feat, triumphant floats,
The dread of infidels, the chriftian's boaft,
Th' ennobled Crofs.   Where'er its glories ftream,
Eternal crimfon paints the blufhing fcene.
The Sword of Juftice, by a Seraph wav'd,
Illumines the wide air, and hung aloft
Th' eventful righteous Balance flames with gold.
Hither, in one diffufive area's fpace,
By fweeping whirlwinds level'd to a plain,
ADAM's colle&ive progeny conven'd,
Myriads on myriads crowd; in number more
Than billowing fands, by winds tempeftuous driven
Thro' LIBYA's treach'rous foil.   How undiftinguifh'd
Thy armies here, proud XERXES, at whofe touch
    Rivers exhaufted fhrunk! What but a drop
To ocean added, and in ocean loft?

X 2

See!

See! how Earth's cedars bow their with'ring head,
Scath'd with the lightnings, which inceffant break
From yon tremendous throne! How quake her CÆSARS,
Her NIMRODS and her BOURBONS, lawlefs chiefs,
Beneath whofe wafteful fword unpeopled realms,
Ambition's victim, bled! whofe laurels bloom'd,
And wanton'd in the widow's flowing tears,
Their guilty joys bought with mankind's diftrefs!
Curft the vain triumph, and the trophy'd Arc,
And all the proud memorials of their rage,
The ftricken heroes mourn, and wifh atchiev'd
Thofe victories, to which th' angelic hoft
Thro' Heav'n's glad courts applaufive Pæans fing,
Immortal victories, and worthy Man,
O'er paffions conquer'd, and o'er felf fubdu'd.
Not fo the potentate, whofe fpotlefs life,
Pure as his ermine, fhone; who ne'er the fword
Unfheath'd, but when Religion afk'd its aid,
Or his lov'd Country, groaning under wrongs,
Bade him Oppreffion's infolence chaftife:
Flufh'd with gay hopes, and panting for the palm,
He views th' unfading crown, for which he toil'd,
Amidft the foft allurements of a throne
Firm and unfhaken, when Earth faw him fhed
Balm from his fceptre o'er a fofter'd realm.
Ye virtuous ALFREDS, GEORGES, ANNES, ELIZAS,

Protectors

Protectors of your country and mankind;
Lift up the brow of confidence; assume
Th' unblushing mien of grandeur, and behold
Th' exceeding weight of glory, which your King
Awards to all, who made the throne a step
To mount their bleft ambition to the ikies.

The world's diftinctions, and its gloffy plumes
Are vanish'd.   Here the goodnefs of the heart,
Exuberant in fruits of holy life,
Gives man the juft pre-eminence o'er man.
The Monarch; if, to ev'ry luft a flave,
He bruis'd his fubjects with an iron rod,
And iffuing from th' imperial den; on blood
And rapine bent, with ruin mark'd his way,
Outcaft from light, and to congenial fiends
Confign'd, reverfe deplorable! furveys
The beggar diadem'd, and thron'd in blifs.
All greatnefs, but what aggrandizes man,
Diminifht fhrinks.   Pale Beauty hides her face
Once prais'd, than loath'd Deformity more foul,
Unlefs fair Virtue, beaming from within;
Sheds a celeftial radiance o'er the mien.
Proud boaftful Science; o'er the midnight lamp
So oft in vain refearches poring; droops
To fee the fage now dwindle to a fool,

X 3

Who

Who ne'er in ZENO's porch, or PLATO's grove,
Explor'd the path to happiness and GOD.

None more exult, or with more heighten'd bloom
Impurpled, on the dread tribunal fix
The eye serene uprais'd, than those whose breast
Glow'd with extensive charity, and bade
The stream benign in widen'd channels run,
To distant ages circulating joy,
And solace as it flow'd.   Lo! HENRY leads
'Th' illustrious band.   The clouds, which here o'ercast
His pensive brow, the storms, which vex'd his reign,
Are dissipated all.   Immortal Hope
Distends his heart, and glitters in his eye.
Blood-stain'd usurper, how the scorpion whip
Of Conscience ulcerates thy bleeding soul!
How dost thou wish BOSWORTH's less dreaded plain
Had giv'n the last decision to thy fate!
Hail, pious prince! and to thy virtues due
A crown receive, which no rapacious hand
Shall ravish: view a moment's woes outweigh'd
By an eternity of solid bliss.

Now palsy'd Fear the whole assembly shakes,
And bursting sighs o'er all the void resound:
Now e'en the Good misgivings feel.   For lo

The

The feal of adamant is broke, and open'd,
Big with the fate of man, th' eternal book.
The Angels, anxious for this hour which clears
The mazes of the moral plan, unveils
Myfterious depths, which erft intent to fcan
They ftoop'd, and of their wand'ring found no end,
Throng round the Judge unnumber'd, and behold,
Aftonifht, ev'ry dark enigma folv'd,
And providence afferted in his ways.
The marfhal'd world, obedient to command,
Forms a two-fold divifion; on the right
The Juft, the Wicked on the left are rang'd.
So when the genial fpring the turgid gems
Unlocks, and breathes a verdure o'er the meads,
The fhepherd, fedulous to pour his flock
O'er the frefh pafture, the mixt troop furveys,
And bids the fetid and lafcivious herd
Graze from the bleating innocents disjoin'd.
Sufpenfe awhile, and dread Amazement holds
The ftill creation motionlefs: when lo!
The founding Alchymy, by breath infpir'd
Of Archangelic Herald, rings a peal
Of fummons to the righteous, to attend
The Judge, and hear enounc'd their final doom.
Thin fhades of doubt amidft the confcious gleams
Bright'ning their front are interpos'd. As when

X 4

A ROMAN

A Roman chief, from the well-foughten field
Returning, felt alternate passions sway
His breast, now hoping, fearing now left all
His labours might disparag'd sink below
The envy'd prize of Triumph's festal pomp.

With placid brow, at which the æther smiles
Flush'd with redundancy of light, the Judge
Surveys the chosen flock, and sheds abroad
Peace o'er their hearts, and lustre o'er their mien.
Meek dove-ey'd Innocence, with Slander's darts
Oft here transpierc'd, and in the shuffled crowd
Of accidents with Guilt confounded, pure
And spotless as the recent snow appears.
Her stern accusers wither at the sight,
While Cherubs, with benevolence o'erflowing,
Clap their exulting wings, rejoic'd to view
Effulgence of their sanctitude, and long
To waft their sister spirit to the skies.
Omniscience pleas'd the honest heart inspects,
His noblest work; and bares the deep recess,
Where Charity and Virtue sit enshrin'd.
Each unambitious grace, which, like the rose
That paints th' untrodden wild, in secret bloom'd,
Too delicate to bear the ruffling breath
Of worldly praise, now beams in open day,

And

And its unfolded beauties ſpreads before
Applauding angels, and a ſmiling GOD.
The ſtains, which to the beſt below adhere,
Moles in a well-ſhap'd body thinly ſown,
Are by the candid Judge, without a frown,
From Heav'n's memorial books eras'd for ever.

O glorious trial ! where the Juſt, like gold
By friendly fire refin'd, with added weight
And ſplendor ſhine conſpicuous, on the ſtage
Of an aſſembled world proclaim'd aloud
Their merit, and by liſt'ning ſaints extoll'd !
See ſuff'ring Worth exult, her utmoſt wiſh
Now more than gratify'd ! the weighty meed
O'erpays her woes, and with a boundleſs tide
Perennial pleaſures burſt upon her ſoul.
How glow Religion's Chiefs, whom threats nor flames
Could e'er ſubdue ; nor all the ſtudy'd pains,
Which witty Malice forg'd, could ever ſhake
From the firm baſis of their high reſolve !
Their gracious GOD inclines his head, and nods
His approbation, in their ſorrows pleas'd
To recognize his own : the heav'nly Band
The victors greet with pæans, and rejoice
To add the ſteady phalanx to their roll.

Huſh'd

Hush'd be ye winds ! and Earth and Æther, wrapt
In silence, listen to your Maker's voice
Mellifluous, which aloud the mild award
Enounces thro' your regions.   " Come, ye Blest,
" Share the unfading pleasures of my realm,
" Coheirs of blifs, my fire's adopted fons."
Rapt at the found the Just, a shining train,
The yielding clouds divide, by angel wings
Convoy'd in triumph thro' th' aerial space,
With Hallelujahs, and the dulcet strain
Of harps refounding.   Round his throne the Judge
The gather'd Faithful ranks in sev'ral files
Proportion'd to their worth, all stars ordain'd
Orbs to relume by Satan and his crew
Rebellious voided, but in glory each
From each now diff'ring, as on earth their deeds,
How vast the rapture, infinite the joy
From breast to breast rebounding ! how inflam'd
With love ineffable the bridegroom burns,
To meet the pure unfpotted fpoufe, in all
The heighten'd charms of Piety array'd !
How the Redeemer with complacence hails,
The glorious ranfom of his precious blood,
His faints, from ev'ry quarter of the globe
Conven'd, affeffors of his throne, to hear
Guilt fentenc'd, and applaud her righteous doom !

See

See! on the left what confternation broods
O'er all the louring profpect! how defponds
The mifcreant throng! how frantic ev'ry look,
And fpeaking gefture! what a burft of groans
Declares the direful bodings of their foul!
For now the Wicked, like a rufhing fea
Turbid with ftormy gufts, their cited numbers
Pour round the bar, and deluge all the plain.
Luft, Murder, Avarice, and rancour'd Hate,
And Perfecution, varnifht o'er with zeal,
And foul Hypocrify, beneath the veil
Of fair Religion lurking, grifly forms,
Touch'd by a ray, quick flafhing from the throne,
Start up in native ghaftlinefs reveal'd.
How vain the caitif's artifice, which oft
O'er baffled Juftice triumph'd, now the Judge
Omnifcient fcans his life, and brings to light
Each hidden purpofe, each unwitnefs'd deed!
Th' invenom'd heart, its mazy folds evolv'd,
And ev'ry cell difclos'd, where Malice fate
Hatching dire treafons, maffacres, and ills,
Trembles beneath a fearching God.   Appall'd
Heav'n's habitants look down, with horror viewing
Humanity degraded to a fiend.

Ah!

Ah ! how they writhe their limbs, and gnafh their teeth,
With tortures inly rackt, afham'd to view
Blazon'd their crimfon fpots, afraid to meet
The glances of Omnipotence enrag'd,
Th' offended JESUS to confront, whofe laws
They trampled under foot, whofe name they mock'd,
And glorying in their fcandal, ftill rebell'd,
By all his gracious offers unreclaim'd !
In vain to rocks they call, in yawning depths
To whelm their heads abafht.   Alas ! the rocks
Soon will their fuel'd entrails fcatter wide,
And nought remain a monument of wrath
Divine, but Man, apoftate Man, condemn'd
To feed th' undying worm, to howl in fire,
His torments coextended with his being.

And now with afpe&, kindled into rage
Tenfold, at which earth, air, and fea around
Float with redundant flames, with voice, at which
Trembles Heaven's wide circumference, the Judge
The ftern award enounces.   " Go, ye Curft,
" To fire, as everlafting as your fouls,
" For Satan and his impious hoft prepar'd."

Strait at the found deftroying Angels pour
Their wrathful vials o'er a world profcrib'd,

A guilty

A guilty world! which faw its Maker bleed.
Inceffant thunders thro' th' aerial vault
Roll the big mutt'ring peal, and lightnings glare
Terrific thro' the gloom.   The fun, the moon,
With blood difcolour'd, o'er the darken'd foene
Scowl horror and amaze: ftars from their fphere
With hideous ruin and combuftion rufh.
Convulfive tremors rock the reeling earth,
And from her riven womb, where prifon'd flept
Till now, in min'ral or metallic beds,
The vengeful minifters, embody'd flames
Shoot the long fpiry trail, and billowing pufh
O'er many a fpacious realm and region wide
The ruddy torrent.   Ah! what havock reigns!
How Defolation o'er the proftrate globe
Furious her fcythe-arm'd chariot drives, and all
Its boafted fplendor levels with the duft!
Where are the giant-fons of Earth, the ALPS,
And APENNINES, the PYRENEAN cliffs,
Proud boundaries of kingdoms? Where huge ATLAS,
Who frown'd tremendous o'er the fubject furge?
All, like the fnow which glitter'd on their tops,
Melted before the prefence of the LORD,
Are perifh'd, and no veftige left behind.
Ah! vanifh'd is that fpot, for juftice fam'd,
Of injur'd ftates th' Afylum, Queen of Ifles,

BRITANNIA.

BRITANNIA.   Oh! my country! there she sinks
Whelm'd in the fiery flood, and ambient seas,
Once her strong bulwark, but augment the blaze.
Empires renown'd, where erst contention rag'd
To add fresh laurels to the victor's brow,
Join'd in one fate, an undistinguish'd mass
Of ruin lie, a monument to shew
How vain Ambition's most successful toil.
The raging tumult thickens, and Uproar,
'Midst Nature's groans, and crush of elements
Holds her licentious anarchy.   The pow'rs
Of Heaven are shaken, and yon unpillar'd arch,
Earth's gorgeous canopy, with fervent heat
Melts, like a scroll convolv'd, to viewless air.
Th' august assize now finish'd 'midst the loud
Plaudits of wond'ring Angels, darkness drops
The curtain o'er Creation.   Oh! what plaints,
What yells resound, while rolling in the surge
Sulphureous, kindled by the Almighty's blast
Th' eternal Tophet, Myriads howl and wish
They in the gen'ral wreck cou'd lose their being!

His ways asserted, and unerring right
In each proportion'd recompense display'd,
The Judge all-glorious rises from his throne,
And with his bright retinue wings his car

Triumphal

Triumphal thro' the ſkies, to heavenly Sion
In radiant pomp aſcending. Angels ſtrike
Their golden chords, and melody divine
Exulting thro' the ætherial region floats.
On their gay foreheads amaranthine crowns
Of joy, immortal praiſes in their mouths,
The ranſom'd ſaints their Saviour hail, and loud
Hoſannas from unnumber'd voices pour'd
Swell the glad jubilee. Heav'n's op'ning portals
Shook with the feſtive acclamations ring.

THE

THE

REDEMPTION:

A

MONODY.

BY

J. SCOTT, M. A.

Τον οντα παντων Κυριον γενικωτατον,
Και πατερα, τετον διατελει τιμαν, μονον
Αγαθων τοιετων ευρετην κτιϛορα.

Frag. Menand.

M DCC LXIII.

ADVERTISEMENT.

*THE Reader need not be told that the following Poem
was written for* SEATON'S PRIZE, *and rejected. It is
not now published as an appeal to the Public from the sentence
of the Judges; but as it may afford half an hour's innocent
entertainment to the Reader.*

*The Author chose this contracted plan for two reasons:
one was, that he might keep clear of Arguments pro and con,
which if unskilfully handled are as ridiculous in poetry, as
wooden swords in skirmishes at a puppet-shew; and the other,
that he might not trespass upon the Reader's patience by enter-
ing too prolixly into a subject, which is better suited for a
large volume, than a small pamphlet.*

*The poetical Reader need not be told that the Metre is
an imitation of that, which* Milton *hath used in his Ly-
cidas.* ———

Y 2

THE

THE

REDEMPTION.

D AUGHTERS of Jove, no more!—Adieu, ye
  Maids,
Whofe vifionary forms have met my eye;
Whether I mus'd by Anio's headlong fteep,
Or by the fabled haunts of Caftaly,
Or where Cephifus joins the billowy deep;
Or where thro' groves, and olive-woven fhades,
Iliffus rolls his ftream;
For now a loftier theme
Demands my fong, REDEMPTION's wondrous plan,
And thy fad fufferings, O my God, for Man!

  But come, O Virgin-mufe of Sion, come,
Come gently, and my breaft infpire
With fome faint fparks of that feraphic fire,
Whofe beams refulgent glow'd,
When burfting thro' the womb
Of dark futurity, " A God, a God,"

Y 3

Proclaim'd aloud the heav'n-enlighten'd Seer,
" From Bofrah lo he comes mighty to fave,
" Mighty to triumph o'er the grave ! "——
And all the oaks of Bafhan ftoopt to hear,
And Lebanon's attentive cedars bow'd.

    But turn, O turn thine eyes
To where with groves of Palm, and Olive crown'd,
On the fair bofom of the mountain lies
The Garden's holy ground !
For there my Saviour's bitter agonies
Began ; there from th' Abyfs profound
Of blackeft Hell, a ftream of horrour flow'd,
And overwhelm'd his pure and innocent foul ;
Or ere his facred blood
Had wafht, had cleans'd us from pollutions foul,
And feal'd anew the League 'twixt Man and God.

    Dark rofe the dreadful Night,
And not one fprightly note, or pleafing found,
Was heard to breathe around :
The Shepherds fat with filent horrour mute,
And charm'd no more their pipe or jocund flute ;
And Philomel her wonted ftrain forbore :
How could fhe fing, while from the blafted oak
The hoarfe night-ravens croak,
And Screech-owls moan aloud in dire affright,

And

And fcreaming from the pool with hideous cry
Aloof the Bitterns fly ;
While clouds impetuous burft with horrid roar,
And Spectres fhriek, and Ghofts unholy yell,
And mutt'ring in the black and turbid air
Dæmons and fiends of hell,
Array'd in livid flames, terrific glare ?

    Earth to the center fhook,
And univerfal Nature quakt for fear,
As if her end was near ;
While ev'ry pale Star, with diftemper'd look,
Shot from the fky :—and well, O well they might
When he was doom'd to agonizing pain,
Who bade them flame on high,
The faireft gems in heav'n's fair canopy,
And fill'd their orbs with everlafting light.
But now fee where he lies
On the cold ground, expos'd to thick dank air,
And all the fury of the madding fkies !
See how each nerve and vein
Trembles and throbs with torture ; how his eyes
Start from their feat with anguifh and defpair !
What drops of fanguine fweat roll down amain
From his fair limbs ! " O Father, O remove
" If poffible this cup ; yet not my will,

Y 4

" Bat

" But thine be done !!" O agonizing Love;
O Grace beyond compare!
Swift thro' the yielding air
The words upflew to heav'n, and all the Quire
Of bleſſed Angels ſtood in ſpeechleſs trance :
Aſide they flung their harps of golden wire,
And in their bow'rs of amaranthine ſhade
For one ſhort moment ſtay'd
Their ardent ſongs of rapture and of praiſe,
While wonder-ſtruck they gaze,
O King of Suff'rings, on thy conflicts dire !

    But ſoft ! Am I deceiv'd, or doth a ray
Of light ethereal burſt thro' yonder cloud,
And gild the mountain top with its fair beam ?
Lo down the lucid ſtream
An Angel glides ! he leaves his cryſtal ſphere,
And cuts with nimble wing his liquid way
Thro' the rank vapours of this murky air ;
Sent, O my Saviour, from thy lab'ring breaſt
To drive away the horrours of deſpair,
And give thy ſorrow-ſick'ning ſoul to reſt.

    And hark, while ſwiftly from th' ethereal he
This harbinger of light
Deſcends, what awful ſilence reigns around !

No

No more their ruftling heads the Cedars wave,
And each aërial Sound
Creeps foftly to its cave :
The dark Clouds flumber on the mountain's brow,
And Nature ftands abforb'd in dread fufpenfe ;
While thus the Angel cheers his drooping fenfe,
And bids full ftreams of heav'nly mufic flow.

THE HYMN.

Hail * Sun of Righteoufnefs, whofe healing ray
Can pierce the darknefs of Egyptian night;
Tho' now fome earth-born clouds obftruct thy way,
Soon fhalt thou blaze in thy meridian height;
And beaming, with celeftial love,
Deftroy the † covering, and the veil remove,
And guide the nations with thy friendly light,
To the bleft regions of eternal day.
Then, O ye Hofts on high,
Cherubs and Seraphs, that excel in might,
Ye that encircling guard the faphyr throne,
And fing Hofannas to the great THREEONE,
O praife him, praife him everlaftingly !

When Man rebell'd, and from th' abyfs profound
Thofe mifcreated monfters Sin and Deatn

* Malachi iv. 2.   † Ifaiah xxv. 7.

A way

A way to Eden found;
There blasting, with their pestilential breath,
Each herb, and fruit, and flow'r,
Of Eve's * delicious bow'r;
Thou saw'st the havoc, saw'st with melting eye
† The sad Earth labour under the horrid doom
Of guilt, and misery;
Saw'st all her beauty, all her vernal bloom
Like flow'rs frost-smitten die;
While heaving with convulsive pangs, and groans,
She op'd her jaws, and yawn'd the general tomb
Of her once happy, once immortal sons!
At that dread hour, when statue-struck with woe
Stood the primæval Pair,
And wept, and loaded with their sighs the air,
We ‡ lookt around—but lo
Not one to pity them, not one to know!
No Son of light, no Angel dar'd to plead,
No Seraph intercede:
Till Thou, the high priest, heard'st the wretches moan,
And off'ring up their incense-breathing pray'r
In golden censer at th' eternal throne,

* Paradise Lost, iv. 690.

† The Author purposely left this line thus unharmonious, that the
sound might be in accord with the Sense.

‡ Psalm lxix. 20, & Isaiah lix. 16.

" On

" On me their Shepherd, me thy wrath employ,
" But spare these haplefs sheep, O Father, spare,
" Let me with agonies their grief atone,
" And all their sins, and all their sorrows bear."
Then sang the morning Stars their hymns of joy,
When thou, the Father's uncreated Son,
The promis'd * Shilo, quitting thy abode,
That heaven of heav'ns the bofom of thy God,
And stript of all thy blifs, and all thy glory,
Began'st, O wondrous story,
The tafk of Love, and voluntary Woe.
Hail Word eternal! Hail creating Mind!
Then did the Hills, then did the Vales refound ;
The Vale of Arnon, and the purple brow
Of beauteous Amana, and Shenir rang,
And all the forefts of thy Carmel fang,
When Thou, in flefhly † Tabernacle fhrin'd,
'Ganft pour the ftream of bleffings all around,
And brooding over teach thy helplefs care,
As the fond Eagle doth her young, to try
Their fcarce-fledg'd plumes, and thro' the bafer air
Affert the manfions in their native fky.
‡ O goodly Vine, beneath whofe cluftring boughs
The weary flocks repofe !

* Gen. xlix. 10.　　　† a Cor. v. 1.　　　‡ John xv. 1.

O * Rofe of Sharon ! O † Enclofure fweet
Of chief perfumes, of fpices frefh and rare !
Wake, wake ye winds, and o'er the Garden blow,
That all the foul-delighting fcents may flow ;
And ye, O Spirits of air
Catch the rich odours, and to heav'n repair,
That angels may diffolve in raptures meet !
O ‡ Phofphor ! O effulgent Son of Morn !
But ah how fallen, faln ! how chang'd from Him,
Who led to war th' embattled Seraphim, .
And all the Youth of Heav'n ; whofe flaming hand,
With thunders arm'd, hurl'd from th' ethereal fky
The arch apoftate and his rebel band,
Hurl'd them with ruin, and combuftion dire,
To bottomlefs perdition, there to lie
Weltring in lakes of everliving fire !
Yet, fpotlefs Lamb, tho' now with wrath divine
Thou feel'ft thy adamantine foul oppreft ;
Tho' Adam's fins are by adoption thine,
And crufh with heavy load thy lab'ring breaft ;
Yet quickly fhall the mortal coil be o'er,
And grief, and pain, and anguifh be no more ;
Soon fhall the brightnefs of thy Godhead fhine :
Ev'n now methinks thy § robes with fanguine red

---

* Solomon's Song, ii. 1.   † Solomon's Song, iii. 12. & infra.
‡ Re. xxii. 16.   § Ifai. lxiii, 2.

Are

Are ftain'd, like thofe that in the winefat tread ;
I fee, I fee thee rife.
How bright, how glorious, o'er the ftarry fkies,
And Sin, and Death are led
Chain'd to thy Chariot wheels ! Hark, hark the Song
Begins, the Song of triumph and delight,
Which erft we fung, when from the dreadful fight
Returning Victor all the rapturous throng
Of Saints and Angels hail'd thee, wond'rous King,
Almighty Lord, Heav'n's fole eternal Heir :
Lift up your heads, ye Gates, and O prepare,
Ye living Orbs, your everlafting doors,
The King of Glory comes !
What King of Glory ?——He, whofe puiffant might
Subdu'd * Abaddon, and th' infernal pow'rs
Of Darknefs bound in adamantine chains :
Who wrapt in glory with the Father reigns
Omnipotent, immortal, infinite !

    The Angel ceas'd, and from his flinty bed
The God-redeemer rofe :
Lull'd was his care in heav'n-infpir'd repofe,
And his fick foul with airs ethereal fed :
Content he rofe, O Father, to fulfil
Thy fixt eternal will.

* The Angel of the bottomlefs pit is fo called in Rev. ix. 11.

And

And now the madding crew their Saviour led
Mild as a Lamb to flaughter, like a fheep
Before her fhearers dumb —— But, O my Mufe,
Forbear !——Ev'n gnarled Oaks for grief would weep,
And the rough rocks their briny tears diffufe,
Should'ft thou to Calvary's cleft fummit rife,
And there, in colours fuited to thy woe,
The torments and ftupendous forrows paint
Of the great fuff'ring Saint.——
Oh ftop, and from the humble bafe below
Caft up thy tearful eyes
To where thy Lord, and * Love was crucify'd ;
So fhall the World, and all its vanities
Appear like drofs——Ambition, Luft, and Pride
Shall far, far off their baleful pow'rs remove,
And in the pure unfpotted mind
Nothing remain behind,
But Adoration, Ecftacy, and Love.

    * Cyp. Ερως εμος εσαυρωται.

F I N I S.

www.ingramcontent.com/pod-product-compliance
Lightning Source LLC
Chambersburg PA
CBHW031132120726
47905CB00006B/1660